Finding Renee

ANDREA R. PARKS

ARENEE PRODUCTIONS

Library of Congress Cataloging-in-Publication Data has been applied for.

ISBN: 978-0-578-36198-7

Contents

Dedication

To Colbi Mishale Holliday, the best daughter God could ever create for me. Thank you for always supporting my creativity and giving me honest feedback. To Alonte Holliday, my son-in-love, you have blessed our family.

Mom and Dad, thank you for always encouraging and listening with an open mind to anything I have written, Rest in Heaven, Mildred, and Rudy Parks.

Acknowledgment

S o many to thank…

My best friends and Godmothers to Colbi, Kimberly Luttery, and Gretser Rush: You've been there for and with me at my worst and best. I will forever keep you close to my heart. You taught me how to become a better friend, and I thank and love you, my sisters.

My dear friends and family: Regina Hayes, Kelly Forrest, Shawn Gillespie, and Gretser Rush, took the time to read my novel and give their honest feedback; you kept me going and helped me sharpen my skills. Thank you, Lisa Green Kelsaw, Rachel Jackson, Mr. and Mrs. Duane, and Luna Parks, for your support and belief in me and my dream. Valerie Hanserd, my friend/sister, thank you for all the talks we've shared. You have been my support from day one. Thank you for keeping it real with me through the years.

To my friends, Vivian Bamberg, Michael Williams, Amanda Wright, and Dawn Hardwick; we've developed a friendship over the five years since we met at work. Thank you for your friendship and thank you for supporting my dreams.

Colbi and Alonte Holliday, you are my sounding boards and game partners. You keep me youthful and knowledgeable. You have encouraged and balanced me. My siblings, Le, Curtis, Duane, Ricky, Larry, and Ardell, thanks for being who you are because it helps me be me. I can always count on you to hold me down and have my back when necessary. Thanks for strengthening my character. I enjoy our conversations; a girl couldn't ask for better brothers. Thank you to my nieces and nephews for their encouragement and support, along with the McClain/Parks family, in general. It means the world to me. I have the best family in the world. A special thank you to the following: Jeanine Hayes, my hairdresser, cousin, and friend. Finally, I can't move on without mentioning Kim Thomas and Valerie Jackson, Vicki Scott, and Anitra Parks who are more than my cousins; they are my sisters. You were there when I needed advice and support. Thank you.

To my cousins, Adrienne and her late husband, Carlie, Murphy; always there for me in many ways. Thank you for our relationship. It wasn't always easy, but worth the growth. I've learned so much from our relationship as cousins and friends. Rest in peace, Carlie.

Thank you to those I met along the way who have encouraged me. This has been an exciting adventure that I loved from my first thought, character, and word. This has given me life in so many ways, and for that, my Heavenly Father, I'm humbled and grateful… Thank you!

Finding Renee

Finding Renee is a novel about a woman in her fifties who develops into the woman she was destined to become once she steps out of her comfort zone. She re-invents herself by stepping away from her corporate job to do what she loves, making jewelry. Renee's life changes from dull into a vibrant woman who embraces excitement. The journey starts when Renee meets a man twenty years her junior. Through that relationship, she evolves into a confident woman loving who she is physically and sexually.

She learns that being spontaneous allows her to release her inhibitions in the bedroom and enjoy every sensual moment. But as she evolves, Renee finds herself torn between her soulmate and her former best childhood friend, Monique. Her secrets reveal a hurtful history that will destroy relationships. A high school reunion allows Renee to reconnect with old friends and confront new enemies. Losing a lover can be heartbreaking but losing them to your best friend is devastating. Finding Renee is the first novel in a trilogy that will only have you asking for more.

Meet the Author

Andrea Parks started writing when she was 17. Her first work was a poem expressing her broken heart over a breakup with an old boyfriend. She couldn't verbally express how she felt, but within days of the split, Andrea was able to articulate her feelings in a poem. She also wrote her first play for her local church at 17. Andrea fell in love with the literary world when she was first introduced to the novels "The Count of Monte Cristo" and "A Tale of Two Cities" in her senior literature class in high school.

She fell in love with the theater when she went with her church youth group to the "Wiz". From that moment, she was hooked and never looked back. Andrea has written poetry for various events, both personal and professional. But it wasn't until she raised her daughter that Andrea developed her voice to create her first novel. She wanted to write stories about women who lost themselves, often taking care of others, but who finally "find themselves", and re-invent their lives while finding their voices.

Renee Morgan

She was a mocha shade with brown, beautifully almond-shaped eyes that sparkled when she smiled and changed to a shade of hazelnut hue in the spring. Her smile drew you into her beauty, and her walk effortlessly allowed her body to dance to a rhythm that delighted most men. She had beautiful, curly black hair with streaks of gray framing her round face perfectly. Time had added pounds to Renee Morgan's 5'4 frame, but one could see that beneath her thickness was a shapely frame waiting to be revealed. Her voice was slightly raspy when she spoke; one couldn't help but be captivated. Although attractive, Renee didn't recognize her beauty. But Renee was learning about herself as a woman.

As a single mother, she discovered some hard truths. Single parenting, and raising twins, AJ and Kiana, was a struggle; Renee could provide for them financially, but she couldn't give AJ the father experience of teaching him how to become a man or give Kiana the experience of feeling the love of a man. Renee did her best, though, and prayed it was good enough to provide them with a healthy and stable adult life. Renee never married and after the break-up with her children's father, Eric Coleman, who wasn't around much to offer help. She decided to focus on financial stability for her and the twins. Renee never held Eric's issues against him; she understood that he was battling his demons and didn't want his children to see him struggle. Renee worked as a supervisor at a Fortune 500 company, working her way up from the mailroom. Before the twins, she was like any other 20-year-old searching to find themselves. Renee's parents always wanted her to go to college, but finding a job after high school that paid her $13.50 an hour was good enough for her at the time. Once the twins arrived, Renee decided it was time to build a career.

Renee took night classes to get her degree in business and graduated summa cum laude by the time the twins turned six years old. She moved up the ladder, making connections at every level, letting everyone know that she was determined; she just needed a shot. And when she got it, Renee never looked back. Initially, Renee told everyone that her children were her motivators, and as they grew older, they became her biggest cheerleaders. But she focused so much on her career and her kids that Renee forgot about focusing on herself.

Renee learned early in her career just how tough climbing the corporate ladder can be. There is always someone out there who wants your job and thinks they can do it better. Her first mistake in her new role as a supervisor was to go to work wearing her hair in its most natural state: kinky, coiled, and curly. Her boss, who was also black, never mentioned acceptance or, in this case, non-acceptance. But from her specific comments, Renee understood not to wear her hair like that again. One of the comments was general but telling. "What made you want to wear your hair like that?" The question and tone in her voice rubbed Renee the wrong way because, in her mind, it meant that her boss saw her as an unprofessional Black woman. So, she never wore her hair in its kinky, curly, natural way at work again. It wasn't because Renee was intimidated, but because she understood the politics in the white-collar world that her boss so transparently revealed. Renee wasn't so in love with her hair in its natural state that she would allow her appearance to get in the way of moving up the corporate ladder. So, she kept her hair straight for the time being.

Her boss, Cassandra Newhouse, was on her way to a huge promotion, becoming the first African American woman at their company to wear the title "Vice President of Operations". This would mean Renee replacing her boss as director of operations, putting her in the six-figure status. So, for Cassandra Newhouse, the presentation was everything. She always reminded Renee that Black women need to get a seat at the table while still available. Cassandra was 5'8, full-figured with shoulder-length bone straight hair, and a flawless, smooth, dark-skinned complexion. Cassandra was also single and had never married, nor had any children. Becoming a wife and mother was optional. And she was driven to climb the ladder as high as it could take her, breaking whatever glass ceiling standing in her way. But Cassandra was the kind of boss who never wanted to block anyone's journey to success if it didn't interfere with her own. She continued to press Renee hard to keep such a professional image. Renee played the game because she thought moving up was what she wanted, to be considered a success. All her friends were tied to the corporate world and were on the same journey. Renee was behind in climbing the corporate ladder because didn't attend college until several years after high school.

Her boss did get promoted to "VP of Operations", and as expected, Renee became the new director of operations. But by the time it happened, Renee wasn't excited and didn't understand why. She kept up the pace, though, with the new role. Years later, after the twins graduated from college and moved to different cities, Renee realized it was time for a change in her life. Cassandra was still climbing the ladder and now was the president of operations. She wanted Renee by her side, replacing her as vice president of operations. But Renee knew in her heart that her next step on the ladder of success would not include Cassandra or any other boss. Renee had her dreams, which she had pushed to the side for far too long.

She began making the necessary plans to step out on faith and focus on the one thing she was damn good at, and she enjoyed doing; she loved creating jewelry and people often complimented what she wore. Renee spent the following week putting together a business plan. "Simple Touch of Elegance", Jewelry by Renee Morgan, would be her business name. She told Jessica Palmer, her best friend, and Godmother to her twins, that she would quit her job and focus on that. Jessica felt it was too risky and suggested perhaps Renee should focus on meeting someone who could become a future husband. Renee's daughter, Kiana, had been on her about getting out more and making herself available; this would be a great time to start. They even suggested trying online or speed dating. But Kiana warned her mom if she decided to try online dating to avoid getting catfished.

Of course, Renee had no idea what catfished meant, and Kiana was trying to explain in between pauses of laughter and a comment about "old people". Renee then chuckled and responded: "I'm not old," she said, giggling again.

That was when Kiana reminded her mom of that time two years ago when they were texting, and Renee's response to what Kiana had said caused Kiana to text back with an "SMH". In between both of their giggles, Kiana continued her walk down memory lane and reminded her mom that she had called to ask what "SMH (pronounced smaaa)" meant. When she told Renee that "SMH" stood for "shaking my head", Kiana knew she could rest her case. They laughed so hard that Renee's abdominal muscles were aching.

Renee finally took her daughter's advice and found an online dating site called "Love Match". After filling out her profile, she began receiving messages and flirts. It was exciting to see all the interest so quickly. As Renee scrolled through the many faces of possible suitors, she noticed a pattern after a few days of responding to her messages. First, the men would send her a note telling her they found her attractive and would love to hear from her. Next, she responded to those who caught her eye, but no one answered. Then, finally, someone went a little further in responding and their conversation back and forth was great. A couple of days later, he decided to flirt a little more but sexually. He explained just how he loves to taste the fruit of a woman. At first, Renee paused and stared at the screen because she didn't know how to respond. "Is this what they do now?" she mumbled. Renee could see him typing and asking her if she was still there. She thought that he would get the hint if she changed the subject. She asked him if he loved to travel. He responded by asking her if this was an invitation to visit her. "What the hell," she thought to herself. She typed, "LOL," and "You are too funny; we don't know each other like that, anyway."

His response was, "What better way to get to know someone other than in such an intimate way?" Then he sent an emoji of an eggplant. Renee couldn't believe how bold this guy, Carl, was to send her an emoji version of a "dick pic". She was texting Jessica to tell her about this Carl when Kiana called to see how online dating was. She told Kiana about the conversation with Carl and the image that he felt comfortable sending her. While she was on the phone with Kiana, Carl continued to ask if she was still there, and eventually, he stopped asking and left their chat. The next day, there was a message from Carl asking what had happened.

"Had a call from my daughter, and it took longer than I thought," she typed.

Without any apologies, and just like that, he blocked her. Renee continued using the online dating app for a few months, especially since she paid three months in advance. She had met some attractive men, but most of the men would do drive-by hello's and then disappear. She was sure that a few of those profile pictures in her inbox must be on the FBI's most-wanted list and quickly removed their messages. Then, just when she was ready to give up, she received a message. She was taken back a little as she read the note.

Hello, my name is Michael, and my best friend, Thomas, who is new to online dating, noticed your profile and was quite taken with your beauty. Unfortunately, he isn't a member, and today is my last day on this account because I found the love of my life. I know this goes against the rules, and I don't know if you believe in God, but I don't believe in things happening by chance. I hope that you don't think that I'm creepy. Just trying to help a friend out. If you are interested, and I hope you are, here is his email address: Thomas.Bradley@email.com."

Renee decided it was a hoax and initially wasn't interested in wasting her time. But a few days later, Renee chose to email this stranger, and to her surprise, he responded. For a few months, she had a wonderful time communicating with Thomas. She opened her heart in such a way that it surprised her. His emails were timeless and beautiful, and Renee felt like this was an old-school courtship. Renee was a little surprised by the photo he sent her because she had never dated nor desired to date a white man, but here she was falling for this man. A man so different than what she was used to dating, she wouldn't have given him two seconds of her time if they had met face to face because he wasn't her type.

But on paper, his words made her heart smile, and that was worth taking a chance. Since Thomas didn't live far from her, Renee felt it was time to meet after three months of phone, text, and email communications. Things seemed to be working out fine, and she was excited to meet this man who was sweeping her off her feet. They set a date, time, and place to meet, and she called him the day before to make sure everything was still on, but there was no answer. She texted him, but no response. It had been a week since Renee last heard from Thomas. She felt this was what Kiana warned her about and that she was indeed catfished. Her first thought was, "I know this punk ass just didn't catfish me." She chuckled as she blocked his number, removed her profile, and canceled her subscription.

Ordinarily, she would be upset, but instead, she looked at the positive side: her heart was ready to find love for the first time in years. Renee never realized how lonely she was because the twins filled her days and nights until she became an empty nester. The overwhelming realization of being alone swept through her body like an intense chill, and she couldn't help but break down and cry.

After her breakup with Eric, the twins' father, she never really dated anyone else seriously. After wiping the tears from her face, she thought there was no sense in crying over what could have been but to instead focus on what could, which was her jewelry business. Then, just as she started to research on her cell phone, Renee received a text from Jessica.

"Did you get your invitation to our high school class reunion?"

Renee got up from her sofa and walked outside to her mailbox to see if she had any mail, and there it was, this white envelope addressed to her. After opening the invitation, Renee responded to Jessica.

"Yes. I just opened it up, but I don't think I'm going."

Renee waited for Jessica's reply as she walked back into the house, but there was no text. Then, her phone started ringing, and it was Jessica.

"Hello," Renee answered.

"Girl, are you crazy? Of course, you are going to the reunion. It's our 37th reunion, and you haven't been to one. You have a lot of catching up to do, and I understood all those other times because of the twins, but you have no excuses now. The kids are grown and minding their own business. Now, it's time for you to breathe life into the slowly dying thing you call your life!" Jessica yelled at her.

There was a pause, and then Renee responded to Jessica and explained that it had been an exceptionally long time since she had been out to a social event. She was happy and content staying home if it wasn't a business dinner that had taken her out of the house and away from the kids. She continued to explain that she did not need to be active in mingling with people. All she wanted to do was come home from work, eat dinner, have a glass or two of wine, and then go to bed after watching one of her favorite reality shows. She pulled her ear away from her cell phone after hearing this loud shriek that sounded like Jessica was screaming the word "What?" into the phone.

"Listen, Renee, you are one of my oldest and dearest friends, and you know how you are always saying, keep it "one-hundred" with me; don't sugarcoat it because you are trying not to hurt my feelings. Well, girl, I'm about to keep it "one-hundred"! You must be the most boring friend that I have. You don't date or go out with friends, if you're not going to work or church, you are at home. Hell, do you even go to church anymore? You shop online, so you don't have to go to the mall!"

Renee interrupted. "Wait now, Jessica!"

"Renee, don't get upset with what I'm saying because it's coming from love. I worry about you. You act like you're eighty-three years old and waiting to die. You have so much more life in you, and you are wasting it, and for what?" Jessica calmly said.

There was silence for what felt like an hour, but it was only five seconds. Then, Jessica realized that Ms. Keep It "one-hundred" never kept it "one-hundred" with herself, and she was now in her feelings.

Renee broke the silence first. "I know it's all coming from love, but damn, girl!

Jessica laughed, explained that life was too short, and reminded Renee now was the time to live her best life. Renee laughed and agreed, conceding that she would give going to the reunion some thought. Finally, Jessica decided and then mentioned that she heard that Byron "Moses" Banks would be at the reunion.

"Moses?" Renee shrieked.

"Yes. Moses." Jessica responded. "Remember when he parted your thighs at our senior homecoming game?"

Jessica and Renee laughed in concert for what seemed like thirty minutes. Their laughter was interrupted when Jessica received another call on her other line. They both said their goodbyes, but not without Jessica making Renee promise to give going to the reunion some serious thought. Renee poured herself a glass of her favorite Moscato in her stemless wine glass and sat on her sofa, looking at the invitation to her 37th high school class reunion. She favored this wine because of its sweetness; there was a note of pineapple, peach, citrus, and red fruit. It had a smooth, almost velvety mousse that excited her palate. No matter how she felt, her mood seamlessly changed into pure happiness after one sip. She softly mumbled aloud, "37 years ago, I was a high school senior… Damn, I am old!" she chuckled.

The invitation was plain-looking with red and black lettering, which were also Garrett's High School's colors. The invitation read: "Raymond Garrett's High School Class of 1983 cordially invites you to its 37th high school reunion." Renee reminisced on her senior year and Moses; he was the love of her life back in high school. He was intelligent, funny, and happened to be very attractive. Moses had a caramel complexion with gray eyes. He was one of the most popular boys in school, not just because he was good at sports or had a car, but because he had gray eyes. Black folks weren't used to seeing a different eye color than black, brown, or sometimes hazelnut. Every girl wanted to be his girlfriend and every boy wanted to be his wingman! As Renee pondered whether to go to her class reunion, Kiana called and interrupted her walk down memory lane.

"Hey, sweetie!" she answered.

"Hi, Mom. Were you busy?" Kiana asked.

"No. I was just looking at an invitation to my 37th-year high school reunion." She didn't want to talk about it with Kiana and listen to another sermon about her life or the seeming lack thereof, but it was too late because she could hear the smile in Kiana's voice.

"That's great, Mom, and I hope you plan to attend?" Kiana exclaimed.

She swallowed the last of her wine before responding.

"I'm thinking about it, and before you give me your speech about how I never go or do anything, I already heard it from your Auntie Jessica."

"Well, I hope that you will go. You don't have any excuses now, and maybe you'll run into an old single boyfriend while you are there," Kiana said with a chuckle.

Renee rolled her eyes and said nothing. She could feel her concerned daughter revving up to give her that stern talking as if Kiana was the parent, and she was the child. Kiana listed all the reasons why her mother needed to get a life. Renee understood her concern and agreed that it was time for a change.

The next day, Renee decided to go to the gym to see about collaborating with a trainer. She grabbed her purse and headed down to the gym. Since Renee decided to attend the class reunion, a little work getting back into shape was necessary. As she headed toward the gym, she began to think about her move to Tampa, FL. She smiled, thinking this was one of the best decisions that she had ever made. After walking into the gym, her eyes locked with this brown-haired young Spanish guy who looked the same age as AJ and Kiana. Renee smiled as she walked toward the young man and said, "Hi, I would like to meet with a trainer to discuss a weight-loss program."

The young man smiled, introduced himself as Carlos Rivera, and told her he was a personal trainer and would love to discuss her goals. They both walked to a table where they could talk privately. She had a trainer when they finished talking. Her new trainer was cute in an exotic kind of way. He was not so bulky that his arms looked like the "Hulk." His skin was caramel, not from tanning, but from being of Spanish descent.

For a few seconds after signing up, she wasn't sure she wanted Carlos to train her. She felt a little intimidated because he was so young. She felt old as she mumbled, "Too late now; you signed on the dotted line." She left the gym and headed to the store to buy some workout clothes and equipment necessary for her workout with Carlos the next week. They both decided that hour-long morning sessions would be better, starting at 7:00 am., and that they will meet every Monday, Wednesday, and Friday. Renee had six months to complete her weight-loss goal, and Carlos agreed it was doable. After her meeting, she felt excited about doing something other than work and watching church on the television.

As Renee pulled out of the parking lot, an oldie-but-goodie song came on the radio. Renee turned up the volume and began singing Prince's "1999" song. Every time she heard this song, she thought about her senior prom. There were so many great high school memories (before her break-up with Moses and betrayal from her best friend, Monique Jones). Reminiscing about her senior year made Renee excited about attending the class reunion. She parked her car at her favorite store, Target or Targé (as some of the bougie people continue to call it), to look for some workout clothes. It'd been at least twenty years since she worked out, other than cleaning her house and occasional walks around the neighborhood. Now that she had more time on her hands, Renee wanted to focus on herself, inside and out. But, as she rummaged through the clothing, she felt somewhat discouraged because there weren't a lot of cute workout clothes in her size.

"Damn," she mumbled to herself. "Did I gain that much weight?"

Renee walked over to the plus sizes and found a few cute outfits but was embarrassed that she could easily fit a size twenty. She was still in denial about her clothing size and realized that she had been wearing too-small clothing, hoping to return to her average size. She did not understand that size twenty had been her size for over ten years. The reality of how much weight she had gained brought Renee to tears. She was glad she signed up with her cute trainer because she had a lot of work ahead of her but wasn't sure if she had enough time. She wondered just how many pounds she had gained. Before the twins, Renee was a size eight, her largest size ever. She took a deep breath and decided that she wouldn't waddle in self-pity. Instead, Renee viewed this as a challenge to push herself physically and emotionally beyond her comfort zone. After paying for the few clothing items to jump-start her workouts, she was on her way home. As she pulled into her garage, Jessica texted.

"Hey, girl, just checking on you and making sure you haven't changed your mind about the reunion."

Renee smiled and replied.

"Girl, I'm good and yes, I'm still going to the reunion. I'm excited about seeing everyone. Do you know if Monique is coming?"

Jessica didn't respond immediately, so she went into the house and grabbed her favorite comfort food, chocolate chip ice cream with a slice of chocolate cake and a glass of wine.

"I guess you haven't heard the news," Jessica responded.

"No. I haven't," Renee replied.

Her phone began to ring, and it was Jessica calling. The tea was too juicy and too long for a text whenever Jessica called.

"Girl," Jessica said in almost a whisper, "Monique's brother-in-law Mark Harris decided to run for Governor of North Carolina. They were vetting every member of his family to ensure they didn't have any embarrassing skeletons in their closet that would hurt his chances of winning. Soon after his announcement, Monique told me that she had received an email telling her that her husband isn't the father of her son."

"WHAT THE HELL!" Renee screamed, not in horror but in joy. She mumbled, wondering when the chickens would come home to roost, "I wonder, who is the baby daddy? Do you know, Jessica?"

"No, I'm glad I don't know," Jessica responded.

There was a brief silence between the two women as if they both had the same thoughts but didn't want to share them aloud. There was a rumor circling their friends that Moses and Monique hooked up that year he was to be in town for his father's funeral. Renee continued her rants about Monique as she basked in her childhood friend's soon-to-be downfall, who was only on friend status because of Jessica. She then took her glass of wine to the head and let out a loud burp, followed by an "Excuse me, girl." Jessica ignored Renee's behavior and knew why she was acting like this, but she was slightly annoyed.

"Monique isn't doing so well; she is freaking out, as I'm sure that you can imagine. This will be a PR nightmare, and I'm unsure how she would manage things at this point," Jessica blurted out.

Renee couldn't take the poor-Monique attitude that Jessica was displaying and told her that Monique was getting just what she deserved. She explained how Monique would now know how others felt when they got screwed by her. In her explanation, she broke down how Monique was freaking out, which meant that her husband and his namesake Christopher Jr. (affectionately known by everyone as CJ), had no idea what bomb was about to drop. All the country will know their truth. All Jessica could do was agree with her but warn her not to celebrate in someone's misery. She knew that Jessica was right, but she wasn't at that level of forgiving Monique after all these years. When Monique got pregnant, Renee had her suspicions but no evidence of who the real father was. Renee's and Monique's long-strained relationship left very little love between them, and Renee only felt sorry for Chris Sr. and Jr., who were innocent in this soon-to-be tragedy. Renee didn't feel sorry for Monique because it was her turn to feel some pain; however, for a split second, Renee considered putting the past in the past and being the bigger person by supporting her childhood friend. She picked up her cell phone and began to dial Monique's number. Before she could hit the send button, Renee had a change of heart and mumbled, "Bigger person, my ass; I hope that she catches all the hell coming her way." She threw her phone on the sofa and poured herself a glass of wine, smiling at the thought that Monique was getting what she deserved.

She remembered the last time they had a conversation. It got heated when Monique accused her of trying to remain the victim. High school was over, and everyone had gone their separate ways. If Moses wanted Renee, he had plenty of time to win her back. Instead of moving on with her life, it was easier for Renee to cling to the only thing she felt made her the happiest, and that was Moses. Monique told her that she was a sad and pathetic woman who put all her identity in a boy who could only think with the head that resided inside his pants.

When Renee met Eric Coleman, she thought that she had another chance at love. Things were going great for a year, and Renee felt that she was finally putting Moses behind her, but often wondered what would have happened if they had stayed together through high school. After Renee and Eric celebrated their first year together, their relationship turned ugly after Eric was fired for failing his drug test.

Things became financially tricky, not to mention their arguments were becoming borderline abusive. A few months after their breakup, Renee found out that she was pregnant and with twins no less. She told Eric that they were going to have twins, she knew that he wasn't ready to be a father, but she wasn't going to end her pregnancy, they would have to figure it out one day at a time. Eventually, the pregnancy was too much for Eric. He explained to Renee that he just couldn't imagine having his children see him as a drug addict, he packed what little things he hadn't pawned and moved out. Looking back it was the best gift that he gave Renee and their children. Renee heard that his drug problem had gotten the best of him and that he was homeless wandering in the streets of Rockford. Renee raised the twins on her own and her fond memories of her love for Moses kept her sane. Maybe Monique's harsh words had some truth, because at that point, pathetic and sad were where Renee felt contentment. Not even her favorite wine could cheer her up at that moment, forcing her to look at herself. She began to sob a little over the prospect that she may never love another man like she loved Moses.

Yet, she could never shake the undeniable love for him. Their connection was strong from the moment they met. It was something of a magical force that drew them together. She couldn't explain why such a short experience had such a lifetime emotional effect on her. Jessica would always say that because he was her first love and her first sexual experience, Renee would always have a special place in her heart for him. What they shared, however short of a time, was love. She knew that he felt the same way she did because the first and only time they made love, it was like their souls connected, and until prom night, they lived as one soul.

The following day, she stayed in bed a little longer than usual, surfed what was on TV, and stumbled across a rerun of an old television show, "Columbo". It'd been years since she watched this show, and Renee remembered how she and her mom would sit on the sofa watching and guessing who the murderer was. Of course, now, looking at the show, it was obvious who the killer was, but it was still a good show, so she kept watching it. Renee loved watching old murder mysteries from the past, and Columbo was still one of her favorites. She loved how Lt. Columbo works the nerves of the suspects by asking annoying questions, knowing they are the murderer. After Columbo was over, she got up and dressed for the day. Renee decided that it was time to revamp her life. She started by creating a vision board from an old poster board that Kiana had left in her room after graduation years ago.

When she finally added what she wanted on her board, Renee took a step back to see what she had put together. Put God first, use your God-given talent, get out of the box you're in, and lose weight. Then, go do something by yourself at least twice a month, see all of Florida, travel more, meet men and date, and stop finding fault with every man… husband. She added her husband there because she decided that marriage wasn't off the table. Giving up on love and meeting the man she would call her husband one day was still possible. Satisfied with what she had, she decided it was time to put her words into action by cleaning out her kitchen. It was time to rid her pantry and refrigerator of all the unhealthy foods that would ultimately comfort her each day. She was glad that trash day was the next day in case she changed her mind. Out went cakes, chips, soda, ice cream, and candy. She left and went grocery shopping for everything she needed for her meal.

Jessica Palmer

S he was 5'8 and a red-headed firecracker. She had big eyes like a deer in headlights. In Jessica's first year of high school, she was built like someone's little sister with no boobs, no butt, and no shape. She entered her sophomore year without any physical growth. During a pep rally, she was heading to her locker and noticed several students surrounding her area. One of the guys on the football team had taped a note with a scripture that included these words: "We have a little sister, and she has no breasts." Song of Solomon 8:8. The boys made fun of Jessica by following her around the rest of the school year, quoting that scripture. Jessica never found out who that boy was, but his effort to trigger laughs started the nightmare her sophomore year, Jessica found out who that boy was later in life when she married him.

His name was Richard Palmer. By her junior year in high school, Jessica had developed into a lovely teenager, and as an adult, she was even more stunning, with curves in all the right places. But Jessica still had the scar above her right eye from a childhood fight with Diamond Brooks. She hated the freckles that dominated her entire body and had the thickest lips ever seen on a white girl they hadn't bought. Nevertheless, Jessica had a kind soul and could handle herself when tested. She was sweet with a touch of roughness.

Since grade school, Jessica, home girl extraordinaire, had been best friends with Renee Morgan and Monique Harris (whose maiden name was Jones). They all lived on the west side of Rockford, IL, the "west end", as it was still called today. She and her family had just moved into the projects nearby and were the only white family to assume residence. Jessica, being Jessica, didn't know to be scared, and made friends quickly – except with one little Black girl named Diamond Brooks. Diamond was the schoolyard bully. She was a big girl and mean to the core. She would beat up boys and girls as if it was a sport. One day during recess, Jessica innocently asked Diamond if her mother was a stripper and gave her that name so she would follow her.

The laughter grew throughout the playground. All the boys took advantage of the innocent question and began to ask Diamond for some dollar bills, including the boy named Richard Palmer. Diamond's only reply was a fist to Jessica's right eye, later creating a scar. Her eye turned black and blue with a cut above it, compliments of Diamond's flower ring, and right before Renee's and Monique's very eyes. Monique shook her head at the sight as Jessica slowly stood back up after falling to the wet ground. She didn't cry. She just asked, "What did I say that was so wrong?" Renee and Monique walked over to Jessica after Diamond left and laughed so hard that Jessica also began to laugh. That day, Renee and Monique decided to be friends with Jessica and show her the ropes so that Diamond wouldn't kill her. Later that year, Jessica's father met a younger woman and left his family. He later admitted to Jessica that he wasn't in love with her mom anymore and seeing her with all Black girls hurt his stomach.

His fear was that she would grow up to marry a Black guy and be hated by both Black and White people because the world wasn't ready for interracial couples. That was the last time that Jessica ever spoke to her father. Three years after her parent's divorce was completed, her mother married a man by the name of Gordon Everett, an African American and a deacon at Renee's and Monique's church. He treated both Jessica and her mother like they were queens. Jessica never wanted anything, and they moved out of the projects and closer to where Renee and Monique lived.

This made their friendship closer, a bond that would never be broken amongst the three, or so they thought. As time passed and the three girls made it to high school, they all were beautiful young ladies. Jessica was so striking that every athlete wanted to date her, but Mr. Everett wasn't having any of that nonsense. He kept a close eye on Jessica. Any boy, regardless of color, who wanted to date Jessica had to come through him, and very few were successful in dating her unless it was done in secret.

Jessica became good at hiding things from her mom and stepfather. The girls would make sure they covered for Jessica and asked if she could spend the night at either one of their homes every Friday so that she could attend the games with them and have a little freedom, especially during football and basketball season. Mr. Everett wasn't a fool and knew that both Renee's and Monique's parents were strict but not as tough as he tended to be towards Jessica. He would often tell the two girls how good it was to see nice Black church-going girls befriending his daughter. He respected the girls seeing Jessica as a person and not simply as a white girl as many of his family members saw her. How his family treated his new wife and daughter often bothered Mr. Everett. Jessica wasn't the stereotypical white girl you'd see in the movies. She wasn't trying to be black; she was her true White self with a dab of Blackness. She picked up some black mannerisms, which caused many Black girls who were jealous of her to pick at and bully her.

They gave Jessica a nickname in elementary school. To the mean girls, Jessica's new name was "Moo-Moo." Jessica hated it. Diamond gave her the name as payback. Their teacher at the time was reading various books to the class. It was unfortunate that when she read the story about

"Stella the Cow who said Moo," Jessica just happened to have on a black and white outfit with black and white spots like what you'd see on a cow. That was the first time that Renee and Monique saw Jessica cry and the first time they all got into a fight with most of the Black girls in the class that year. It got so bad that all three girls were suspended for fighting, and that was when Jessica's mother, Tami, explained to all three girls that they couldn't fight ignorance with their fists. She explained that those girls are the losers because they couldn't see past their ignorance. She then told the three girls that they didn't need a lot of friends if they had each other. What they all had in common, was that none of them had any siblings, and what they had was each other. Sisters for life!

Jessica married her high school love, Richard Palmer, and lived on the north side of Rockford. They had a comfortable life. Richard was a professor at a local college, and Jessica was a Registered Nurse at one of the hospitals. They didn't have any children because Jessica was having trouble keeping a viable pregnancy. She would conceive but miscarry around the fifth or sixth month. This put a strain on their marriage. Richard desperately wanted to become a father, but after the fifth miscarriage, he couldn't take the disappointment anymore and decided that having children wasn't in the cards.

Their lovemaking felt more like a chore, and he was beginning to resent Jessica for wanting to continue to put them through this heartbreak. Richard didn't have the heart to tell her that it was no longer an option for him to try to have a child. She wanted to adopt, but he would make excuses whenever she brought up the subject. Finally, it reached the point that she just gave up and put all her love into Renee's children. After a time, they both grew further apart once the children were off the table. They began to live more like roommates with benefits than as husband and wife.

Jessica would come to Florida and stay a few weeks with Renee and the children yearly. She would call it her home away from home and schedule her trips during the fall when it wasn't so hot, and she could enjoy the beach without burning. Jessica would also catch a few wandering eyes from various men. However, Jessica would never treat Richard like her biological father had treated her mother. She knew her marriage wasn't working, but she wasn't ready to live as a single woman. To her, it meant failing as a woman and hearing her father's voice saying that Jessica should have never married a Black man. All they would do was disappoint her, and she just couldn't give her dad that satisfaction. Although her father died 10 years ago, his harsh words still haunted Jessica.

Out of the blue one day, after a long shift at the hospital, Jessica came home to an empty house, and a note from Richard taped to her favorite wine, where he knew she would find it. The note read…

"Jessica, our marriage hasn't worked for a long time, and I want out! I love you, and I'm still very much in love with you, but this isn't working for me, and if you are honest, it's not working for you either. Maybe we have grown apart, I don't know what it is, but I know it's not working. It has been a marriage of convenience; honestly, I no longer want to live my life like this. The divorce papers are in the manila envelope on the kitchen table. Please sign so that we both can move on with our lives.

I called a realtor, and she will be stopping by tomorrow to look at the house. I have moved most of my things out and have temporarily moved into an apartment until we can settle things. Before you ask, NO. I'm not seeing anyone else. I just can't live like we are roommates. I tried to talk to you several times, but you never wanted to discuss our problems. We haven't had sex in a year, and I respected our marriage, but a man has his needs, and I no longer want to wait to see if we will ever become intimate again. You probably think this is a weak move, and perhaps it is, but it's the only way I could get your attention. I know that this isn't the best time to ask for a divorce, especially when you are preparing for our class reunion. Don't worry, I won't be attending. You need to find yourself a divorce attorney. I have one, and when you find one, they can contact Henry Maxwell at (815)999-0000. I wish you the best in life, and yes, I know… my black ass is a mother fucker!"

Suddenly, Jessica felt sick as she grappled with what had just happened to her life. She tried to cry, but no tears would come. Instead, Jessica made a moaning noise that mimicked a crying sound, but it sounded like those actors who couldn't cry on the spot. Jessica opened a bottle of wine and drank straight from the bottle. After drinking half of the wine, Jessica yanked the nicotine patch off her right arm. Then, she found the hidden stash of cigarettes and decided that this wasn't the time to stop smoking. Richard didn't like her to smoke, especially in the house, so she had decided to finally quit. That was two months ago. She couldn't find any lighters, so she turned on the stovetop and lit her cigarette from the fire of one of the burners. Jessica took a long draw and held in the smoke for what seemed like minutes, then she blew the smoke out as she screamed the words… "Mother fucker."

Those words echoed throughout the empty house, and as Jessica closed her eyes, she began to cry uncontrollably. Jessica knew her marriage wasn't perfect and that wasn't all Richard's fault. After all, she decided to stay when she knew it was over. She hated herself for not pushing for adoption. Having children was important, especially after not having any siblings growing up. She dragged herself up the stairs and into the primary bedroom only to find that the king-size bed was gone. She didn't have the strength to scream, so she walked into the guest bedroom, laid down on the bed, and cried herself to sleep. The following day, Jessica managed to pull herself up to call her boss to let her know that she would not be coming to work and needed another week off. When her boss asked her if she was sick, Jessica responded, "No, I'm not sick, Becky. I have an urgent matter to take care of, so can you please extend my vacation for this week?" Becky started to respond, but the tone in Jessica's voice prompted her to softly say, "Okay. Please take care of yourself."

After slowly hanging up, Jessica took a shower to clear her head. Then, she went downstairs to make a cup of coffee. While waiting for it to brew, she finished off the now stale bottle of wine she left on the counter last night. She then heard the front door open, and a woman's voice yelled, "Hello, is there anyone here?" As the woman walked inside the house, it reeked of stale cigarettes, she was startled when she saw Jessica with a lit cigarette in her right hand.

Jessica harshly asked, "Who the hell are you?"

 The woman managed to introduce herself as Richard's realtor, Karen Sherman while choking on cigarette smoke. Ms. Sherman explained that Richard had hired her to sell the house. She then commented in a some-what snarky tone, "I had assumed that Richard informed you that I was coming over, and do you mind not smoking (she waved the smoke away from her face)? I can't get either of you a good deal if this house smells like disgusting cigarettes!"

Jessica paused, looked the older woman up and down, and took a long drag from her cigarette. Ensuring that there would be so much smoke when she exhaled that the ladies wouldn't be able to see each other until it cleared. Once it did and Karen Sherman's cough subsided, Jessica informed her that the house wouldn't be going up for sale today, tomorrow, or the next day, and she could find her way out the same way she found her way into her house. The realtor became infuriated and tried to criticize her rude behavior and tone. Jessica interrupted and told her it was time for her to leave before it got ugly. Again, Karen was trying to over-talk Jessica, and again, Jessica interrupted the realtor and yelled, "Get out!" When Karen didn't move fast enough, Jessica screamed, "BITCH, GET THE HELL OUT BEFORE I HURT YOU!!!"

Karen ran out of the house and never looked back. Thirty minutes later,

Richard was calling her. She didn't pick up. Then she screamed, "Bitch, if you want to talk to me, bring your ass over here like a man."

Moments later, the phone was ringing again, and this time, Jessica decided she would answer it and cuss Richard's ass out. But to her surprise, the caller ID showed that it was Renee calling. It didn't matter; she didn't want to talk to anyone, so she let the call go to voicemail. Then, as she headed up the stairs to go back to bed, the doorbell rang. At first, she ignored it, but it kept ringing, which irritated Jessica more. So, she quickly walked to the front door and swung it open, and screamed, "Go," but couldn't finish her sentence because it was Renee standing on the other side. She could tell that Renee knew what was going on because the look on Renee's face said it all.

Renee said softly, "Richard called me yesterday to tell me what he had done. So, I jumped on the next plane out of Tampa to check on you."

Jessica fell into Renee's arms and cried. Renee couldn't understand everything Jessica was saying except for her favorite words, "Mother fucker." Renee walked Jessica into the house and was hit with the haze of smoke lingering in the air from a recently lit cigarette. They walked into the living room, and Jessica laid on the sofa and began to sob again. Renee just held her until her crying stopped. Jessica wasn't your typical woman who was emotional. Renee expected to see the house torn apart and Jessica in somewhat rage but not in tears like she or Monique would have been if this were happening to them. Jessica was their pillar of strength when life kicked them down, and they never had to worry about Jessica. Renee was worried about her best friend, and it was time for her to be that pillar of strength.

Jessica finally fell asleep on the couch, and Renee started to put the broken house back together. She opened the windows to let in some fresh air and to rid the home of the smell of stale cigarette smoke. She found Jessica's stash and tossed them into the garbage. Jessica woke up while Renee was cooking. Since there wasn't much to cook, Renee thawed out a chicken she found in the freezer and fried it with her famous ingredients along with some salad. Jessica walked into the kitchen and smiled. They embraced each other, and Renee knew Jessica would be okay without words. Finally, Jessica said, "Hey, aren't you on some clean eating shit or something?" as they sat down to eat.

Renee smiled and said, "Yes, and aren't you on some I stopped smoking shit or something?"

The two ladies laughed and sipped on the last bottle of wine in the house. After a few weeks, Renee was on her way back home. It was tough seeing her friend so sad. It made her reflect on her life and what she could do to revive it. So, Renee promised herself that when she got back, she would stick to what she was putting into place before the "Jessica crisis". But, of course, she wasn't home yet, and couldn't resist picking up her favorite Garrett's Chicago mix popcorn at the airport. Renee made sure she visited all her favorite eating spots in her hometown. She loved Tampa, but their pizza is pale compared to the Chicago-style pizzas she grew up eating, and still swears that it's the best. She also had time to see her family, who were upset that she didn't tell them she was in town until it was time to leave. She explained that she was there for Jessica, who had an emergency and needed her help.

She was happy to see one of her aunts cooking fried green tomatoes, and her cousin was making Oxtails and rice. She grabbed a plate, a fork, and a knife and started piling food on her plate. The food was so good that Renee returned for seconds, and both her cousin and aunt burst into laughter. Her aunt told her she had never seen someone stuff food into their mouth so fast and chuckled while telling her that she never got to taste the food. For a split moment, she was looking at her mom. Her aunt resembled her mom so much that people wondered if they were twins. Renee laughed and told her aunt that she hadn't had this type of food in a long time, and it would be a long time before she ate like this again.

32

The Pick-up

On her way home from the airport, Renee decided to stop by Target. While shopping, a nice-looking man walked up to her. "You dropped these," he said, then gave her a pair of socks that fell out of her shopping cart. She smiled and thanked him. He complimented her beautiful smile, which made her blush. There was a little awkwardness in the air, but she didn't care. It was the first time in a long time that a man had paid her some attention. He was taller, thinner, and younger than she was, and he introduced himself as Gerald Foreman. She gave him her name, Renee Morgan. They chatted for a few minutes, and then she thanked him again and walked away. She could sense that he was trying to work up the nerve to ask her something and her guess was that he would ask if he could call her. The thought made her smile that someone was checking her out after a long time, and it felt good. As she walked around the store, she had a little more pep in her step, her shoulders and back were straight, and she walked through the store confidently like a queen. She made it through the long register line and was finally out of the door. As she was walking out, Gerald was standing at the entrance, smiling.

She returned the smile and jokingly said, "If I didn't know any better, I'd say that you were waiting for me."

Gerald tilted his head to the left as if he were blocking out the sun and slowly said, "I was," as he walked towards her.

"I didn't want to leave without asking you out for a drink or dinner," he said in the sexiest bass voice she had ever heard.

Her mouth dried up, her knees buckled underneath her, and her panties became somewhat moist. She couldn't tell if she had gotten sexually excited or if her bladder was leaking when she tried to suck in her round belly. Either way, she needed to leave before she embarrassed herself. So she quickly said yes, she would love to have drinks, and she started to go, but he stopped her.

"Unless we are going out for drinks right now, that would mean we would need to exchange phone numbers," Gerald said with a soft chuckle.

Renee laughed and said, "You're right. Where is my head?"

They both exchanged numbers. Then he walked her to her car and put her groceries inside the vehicle. She extended her hand to thank him.

Gerald shook his head and said, "Where I'm from, we hug."

"All right," Renee said, as she smiled.

They hugged, and she got into her car and left. As Renee drove down the street, she wondered aloud. "Am I dreaming, or did I just get picked up by a guy?" Renee sang every song on the radio until she drove into her garage. She was excited and scared at the same time about what had just happened. Renee had never had anyone hit on her at the grocery store and thought that stuff only happened in the movies or on television. It seemed a little romantic or creepy, depending on if you're a cup-half-full or half-empty type of person, but she decided that their chance of meeting was very romantic. Out of fear, a small part of her hoped that he'd never call, and the other part hoped he would. She knew he didn't check all her boxes on the surface, mainly because she could tell there was an age difference. But Renee decided that being a man was enough for now. It's been a long time since anyone showed interest, and she wanted to feel attractive and desired. Renee had to remind herself that her happiness was overdue, and if she didn't get out of the house, she might as well start collecting cats. She thought about all those years she had allowed herself to lie dormant and only exist without ever living. Her children were her excuse to hide from the world and not deal with relationships.

Renee never entertained the idea that she could meet someone who would accept her flaws. It was beginning to sink in that she wasted many years not pushing through and dealing with the hurt from previous relationships. Renee prided herself on being a strong, independent, single mother who could do whatever she set her mind to do. Still, Renee was also a hurt woman who pushed the pain endured throughout dating and from life deep down into her soul, where no one could ever uncover and use it against her. She ended the night writing in her new journal, and the last thing she wrote as a reminder was that tomorrow was another day, "and I smiled."

Renee woke up the next day with a smile. She was still thinking about her encounter at the store. She wanted so badly to call Jessica but decided to keep it to herself with all that Jessica was going through. She won't tell Kiana because she can hear her saying it now. "Mom, seriously?" It was fun to keep this a secret for now. Later that day, Gerald called, asking her out for drinks on Friday. After he asked where she wanted to go, she told him, "Sunset on the Beach," the one on the Causeway. He said that was one of his favorite spots. He suggested she wear something comfortable so that they could walk on the beach afterward. After she hung up, she told Alexa to play, "I Got a Feeling" by the Black-Eyed Peas and then she danced.

The Date

They decided to dine on the patio, looking toward the water. Renee thought the water could be the perfect place if there were any awkwardness or if they wanted to bask in the beauty of the sun setting for the evening if the date was going well. She loves being by the water and was glad that she suggested "Sunset on the Beach".

He mentioned during the date that he had two small children, a boy, and a girl. He said their names as a badge of honor; his daughter's name was Bey-a-Ce (pronounced Bay-a-Say), a twist on Beyonce's name, who happened to be La Shanique's favorite artist, and his son's name was Bugatti Veyron because Jay-Z owns one. All that Renee could think was how ghetto their names sounded. Finally, she realized she was wrong for thinking that and quietly told her inner self to calm down and stop judging. That was one of the reasons she didn't have anybody now. Renee smiled as he continued to speak, and when he smiled, so did her inner thighs. She was taken aback a little by her behavior. She had never experienced this sensation before and wasn't sure what to make of it. The only thing she was sure of was that it was becoming more robust as time progressed. After dinner, they took a stroll out on the beach and talked more. He grabbed her hand as they walked. It was a beautiful scene watching the sunset.

Something about the calmness of the water also calmed her down. She was able to focus on their date and not Gerald's manhood, which she couldn't help but notice. They ended the night with a hug, and Renee promised to call and tell him she had safely made it home. They continued to talk every day and sometimes more than once. It was the usual getting-to-know-you type of conversation. What is your favorite color, food, movie, or music…? Etc. Renee was surprised at how much they had in common. She could sense that their connection was strong and seemed to grow stronger each time they talked. Or maybe she was just breaking out of her shell and enjoying the moment? Whatever it was,

Renee planned to keep going until it ended. Days later, still feeling good about herself, she texted him asking if he wanted to come over for dinner that night.

Immediately after she hit send, she regretted it. What if Gerald was just being kind and really wasn't interested in her like that? Or maybe he just wanted sex? Sex wasn't a deal-breaker, Renee thought to herself. She was okay with just sex. After all, she needed to get her groove back. She dropped the phone after seeing his response. He responded with a yes, a heart, and a smiley emoji. She picked up her phone and started making plans. The first thing she did was make an appointment for a Brazilian bikini wax, just in case. Then she went grocery shopping for a nice dinner and two bottles of wine.

Dinner was set for 8:00 p.m. to give Renee time to get things together, and by the time dinner was done and she had showered and put on a cute outfit, he was ringing her doorbell. When Renee opened the door, she saw this 6'2 chocolate man with deep dimples and lips that would give her imagination a run for its money. She asked him to come in, and as he walked inside, he hugged her and said, "You look beautiful tonight." She stumbled over her words but managed to say thank you, like a shy schoolgirl. Before they released their hugs, she inhaled his scent, closed her eyes, and smiled. Renee asked him if he would like a drink before dinner, and Gerald asked what was on the menu; and she mentioned that she had Moscato wine, whiskey, and other non-alcoholic beverages.

He passed on the wine and settled on a glass of whiskey neat as the drink for the evening. As he sipped his drink, he complimented her on a smooth whiskey and thought how well his favorite cigar would pair well with this drink. They talked during dinner as if they had known each other for years. They laughed and joked about how Alexa was answering their questions. Then he asked Alexa to play "Spend the Night" by the Isley Brothers. Renee looked at him, smiled, and said, "What do you know about the Isley Brothers? You were a child back then."

He smiled and said, "Yes, I was ten years old, and that would make you twenty-eight years old at the time?"

"Yes, I am eighteen years older than you," she said with a concerned tone. He grabbed her hand and asked her to dance, pulling her close to him; he whispered into her ear, "I am a grown-ass man now, and that is all that matters."

They danced slowly, and she loosened up as he softly sang to her. He tightened his grip around her waist, and she could feel things stirring between her legs; before she could push him back, their eyes met as he gently kissed her. The longer the kiss, the more intense it became. Before she knew it, he was touching her in places that would be a dead giveaway that she was ripe for the picking. She no longer cared that she hadn't had sex in years. Tonight, she was throwing caution and that old-school teaching of waiting before having sex out of the window. She was not trying to marry him; she saw this as practice for her one-day husband. She did not want to be gullible or naïve when she seriously started to date. After a few moans and heavy breathing, she grabbed his member, which she was pleasantly surprised and equally afraid of at the same time. He whispered for them to go to her bedroom, and she paused and told him that she hadn't had sex in years. He stopped and looked at her, asking her how many years; she said ten years. He kissed her forehead and said, "I'll be gentle. I promise."

As they walked to her bedroom, she felt like a nervous teenager having sex for the first time. It was that same feeling she had when she and Moses made love and how scary it was because she didn't know what to expect. This time she knew what to expect as far as the act of intercourse, but the size of Gerald's member made her feel like she wasn't ready. Because it had been years since Renee was intimate, she also felt self-conscious about her weight. Renee's anxiety slightly heightened when Gerald wanted to have the lights on to see her beauty, and she preferred them to be off to hide her imperfections. Finally, she gave in and allowed the lights to stay on.

He began kissing her feet; Renee enjoyed how sensual his kissing made her feel. As time progressed, he moved towards her middle, where he took his time cultivating a relationship between his lips and hers. As she moaned, she smiled, mouthing the words, "Thank you, Jesus." His gentleness and attention to her body were so that she couldn't help but explode. He never missed a beat as he inhaled her delicious treat. He stayed there for what seemed like forever, and she was sure that at this point, she had drowned him. As she was about to tell him to stop, he slowly moved toward her stomach. He kissed it as if she had a six-pack instead of a very large rounded belly.

At that point, she felt her sexiest, and from that moment on, she relaxed and enjoyed the moment. As they made love, he hit every spot as if she had drawn him a map, and by the time they finished, she was out of breath and parched. The last time she was that thirsty, Renee had given birth. Finally, she and Gerald were both tapped out, and the only energy remaining was to kiss each other good night. As she closed her eyes, her treasure gave small shockwaves applauding her for giving it life again.

Being the early bird she is, Renee woke up and suddenly remembered what had happened last night. She eased out of bed and turned the water on in her walk-in shower; it was huge and one of her favorite places in the house. A chocolate body walked in, smiling as she began to wash up.

He walked towards her, grabbed her towel, and slowly moved it across her back. There was a second washcloth available, not because Renee anticipated Gerald taking a shower with her, but because she grabbed two by accident. They each took a turn washing one another, and as Gerald went in for a kiss, she held her hand to her mouth, shaking her head and gesturing no. He understood and looked for a remedy; that was when he saw her mouthwash on the sink. He grabbed it.

They both took a swig, rinsed, and spit it into the drain. His kiss was just as passionate as the night before, and she was grateful for the seat and the bar in the shower because she ended up using them both. She took control of his body, and just like that, she was giving him what he had given to her last night. She smiled at the noise he made after she pleased him to the point of ejaculation. It was the first time she had sex in her shower other than what she usually did to herself. After they finished, they washed and got dressed. He had to leave to go pick up his children from his mom. Renee let him out the front door and went to make some much-needed coffee. Surprisingly, Renee saw that her phone still has a 10 percent battery life after grabbing her phone, she was sure it was dead, but she was at ten percent with ten missed calls and fifteen text messages. She plugged up her phone and began looking at who had called her; there were several misses from Jessica and her daughter, and the last one was from Carlos, her trainer. Renee forgot about her Saturday morning session. She started reading her text messages when Jessica called.

"Bitch, why didn't you answer my calls? Jessica screamed.

"Bitch?" Renee responded. "Now you're my girl and all, but you know how I feel about being called a bitch," she spoke, annoyed.

"I'm sorry, I was just worried. You always answer my calls and texts, and when you didn't respond, I reached out to your daughter," Jessica said in a worried voice.

"What?" You called Kiana and got her worried? Renee sternly asked.

"Why are you acting like this, Renee? You are always available," Jessica said, feeling annoyed.

"I had a date last night that ended a few minutes ago," Renee mumbled under her breath.

Her phone started ringing, and it was Jessica, who was now trying to FaceTime her.

"Did you say you had a date last night that ended a few minutes ago?" Jessica shrilled.

"Yes. I had a date that just ended, and yes, you can stop trying to figure out how to ask if I had sex. It was explosive, and I didn't care if I looked like a slut. I needed every bit of what I received last night and this morning," Renee said with the biggest smile that she had in a long time.

Jessica was happy for her friend who finally got laid, and maybe now she would be a little nicer to Monique, which was why she was trying to call her last night.

"I want to hear all about your slutfest, but I need to talk to you about Monique," Jessica said, speaking slowly.

"Because I'm on such a high," Renee said, "we can talk, and I won't even be bothered that you dismissed the biggest sexual night of my life. So, what is going on with Monique now?"

Jessica told Renee that she was going to call her to free her hands. Which was a lie, she knew that what she was about to tell Renee would devastate her and Renee wouldn't want her to witness the emotions that she would display. The ladies hung up their FaceTime, and Jessica called Renee back.

"Monique called me last night drunk and told me things that you and I had suspected were the truth" Jessica whispered. There was a pause as Renee waited for the rest of the story. "Hello, hello, Renee, can you hear me?" Renee responded.

"Yes, Jessica, I can hear you. Why are you whispering? What else did Monique tell you?"

"I'm just going to say it because there is no good way to tell you," Jessica said more seriously.

"Please just say it and get it over with, so I can deal with whatever she said," Renee responded, annoyed.

"Monique told me that CJ is Byron's son. You know, our Moses?" Jessica said in a nervous tone. There was dead silence. "Renee? Renee? That bitch hung up on me," Jessica said out loud. She tried to call Renee back, but it went straight to voicemail. "Now she isn't answering her phone," Jessica said aloud in astonishment.

Renee couldn't believe what she had just heard. Her heart sunk deep into her stomach, and she couldn't breathe. The sounds coming from her mouth were howling and piercing as Renee cried and thought about what she considered the ultimate betrayal. For the rest of the day, she didn't want to communicate with anyone as she lay in bed. Finally, as Renee drifted to sleep, she whispered, "I hope that bitch loses everything she loves."

The next day, Renee woke up feeling like she was suffering from a hangover but without ever having a drink. As she again processed the information Jessica had given her last night, tears rolled down her face. Renee hoped she and Moses would reconnect during their high school reunion, but now there was no way she would ever entertain thoughts or hope of rekindling what they once shared years ago. Renee had to finally accept that she could no longer hold on to those many years of hope that they could pick up where they left off in high school. Holding on to someone who hasn't shown interest in years was crazy, and some would argue sad and desperate. Now that she had time to take off her rose-colored glasses and step into reality, Renee could see from their point of view and agree.

For now, Renee decided to enjoy the sensual nature of her and Gerald's relationship; after all, this was precisely what the doctor ordered. He was a tall, chocolate, handsome man who knows his way around a woman's body. He was the best of both worlds. She needed something or someone who could take her mind off Moses without fear of being hurt by it or him. Gerald was that distraction. She texted Jessica to apologize for hanging up on her and explained that it was too difficult to process then. Renee assured Jessica that everything was good. Now that Renee had a moment of clarity, she was ready to move on with her life. Renee was over the fantasy she developed all those years of her and Moses' unadulterated love; it was time to move on.

Renee was more determined than ever to focus on what she wanted without stopping or apologizing to anyone for whom she didn't have time. Finally, she decided she was no longer hurt, a past victim, or angry; she was a survivor, a boss, no, a beast! Renee convinced herself. One day of crying was over, and she was back on track. Renee continued working out, eating healthy, and feeling great. She was still seeing Gerald, and it was fun right now, and without drama, since neither of them was looking for a long-term relationship. Instead, they both needed someone on the same page to be friends with benefits.

Renee asked Jessica to never bring Monique or Moses up in her presence. She never wanted to hear their names nor cared about what was happening in Monique's life. Jessica, being the friend she was, agreed verbally – but with her finger crossed behind her back. She wouldn't talk to Renee about Monique or Moses right now. Jessica understood that Renee needed to heal; the only way to heal was to move on completely. During Monique's drunk call to Jessica, Monique also mentioned how hurt she was that Renee hadn't reached out to her when her dad passed. Of the three women, Jessica understood each of her best friends' pain, and she knew if they could let the past go and just talk, they would find their way back to a beautiful friendship. Well, that was what Jessica thought until the truth about CJ's biological father came out.

Jessica had to tell Monique about her drunk call to her, confessing that it was Moses and not Chris Sr., who was CJ's biological father. Jessica admitted that she told Renee about the call because she knew how Renee still felt about Moses at the time. To say that Monique was livid was an understatement, losing all the refinement that had been developed over the years as her hood persona swept in like a category-five hurricane.

When Monique cursed Jessica out, there was a pause giving Jessica time to recompose herself, then she spoke quietly and sternly. "Now, I understand you are upset with me for telling Renee your secret, but you should have thought about it before calling me, drunk. I've been a great friend to you since childhood, and as much as you are upset, I don't deserve this, and you know what? You wanted me to tell Renee deep down, so you didn't have to face her. And you knew that I wasn't going to let my girl be out here still crushing on Moses, who knocked your bitch ass up." Jessica was heated, and the more she talked, the angrier and louder she became, and the more hood that came out of her mouth. But she no longer cared. Finally, Jessica managed to calm herself down and explained that Renee never wanted to see her again. Jessica concluded her conversation with Monique by acknowledging that she didn't blame Renee for how she felt about her and then wished Monique good luck with her problems. Jessica hung up.

It felt good to go off and let out some frustration, but at the same time, Jessica felt bad for how she left things with Monique. Jessica wanted to call back to apologize, but she stood her ground. She was the one that always gave in and made up with these ladies, and they both knew it, but not today.

Monique Harris

A chocolate beauty who stood 5'7 with a curvaceous body, thick lips, and naturally long eyelashes; Her hair was long too but she preferred wearing wigs and weaves to match her moods. Her smooth dark skin was flawless, but unfortunately, Monique Harris didn't see her exquisite beauty; she saw ugliness.

Monique was the typical girl-from-the-hood success story. She married someone whose family came from wealth and prestige, but she was a force in her own right.

Monique's mantra was, "If I want it, I'm going to take it," and it didn't matter whose neck she had to stand on to get it. With her intelligence and charisma, Monique knew how to work each of her blessings to her advantage and hide her insecurities.

Those feelings started in Monique's childhood days when the kids would call her monkey and joke about her dark skin. She refused to play outside at night because the boys would say they couldn't find her unless she smiled. The main reason Monique stayed inside at night was because of Richard Palmer, her childhood nemesis. He would joke around with the other neighborhood kids, shouting "Monique, Monique, her skin is

so unique; she's black as the night when the moon is shining bright."
Her family innocently aided her insecurities when they affectionately
called her Pepper because she was "dark and spicey". Monique hated her
nickname and would scowl at anyone who would dare to use it. She
worked harder than everyone because she wanted most to leave the person
she'd become known as back in Rockford, IL., and become the woman
she always dreamt of being. She took her first step by attending a college
867 miles away on a scholarship. Monique wasn't interested in going to
HBCU. For her, attending a college that she knew would take her into the
world that she so desperately wanted to become a part of as a child was
essential.

While a freshman at this prestigious college in North Carolina,
Monique met a sophomore named Christopher Harris; his family and
friends called him Chris. His family was prominent in Charlotte, North
Carolina, and politics ran in their blood. Of course, success was in their
bloodline, and there was no indication that it would ever end. Chris
was the exception; he wasn't interested in building a career in politics.
Instead, he wanted to help his people, so he went to law school, where
he graduated summa cum laude and worked in the public defender's
office in Charlotte, North Carolina. When Monique and Chris first met,
Chris had a longtime girlfriend back home. He eventually terminated his
relationship with Claudia, whom he had dated for five years, and began
to date Monique.

Monique had already researched Christopher Harris and his distinguished family. She was impressed with the long lineage that he came
from, and she could smell old money. "He looked like money," Monique
always said, and status was her desire. Their relationship grew, and she was
on his arm at every family event he was expected to attend. The men in the
family loved her and doted on her. But the women, especially his mother,
weren't so impressed with Monique, and the sister-in-law clearly looked

down on her. The mother was manipulative and determined to rid her son of the girl from the hood and reconnect him to her best friend's daughter, Claudia Thurgood-Moore. All the women belonged to the same social circles, and they didn't like outsiders who lacked the same social standing. So, Monique had to deal with a jealous ex-girlfriend at these events, and Claudia never missed a chance to outshine her by proving that Monique had nothing to offer Chris besides what was between her legs. During one of Claudia's moments of trying to embarrass Monique, she gleefully expressed to other socialites that had she known Monique was one of the recipients of their family's scholarship, she would have asked her father to be a bit more generous.

After all, their family's purpose was to help the poor and under-privileged. That statement received a few chuckles until Monique fired back by thanking her for the scholarship because had it not been for her family, she would never have met the most exciting and handsome man at the college. Monique went on to say that rumor has it that Chris had a girlfriend, but once he laid eyes on "this beautiful, intelligent woman," he quickly dumped his pretentious girlfriend, who had bitten him when she was down on her knees, providing fellatio. She knew she shouldn't have let on that Chris had told her about their sex life, but now she and Claudia understood each other especially since her clap back received a more significant response of laughter, causing Claudia to retreat to her corner.

Monique walked gracefully towards Chris, where she gently kissed him on his cheek, and he grabbed her hand and held it until his group disbanded. That was when Monique showed the women, especially his mother, that she wasn't some little girl in the hood anymore; she was a force to be reckoned with, and Monique wasn't holding back, nor was she going anywhere anytime soon.

Monique knew that Chris was falling in love with her and that she didn't share the same feelings. There was only one man whom she had ever been in love with, and there were times that she regretted breaking up with him. Byron "Moses" Banks. Thinking about Moses brought up a lot of memories and feelings. Her last fond memory was her betrayal of Renee. Monique knew that Renee never got over what she had done, and she knew that deep down, Renee would never trust her again. Monique understood that her relationship with Renee barely existed and was hanging by a red-headed thread named Jessica. At least it was until last night.

She was still trying to wrap her brain around how Jessica spoke to her. Monique couldn't deny anything that Jessica had said last night. She was a horrible friend to Jessica and especially to Renee. Monique cringed at the thought of how deeply hurt Renee must be feeling, learning the truth about CJ's biological father. After so many years had passed since her first betrayal of Renee when she slept with Moses and eventually dated him. Monique and Renee had gotten to a better place. They had been able to go on a few girls' trips that Jessica was insistent about and acted like friends on the mend.

The feelings of betrayal Renee felt were like what Monique experienced with Chris. Monique's senior year in college got complicated when she discovered him in bed with his former girlfriend, Claudia. Chris had lied and said that he had to study. Monique decided that since Chris was deep into his studying, she would cook dinner and deliver it to his apartment, along with dessert. Once Monique was in Chris' apartment, she could hear two voices in his bedroom. Her heart sank at the thought she was about to catch her boyfriend in bed with another woman.

As Monique walked closer to the bedroom, the woman's voice became familiar; that was when a piece of her died because she realized that the voice was Claudia's. Seeing Chris in bed with her and having sex was devastating and humiliating. She had dropped the food on the floor while asking what he was doing. The smirk on Claudia's face enraged Monique, causing her to react by running towards the bed and grabbing a handful of hair as she pulled Claudia out of bed, naked. Chris broke up the fight and told Monique to leave. He saw that he had hurt her and immediately regretted his actions with Claudia. At that moment, Monique realized that she was in love with Chris and obviously more than he had loved her. Feeling heartbroken, Monique immediately understood the devastating feeling and betrayal Renee felt in high school. Monique decided to go home for a few days to clear her head.

Once she was back in the city where she grew up, Monique bumped into a familiar face that she hadn't seen since high school, Moses. Monique had heard of his father's passing and wondered if she would run into him. He was staying at one of the new downtown hotels that had just been built a year earlier. Moses didn't want to stay at his parents' house since other family members were all staying with his mom to give her comfort and help with the funeral arrangements. He didn't feel like being around the family and having to explain why he never married. Monique and Moses both had a little sadness in their eyes and a sense of loss in their body language. Moses asked if she wanted to meet later in the evening for dinner and to catch up. He was running late picking up his mom to take her to the funeral home for a private viewing.

Monique knew from the moment she laid eyes on Moses that she would be in his arms later that night. She convinced herself that it was vital for her to know if she loved Chris or just his lifestyle. After eating dinner at Franchesco's Ristorante, Moses invited Monique to his hotel so that they could sit on the rooftop and continue catching up. Monique agreed. They never made it to the rooftop; she found comfort in the arms of a man who always had her heart. Their passion was intense, the kind that gave a false positive of being in love. That kind of sexual experience sometimes makes a man or woman insane. Many will say it's that "good dick or kitty" that will turn people out and make them do things they wouldn't ordinarily do. Everyone, if they're honest, has had at least one experience that caused them to go crazy over Moses moving inside and around Monique's body was like imagining wrestling between a man and a woman but as a ballet. The movements were graceful and powerful at the right time; they were soft and delicate when required. By the end of the ballet, and the curtains closed, their body vibrations were as if the audience were clapping and shouting, "Bravo, bravo."

When a person experiences such a performance, it's not easy to bypass the opportunity, and if Renee had that same experience, Monique now understood why Renee refused to let Moses go. That one night with Moses was beautiful, but Monique knew with certainty that it was Chris who had her heart. Yet their brief encounter changed the rest of their lives forever. Monique returned to school, and Chris had been waiting for her; he looked miserable. He approached her as she walked toward her dorm, asking if they could talk. She agreed, and Chris followed her to her dorm room. He explained that his mother had interfered in his relationship and trying to please her only caused him sadness because Monique was the only woman he wanted in his life. He asked her to marry him. She, of course, said yes, and they made love. Six weeks after they reconciled, Monique realized that she hadn't gotten her period. She dropped everything and drove to the nearest drugstore to buy a pregnancy test; in fact, she purchased five just to be sure. The directions read to wait until the morning, but the thought of waiting was unbearable. Monique came out of her bathroom with her mouth wide open because it didn't take a minute to announce that she was pregnant; the test results responded in a matter of seconds. She would be excited if it weren't for one thing: she wasn't sure who the father was, Chris or Moses. She knew that Chris would do the right thing, so she never told Moses that he could become a father.

Once Chris' mother found out about her pregnancy and that Chris was the father, she made them get married before she had to explain a bastard child. "CJ" was born seven months later. Monique was only twenty-two years old. When CJ was a newborn, she had a paternity test done on Moses' hairbrush that she accidentally grabbed rushing out of his hotel room. Once Monique confirmed her pregnancy, she grabbed the hairbrush still in her suitcase and put it in a Ziploc bag to protect his DNA. Monique disguised herself under an alias name, Renee Morgan. So, if it was Moses' baby, it wouldn't be that big of a leap for people to accept that Renee and Moses had a child together. She had to keep paternity a secret because it would ruin her life with Chris and tarnish her new influential and wealthy family's name.

Monique had planned on taking the truth about CJ to her grave. That was until she drunk called Jessica and told her everything. Monique's life was slowly unraveling in front of her eyes, and there was nothing to stop it. The two women whom she loved weren't speaking to her. Someone was blackmailing her, and neither her husband nor their son knew the truth, nor did Moses. If any of this got out, Monique would lose everything and everyone. Regardless of how Jessica and Renee may feel about her, they were the only two people she knew would have her back. "It will be a tough road and a hard pill to swallow asking for their help," she mumbled to herself. She wasn't worried about Jessica because that was who she was, a ride-or-die friend, no matter what. She'd cuss you out, but in the end, she would be right there, standing tall with you.

A tear fell down Monique's face because she realized that from the beginning, she was never really a friend to them; she didn't have the same closeness they shared. Jessica had never spent weeks with her and her family as she did with Renee. She used to tell herself that Jessica was doing it out of pity for Renee, but just now, she realized that those two enjoyed a true sisterhood, and she was just the other friend they tolerated.

Monique was interrupted in her thoughts by an unknown caller that she let go to voicemail. It was time to start her day, so she turned on her shower and her music and stayed for what seemed like hours in the hot, steaming shower. Her soul felt heavy since her brother-in-law Mark announced he was running for Governor of North Carolina during one of their family dinners. Chris asked him about the process and how long it would be before they completed the vetting. They were waiting for some information that may be a concern. Chris seemed a bit upset and stated that he should have given us a heads-up that people were digging into their trash to find out about them. Monique wondered why her husband was getting upset; what did he have to hide? Monique wondered if the concern was about her secret. She reassured herself that she and she alone knew the truth, and if they went digging, they would find out that Renee Morgan, her childhood friend, took a paternity test and not her. Monique wanted to tell Jessica many times, but this would've ended all their relationships, and right now, Monique and Renee weren't on the best terms. To be honest, if it weren't for Jessica, they wouldn't have had a relationship at all. Before they all went their separate ways, Monique's sister-in-law Stacy pulled her aside and asked if everything was okay. She mentioned that Monique seemed quiet after Mark explained that he had someone to investigate everyone's past. She hated Stacy, who happened to be that one family member that always tried to one-up you in everything. Her sister-in-law's smirk made her uncomfortable like she knew something and was dying to tell the world. Stacy looked at Monique, and before walking away, said she was thinking about what would crawl out of Monique's hood rat past that may cause her husband to give up his dream of being governor.

After her shower, Monique picked up her cell phone to call Jessica when she noticed a voicemail message. After listening to the voicemail message, Monique could feel the blood draining from her face. The person who left the voicemail message was the unknown caller and there was no way to trace the phone number. The voicemail was a quote from a bible scripture; Exodus 2:10. "The baby grew, and after some time, the woman gave the baby to the king's daughter. The king's daughter accepted the baby as her son. She named him Moses."

Monique started to delete the message but thought she had better keep it, so she placed it in a folder for safekeeping. Monique cringed at what Chris' parents would think if they found out about her secret. She already knew what Mark and Stacy would say and do; it wouldn't take a genius to figure that out. Stacy never hesitated to find a reason to have their father-in-law favor her husband, Mark, and not Chris. It was well known that both Mark and Stacy felt that Chris shouldn't be the "chosen one" in their father's eyes.

After all, Mark, being the eldest, was the one that was walking in his father's footsteps, while Chris wasn't interested in preserving their conservative legacy. It always felt like they were always in some competition. One of the family's traditions was getting into politics after making partners at the family's firm, which wasn't difficult. Chris and Mark were the heirs to the family firm, so, naturally, they would end up as partners. When you think about it, it was a nice setup. The hardest part would be to get into law school and then pass the bar. Chris passed the bar on his first attempt, but Mark had to take the exam three times.

Law school came easier for Chris than it had for his older brother, Mark. Chris didn't have to study as hard, and that was partly where the competition came in. The other part came from their dad, the Honorable Judge, Theodore Harris, or "Judge", the name that friends and family called him. Judge was the nickname his wife, Cora Jean Harris, had affectionately called him since he obtained a seat on the bench over thirty years ago. Theodore Harris followed in his father's footsteps and groomed his sons to follow in his. Neither Chris nor Mark wanted to become a lawyer or get into politics; they both wanted quite different lives. However, they both relinquished their dreams and followed the family legacy. Chris once confessed to Monique that he wanted to be a history teacher. She was glad he changed his mind, she thought to herself, because they wouldn't have been married." But Chris loved history and wanted to teach children how the past affects the future and how it had shaped our country, especially African American history.

Being the youngest child came with certain expectations, following in the same footsteps as his older brother and the rest of the Harris men. That meant Chris would go to law school after college, marry his longtime girlfriend Claudia, and join the family's firm, "The Law Firm of Harris Esquire", and in that order.

Well, Monique thought, her husband managed to meet one of the three family's expectations. She sometimes wondered if her husband pursued her because he would be defying his parents, marrying the poor black girl whose only family legacy, at least in his mother's eyes, was living in the hood. His mother still said to this day that if Monique had not gotten pregnant with CJ while Chris was in law school, he wouldn't have asked her to marry him. Although everyone, including his mother, knew that Chris proposed before they knew Monique was pregnant.

Breakable Bond

Jessica was fuming, and as she poured herself a glass of red wine, Renee called to formally apologize for her behavior. Before answering the call, Jessica took a long drag off her cigarette, then slowly exhaled as she replied with a "bitch I'm not in the mood" tone. "Hello?"

Renee responded with slight irritation, "What took you so long?"

"I don't sit around waiting for you to call; hell, I was busy, Renee," Jessica said, still feeling angry from her conversation with Monique.

Renee could tell that Jessica was angry, but she didn't know why. Just as Renee was about to ask what was going on, she could hear Jessica exhale.

"Please tell me that you aren't smoking, Jessica? You were doing so well. What happened? It wasn't me, was it? Please tell me that you and Richard aren't fighting again?" Renee said in her concerned voice.

"Yes, I know, no, it isn't you; hell no, and that mother fucker better not let me see his dirty ass." Jessica spewed smoke-filled responses from her second drag, trying to calm herself down.

"I just went off on Monique, and it wasn't pretty. She was angry that I told you about Moses being her son's biological father. She started going off on me, you know, cursing and yelling. It was too much, so I called her on her bullshit. At first, I was calm, but the more I spoke, the more I had begun to think about how she played me all these years and the angrier I became," Jessica spoke with regret in her voice.

"Why do you sound like you wished you didn't go off on her? I know good and damn well; you better not have any issues with what transpired. Let's do a recap of what occurred these past few days. She called you while drunk and told you something so damaging about her past and something so hurtful to me, and yet she expected you not to tell me? You and I both know how Monique operates. She knew spilling the tea on herself in a drunken state of mind would give her some deniability.

She also knew that she could never come to me to tell me like a real woman, so she played you by telling you, knowing full well that you would, in turn, as a true friend, tell me. You would have to deal with the fallout as the messenger of the tea, and because of our relationship, she knew I wouldn't be upset with you, but you would get the verbal abuse she wants to avoid. Sound about right, Jessica?" Renee sternly asked.

A few minutes of silence passed before Jessica confirmed all that Renee had said. Renee wanted to say more, but she already knew that her friend was feeling sad about the whole thing. Fortunately, Renee thought to herself, this mess will not fall on their laps; it shall remain with the bitch that orchestrated this entire thing, Monique!

During her conversation with Jessica, Renee began to think how much she struggled with the thought of reaching out to Monique. As she continued to grow into her own identity, the one thing that she had to come to terms with was being her authentic self. If Renee was going, to be honest, she hated Monique with every fiber of her being, she only tolerated this kumbaya shit for Jessica and was suffocating in the travesty they called friendship. Renee decided that she wasn't going to be a part of their life-long friendship because it died in high school. It was going to break Jessica's heart, who had struggled to keep the trio together, but it was something that must be said. She could faintly hear Jessica in the background, disturbing her deep thoughts, and now Renee became more alert when she heard Jessica ask who she was fucking the night she and Kiana tried to call her. Renee's thoughts came to a screeching halt.

"Excuse me?" Renee said in a whisper.

"Nope, we aren't going to do that, my friend. I know that you thought that dealing with this Monique crap I would forget that you told me that you met some random guy and fucked him, or did he fuck you?" Jessica laughed.

It was an excellent way to deflect from their conversation about Monique, which Renee decided to put on the back burner for now. But that was only because she was eager to discuss her long-awaited sexual bliss, extinguishing her ten-year drought (not counting her sexual toys). Renee replied in an annoyed tone, "Do you always have to cuss to describe things? Why can't you say making love or coitus?" Renee asked.

"Bitch… oops, I meant girl, you haven't had sex in ten freaking years, and the proper definition to describe what transpired in your home that night with a man you barely knew would be fucking, pure and simple. By the way, no judgment here, girl; I'm just keeping it real, you know, one hundred percent real. Now, unless he wasn't any good, you could call it coitus, but when did you stop cursing? Please, let me ask which Renee I am talking to, the holy Renee who made love, the professional Renee who encountered coitus, or my homegirl, Renee, who fucked? In my opinion, I'm speaking with my home girl Renee who got fucked!" Jessica burst into laughter.

Renee burst into laughter before she conceded. Jessica could hear her smiling through the phone as she began to tell how they met and how long they had been talking. Jessica interrupted and asked: "How was it? You know, did you feel like a virgin again? You've been without for ten years, and then there's menopause? You know that our asses are going through menopause, and as an RN, I know little about the human body and its workings. So, don't act brand new. Did you need to use you know what?"

Renee chuckled, knowing Jessica was dead serious about her question. As she began to explain, she thought how embarrassed she would have been to clarify if it was anyone other than Jessica. Renee explained that her GYN told her to use vibrators to keep the walls of her treasure lubricated since Renee wasn't sexually active. She explained that she headed down to her local sex store one day and purchased a few toys after asking the salesperson a lot of questions.

Once home, Renee decided she wanted to have fun with her new toys, so she named them after a few of her fantasies. First, Malcolm has a coco-brown complexion and a chiseled physique. His voice had a rough tone, and he spoke with a commanding voice that could buckle a woman's knees. Second, Malcolm was also the sexy nine-inch G-Spot who would, in time, give Renee some of the biggest orgasms she had experienced. She would take her time to allow Malcolm to find that magical spot of hers that, once stroked, would give her the pleasurable delight she craved.

Then there was Moses, a man who needed no introduction or description and had been her primary fantasy since high school. He was the Jack Rabbit who fulfilled in Renee's mind a taste of what it would be like if she and Moses ever made love as adults. Renee's toy Moses was the type that you want to go slow and smooth into the groove, then right into the fast and freaky, leading to a liquid explosion that required a towel before the entertainment. Moses almost seemed as knowledgeable as a real man would be about the inside and outside of a woman's body; how and at any given moment to maneuver around her hidden jewels and her treasures, allowing her to enjoy multiple orgasms until her body would go limp and sleep was her only option. The next purchase was strictly for the clitoral, the one and only Rose, an oral sex simulator. That worked well when Renee was in the mood for just the pleasure of a man's tongue when she didn't have a specific person to fantasize about.

"You have three vibrators?" Jessica asked in amazement.

With a smile on her face, Renee responded, "Yes. I'm having fun while learning what my body likes in different positions and fantasies. I love every minute of it, and I make no apologies for physically loving myself.

"OMG… You are a FREAK!!! I love you even more," Jessica said.

They both laughed for what seemed like five minutes.

"To answer your question, thanks to my doctor's suggestion and extensive research on sex toys, I was well self-lubricated, but I still used lubrication to enhance the process," Renee said proudly.

She continued to disclose her romantic escapades and how happy Gerald made her feel. They ended their conversation with Jessica telling her how proud she was for coming out of that hermit shell. They said their goodbyes, and after all that talk, Renee decided it was time to take a nice long bubble bath and bring Malcolm with her. Afterward, she quickly showered and crawled into her empty bed, sexually satisfied but saddened by the emptiness on the other side. "A sex toy can't hold, cuddle, or spoon afterward," Renee thought.

She admitted she hadn't felt so alive, vibrant, and out of her comfort zone, in years. It was good to experience a man's touch, his breath on her skin, his eyes locked into hers, and their bodies in sync without any words needing to be said. She was aware that Gerald was that proverbial bicycle, and indeed sex was like riding a bike again after all these years, but far more fun. Being in an intimate relationship had given her the freedom to become spontaneous.

The other night just out of the blue, she took a picture of herself caressing one of her breasts as she touched her nipple and texted it to Gerald. He didn't respond right away; in fact, he never responded to her text. Thirty minutes later, she heard a knock at the door, and the moment she opened the door, Gerald grabbed her face and started passionately kissing her. He slammed the door shut with his foot as he picked her up and threw her over his shoulder, carrying her to her bed. Their lovemaking became soulful, and each movement he made was intentional. He caressed every inch of her body, and she returned the favor. She was floating above the clouds and beginning to love the woman she was becoming.

Renee's confidence stood firm, not because some young man paid attention to her (although it didn't hurt), but because she now believed in herself. Renee was a part of black girl magic because she now saw her flaws as strength, her beauty inside and out, and her intelligence as a weapon, not a curse; she realized Renee Morgan was overall, a woman of worth. But this was just the beginning; her amazing physical transformation would help her believe that she could move on with life, releasing some dream that one day she and Moses would be together again. She wasn't interested in having a long-term relationship with Gerald.

As a young father of two, his current situation was more than Renee wanted to handle long-term. She was looking for someone like her, an empty nester. She could entertain someone whose character resembles Gerald, a kind, honest, funny, holding-his-own financially, sexually stim-ulating man, but with no children – or at least adult children. Renee was finding who she wanted to be at her age, and motherhood was not on her vision board. She wanted to travel and have fun. Other than a job, she didn't want obligations. The relationship with Gerald was one of a mutual agreement, so Renee didn't feel like either was using the other. It was the best sex she had had in years, and she wasn't ready for that to end. It was funny because the old Renee would have told the new Renee that she would get hurt and that she couldn't have sex without falling in love or having some emotional ties with their partner. That was still her belief, but at that moment in time, she didn't care. She wasn't looking for love, just lust, in the sluttiest way possible. Renee, in return, would have told her old self to lighten up; life is too short to worry about falling in love or having emotional ties and just relaxing. She liked him enough to give herself to him in the most intimate way, but not before being completely honest about what she wanted and expected.

Gerald didn't disappoint at all. Although they didn't start as friends, their relationship developed into an honest friendship. When he told her about his dates, the only rule was if they were to have sex with someone else, they would have to inform the other before they became intimate again, making it possible to decide if they wanted to continue – even if protection was used. It wasn't long before they decided that they couldn't imagine better sex with anyone else because they were a match regarding intimacy compatibility. He fit like a glove inside and around her body, and she remembered him telling her the warmth and wetness he felt inside her was the best he had ever experienced.

They were so in sync with how they moved with each other, they created a beautiful dance. He knew her body, her G-spot, every curve, how many kisses it took to make her explode, filling his cup until he was full. She was just as attentive to his body. She also knew what spots to stimulate to get him going and which one to make him finish. She knew his member, how it curved inside her, hitting her G-spot just right, how it responded to her hand, her tongue, and inside of her in every way imaginable. She knew how many kisses it took for him to explode, filling her cup until she was full. It wasn't simply great sex between them; there was an unspoken romance. He knew how much in love she was with Moses, and even if he had wanted more in their relationship, he knew that he couldn't compete with a dream from the past. Eventually, they started hanging out, and working out together when she wasn't with Carlos.

After Jessica ended her conversation with Renee, she was happy for her friend but felt sad personally. Her marriage had ended, and not on a good note. She didn't have any children to focus on, and no young man paying her any attention. For years it was she and Monique living a happy married life. Although they both were living a lie in their marriages, they at least had someone to go home to at night. After all, isn't that every girl's dream? Meet a man, fall in love, marry, and have children together. Unfortunately, the values they grew up on were fading away fast. Women chase the men, and the men do not seek serious commitment.

A single woman with "old school values" doesn't stand a chance in this world. They can do everything society deems proper. Maybe if they did what this famous guy said in his books on how women should think and act in dating, they would have more success. Maybe their pastor was correct that not everyone was going to be married. Why did God give everyone the tools and the emotions to love and explore their sexuality if some men and women weren't meant to have a spouse? If that is the case, why was premarital sex, better known biblically as fornication, a sin?

Jessica was feeling the loneliness and pain of going through a divorce. She managed to keep herself busy by working and hanging out with co-workers and her mom. Those things helped keep her mind off going to an empty home where she created memories of her childhood love and now sworn enemy. Where did they go so wrong? Was not having children really the deal-breaker? They both agreed to sell the house and that she wouldn't smoke inside again. Richard paid to have the entire house repainted, and fixed up, removed all the carpets, and replaced them with new carpets. Jessica agreed to get rid of every stitch of furniture that reeked of stale cigarettes, which was pretty much everything. By the time she had removed all the tables, the house looked and felt empty.

The divorce process became petty, with unnecessary and stupid requests from both sides. Richard wanted all her plants, just to piss her off. Jessica requested his golf balls because those were the only balls he had to offer. Finally, the judge had enough and required them to sell the house and everything inside through a garage sale. The proceeds from the garage sale would go to help aid a homeless shelter. They both protested and suggested they could do better, but it was too late. The judge's gavel slammed down and ordered them both to work together. If either of them didn't show up or fought throughout the process, they would be held in contempt and forfeit their ownership. A court-appointed mediator would be there to oversee the garage sale. They had to decide on the time and date for the sale and make the preparations. Any changes would have to be approved by the mediator. Since they couldn't fight, they had no choice but to speak to each other civilly, like it or not, and neither of them did. They managed to talk to each other throughout the process, and they laughed a few times.

Richard apologized for how he delivered the announcement that he wanted a divorce. He said that he didn't think things through. Richard explained how spending one more night under the same roof as husband and wife wouldn't have made a difference. Jessica calmly told him how much he hurt her in so many ways. The most pain came from not having a child. Jessica explained to him that she wanted to be a mother and that it felt like she couldn't breathe, and spending time with Renee and her kids allowed her to feel alive again. Being around Renee's twins was almost like having her own children.

During her visits to Tampa and while staying with Renee, Jessica would assume the parenting responsibilities of taking care of AJ and Kiana, allowing Renee some-much needed "me time". Renee thought Jessica had given her the biggest favor; she didn't understand that Renee gave Jessica the biggest blessing. It felt so good for a few weeks to feel like a mom. In time, her visits became twice a year, and their relationship was so comfortable that even the twins would cry every time she had to go home. She confessed that she would cry on the plane because she missed them just as much as they missed her, if not more. So, when it became apparent that Richard wasn't willing to adopt, Jessica knew their marriage was over; she just couldn't say the words. She had hoped he would see how much it meant to her to become a mom and give in, but he never did. The pain was too deep to let go of. Jessica began to cry, and Richard held her in his arms. The mediator watched from a distance and hoped they wouldn't go forward with their divorce. Still, the mediator didn't understand that Jessica's pain of not being a mother was irreparable to their marriage. Richard knew it, but after hearing her speak, hoped they could eventually become friends. It was clear that they didn't hate each other; they didn't like who they both became, hopeful that would also change.

Richard knew not adopting a baby was selfish, but, in all honesty, he didn't want to have children after so many failed attempts. Jessica never knew that the loss of each pregnancy caused a deep pain inside Richard, and it became so unbearable that he silently began to blame her for their loss. To him, adopting a child would have been like a consolation prize for losing their children. He didn't know how to communicate his pain, so he became distant and resentful of her. He held on as long as he could, but eventually, it was time to call it quits.

By the end of their garage sale, they had agreed, and it was approved by the judge to allow Jessica to live in the house for a year, paying Richard an acceptable rent until she figured out her life. In a few weeks, she will be a single woman. What a scary thought, and she was thinking about making more changes to her life. Jessica admired how Renee decided to re-invent her life by retiring early and going into the jewelry business.

Renee was more outgoing than ever, and the fact that Renee was having sex with a younger man had made Jessica's heart swell with pride.

Monique was still fuming at how Jessica spoke to her. She was indignant at her tone and the choice of words. Jessica chastised her during their call. "Never in my life has this heifer spoken to me like I was a nobody. I shielded her from getting her ass kicked all over the 'Westend'," Monique angrily said out loud. She fixed another glass of wine, emptied the glass as fast as she had poured it, and filled up her third glass. Monique was genuinely scared that her secret might become public and especially not knowing who the person was blackmailing her.

At one time, she thought it was her sister-in-law, but some of the things the blackmailer knew wouldn't come up in a background check. Monique told Jessica to see if maybe either of the ladies knew her secret and never mentioned it to her. Unfortunately, that wasn't the case, and now she may have ruined the only ally she had, Jessica. Monique needed to get ahead of the game before her husband and son learned the truth. Not having either of them in her life would destroy her. She kept her husband in the dark for years, and if her secret came out now, it would mean losing her family, social standing, and reputation.

She envisioned the news of their love child in a much better scenario and not some scandal shit that comes on television every night. Their high school reunion was in a few weeks, and she needed to make up with Jessica before the reunion. She decided it was better if Moses didn't know about the blackmail and about him being CJ's biological father. He would want to talk to his son and explain why he wasn't in his life, which could not happen. She called his mother, who still lived in their hometown, and got his contact information from her.

Mrs. Lula asked if everything was okay because she hadn't heard from her since she broke up with Moses shortly after graduation. Thank God for the class reunion that was happening soon because she lied and told her that the committee needed his contact, and since they dated, they thought that she had it. Monique volunteered to get his information on their behalf. She could hear Mrs. Lula saying under her breath, "Hmm, hmm," as if she already knew that Monique was lying. Mrs. Lula's responses were shady, especially since Monique knew that Mrs. Lula blamed her for Renee breaking up with her son. Monique was thrilled that Chris couldn't attend the reunion with her, and she couldn't think of a more perfect timing just in case Moses went "all my father's rights were taken", crap on her. At least Monique knew that he wasn't trying to blackmail her. She was sure that there would be an issue with Renee.

Perhaps it wasn't a bad idea to let the cat out of the bag that one drunk evening when she called Jessica. At least she finally saw Jessica for who she was, and to be honest, she did Renee a favor. She seriously doubted Renee would embarrass herself even more by attending their high school reunion. There was no way that her fantasy of Moses could still exist, not after hearing the ultimate betrayal. Monique shook her head and smiled as she dialed Jessica's number, then mumbled, "It is time to put the friendship back together." At least until she found out who was trying to blackmail her. After a few rings, Jessica sent her call to voicemail. Jessica was still mad. "I'll give her a few days to cool off before trying again," Monique whispered to herself. She couldn't understand why Jessica would ignore her like this. They had fought in the past, and they would find themselves back as friends and sisters. They weren't as close as she and Renee, maybe because Monique wasn't as needy or insecure as they were to each other. They both fulfilled what was missing in the other person's life. Jessica had given Renee gave her children, and Jessica shared her companionship with Renee. Now that Jessica was getting divorced, Renee must be excited to have her best friend all to herself. Especially now that Jessica wasn't speaking to Monique. There was a twinge of anger mixed with sadness in Monique's eyes as she thought about how close her two friends had grown to each other over the years, leaving her behind.

 She felt betrayed, but deep down inside, Monique always felt jealous of Jessica's and Renee's relationship. Now they had joined forces and alienated her as a punishment for all her successes. "Fine, those two bitches can have each other right after they help me through this mess; then, we don't even have to speak again," she said as she kissed herself in the mirror.

Byron "Moses" Banks

He was a 6'3, medium-built, caramel complexion man with beautiful gray eyes and a devilish grin that held you, hostage, until he was ready to release his power. He was a quiet man who seldom let anyone inside his well-protected wall of emotions. After growing up in a household where both parents should have never been together, much less procreating, he vowed that he wouldn't ruin the lives of any child by having any. He only had one love in his life, but Byron "Moses" Banks destroyed it years ago. He had been trying to recapture it ever since, and to his dismay, left angry and broken hearts worldwide.

He left for boot camp two months after high school graduation and only once returned to Rockford, IL. Little did he know that his short stay would change his life forever. After reading the invitation to his high school reunion, Moses immediately thought about the two ladies from his past. One had his heart, and the other wanted it. So, he stayed away from his hometown to avoid bumping into Renee and facing rejection. This was why, before his father passed, he would fly his parents out to wherever he lived at the time on the premise that they could see the world. It wasn't a total lie.

Now that he had just retired from the Air Force, Moses felt somewhat out of sorts. He'd been in the military for thirty-seven years and wasn't sure how he would navigate the world outside of it.

Many would consider Moses a complicated man. He traveled the world and met a lot of beautiful women. He loved a few and asked for their hand in marriage, but like clockwork, he would call off the wedding before the actual wedding date. Neither his military buddies nor his family could figure out his problem. He seemed so happy with each woman, except when time grew closer to the wedding. It had gotten so bad that no one took him seriously. Moses knew that none of them would have his heart because it belonged to someone else, even if he would never have a chance to have her again. But holding the invitation in his right hand gave him hope. He wondered if she would be there, possibly giving him a second of her time.

Although he was now bald, and his beard had that salt and pepper distinguished look, Moses didn't look his age at fifty-five. He looked at least ten years younger, he thought. He was probably in better shape than most men that would be attending the reunion. He chuckled to himself. Moses called Tampa, Florida, his home, where he could enjoy retirement. He thought about moving to somewhere in the Charlotte, North Carolina area because Moses loved the vibe there, but felt it was too close for comfort. He didn't want any drama. He chose Tampa, Florida, because of the beaches and the weather. He was tired of the cold and no longer wanted anything to do with the snow. Rain or shine, he would always find himself running down the Tampa/Clearwater causeway at the break of dawn. The view was always so calming, and it helped him clear his head. One morning, he stopped along the bridge to just take in the sunrise and how breathtaking it was when he noticed a fever of stingrays swimming towards his way. As he looked further out, he saw a few dolphins playing and smiled. He continued his run as the sun started to rise. On his drive home, he couldn't shake the thought of seeing Renee again. He hadn't seen her since he broke her heart and graduated from high school. He was going to the reunion on a mission because it was time to clear the air and set the record straight. After his dad's passing several years ago, he understood how short life was. He wanted to live and love and be loved just like everyone else. His friends and family thought that he was afraid of committing when it came to matters of the heart, but they couldn't be further from the truth.

He broke off his engagements with Isabella, Sophia, Giselle, and Rachel, all beautiful women from different parts of the world. He loved them all and still did, but he didn't have that deep, forever love a man has for that one woman. The type of love he had back in high school was short, and he knew from the moment he saw Renee that she was the one. Her smile drew her to him, but her kindness and that fat ass, he must admit, were what grabbed his heart. He smiled and chuckled at the fat ass part as if he had just seen it yesterday. He was foolish to think that this woman would ever feel how he felt, especially after the hurt she endured because of him, not to mention that they hadn't seen each other in almost forty years. He decided that the one thing she deserved was an apology, and he would at least apologize for hurting her.

As Moses drove into his garage, he received a text message. He wasn't sure who it came from since the caller ID showed the name as unknown. But after reading the text, Moses instantly knew who it was; he just had no idea how Monique got his number. Then it hit him; it must have been his mom. He hadn't spoken to Monique since he was home attending his dad's funeral and they had a brief encounter. He could feel the tension in his neck tightening. The mere thought of this woman brought back memories that he'd rather forget. He wondered why she asked him to call her when he had a moment.

He texted her back and said, "I'll call you tonight."

While taking his shower, Moses had a bad feeling about the call he would make later. It was never good if Monique was in the picture. He couldn't imagine why she wanted to talk. Later in the evening, Moses decided to call her back to see why it was so crucial for him to call. He started to feel nauseous as his concerns grew into the worst possible things he could imagine. Moses lit his "Montecristo White Churchill" cigar, sipped on his "Maker's Mark Bourbon Whisky", and hit the call button on his cell phone. Moses held his breath while Monique's phone rang. He started to hang up when she answered in a whisper, saying, "Let me call you back in a few minutes."

 His eyes rolled up in his head as he sighed and hung up. He took a draw from his cigar, allowing the smoke to fill the inside of his mouth, enjoying the experience, and as he released the smoke, Monique called him back. He took a long swig of his whisky as he answered her call. Monique apologized for her strange behavior earlier and explained why she couldn't speak when he called. Monique asked if Moses remembered the time they hooked up when they were both home in Rockford. Moses was holding his breath, waiting for the words soon to follow would not be good. Monique continued and said, quite frankly, that he had fathered her son CJ and she had allowed her husband to believe that CJ was his son.

Monique said that she had kept it a secret until now but was forced to let everyone who mattered know the truth. Monique wanted to clarify that Moses was only CJ's father in DNA and that her husband Chris had been and was still CJ's father in every sense of the word. Monique's words seemed to have hung in the air, and Moses tried to understand what she had just said. It stunned him, and he no longer heard another word Monique spoke. She kept calling his name, but it wasn't until she screamed that Moses snapped out of the shock that she had put on him and asked her to repeat everything because he didn't think he understood. She paused for a few seconds and repeated the part that she figured had him all discombobulated. Then she repeated that he was the biological father of her son CJ, and someone found out her secret. There was silence for what seemed like an hour, and finally, Moses calmly spoke.

"Monique, I need you to explain how I have a son and why I am just now finding out about it after all these years?"

Monique could sense a bit of anger coming from Moses. She decided that responding in her usual way would not be productive; Monique explained that she got pregnant when they were both back home in Rockford. Before Monique knew about her pregnancy, she and her recent boyfriend, Chris Harris, got back together, and he proposed before Monique told him about being pregnant. She knew it was a 50/50 chance that Chris was the father. Once CJ was born, Monique had a paternity test, which confirmed that Moses, and not her husband, was the biological father.

Monique felt remorse for her actions for a split second but had things not lined up the way they did, she wouldn't have had the life she and CJ deserved. Monique said it would be in everyone's best interest not to tell the truth. He could continue to stay in the military guilt-free, though he had not been there for his child. Moses told her he needed time to digest this bombshell, and he also wanted to have a DNA test to prove that he was CJ's biological father. She reluctantly agreed to the testing but wasn't sure how she would do it without her family finding out, especially with so many other eyes looking at her.

After his call with his "baby mama", Moses finished his glass, poured himself a double neat, and emptied the glass as if he had been drinking water. He poured himself another and just looked inside the glass as if he was looking for answers. He was a father. He had no clue how the relationship between him and his son would play out. Would CJ be angry at him, even though he never knew until now? Would he call him Dad or Moses? And would they both end up with a relationship as father and son?

"I have a son," he smiled and said softly and then in a loud booming voice, "I have a son!" Then reality hit him. "SHIT. Shit, shit, Renee! He thought. "This will kill her when she finds out, and she will never speak to me now," he said out loud with a regretful voice.

For years, Moses never allowed himself the pleasure of fatherhood, and as fate would have it, he may have the best of both worlds. He would have a son and a wife if he played his cards right. He knew it would take some time to break down Renee's wall and regain her trust, but he was willing to do whatever it took. The class reunion must set the right stage for him to get the love of his life back. Maybe he was wrong, and she would never give him a second thought, especially now that Monique was forever linked to him, but he needed to try.

It never occurred to Moses that she may be married, happily married. But he made up his mind that, no matter what, before the end of the reunion he would tell her how he felt about her. Go hard or go home, and "I'm determined to go hard for this woman," Moses muttered as he downed the rest of his whiskey. It was time to turn in because tomorrow was a long day, so he placed his cigar in the ashtray to let it die on its own and headed back inside to shower for bed.

Like clockwork, Moses headed down to the causeway for his daily run. Something about running by water seemed to soothe his soul, and he couldn't get what Monique told him last night out of his mind. Was it possible that he would get to have a relationship with his son?

He kept in touch with Richard, his best friend throughout the years, and figured that this would be the best time to call him and let him know that he was coming to town so they could hang out. He also knew that Richard and Jessica were married, and he might get some information about Renee from him. It'd been at least five months since they spoke. He would call him after he got into his car after his run. Usually, Moses liked to ride in silence to continue his thoughts, but today, he decided to be on a mission to get his woman back. After his morning run, he returned to his car and sat for a few minutes, gathering himself before calling Richard. After taking a long and much-needed drink of water, Moses took out his cell phone and dialed Richard's phone number. While waiting for Richard to answer, he smiled when he thought about their good times back in school.

"Hey, man, what's up?" Richard answered.

The two men spoke to one another, and finally, Moses asked if he and Jessica were going to the class reunion in a few weeks. Richard cleared his throat and said, "Damn, man, you been gone and out of circulation way too long. Jessica and I are divorced." Richard surprised himself at how sad he felt saying it.

"Awe, man, I'm sorry to hear that; you guys have been together since high school. So, what happened, if you don't mind me asking?" Moses softly spoke.

"We just grew apart. But the deal-breaker was that Jessica wanted children, and I changed my mind after the fifth miscarriage, and after she realized that she wasn't going to become a mother, she stopped being my wife and became my roommate," Richard responded.

There was a little silence with sadness and regret in the air. Moses could sense that this wouldn't be the cheerful conversation he thought it would be, so he tried to figure out a quick way to end the call.

"To answer your question, I'm not going, but Jessica will be there with Renee," Richard said.

"Oh, so Renee is going to the reunion?" Moses inquired.

"Aw man, don't do that; you only called me to see if she would be there and if she was married." Richard burst into laughter.

"I need you to come to the reunion. I need a wingman, a support system. I'm coming to get my woman, my future wife," Moses said with confidence.

"Hold on, partner, Renee isn't going to be excited to see you after discovering your secret love child with Monique," Richard said more seriously.

"Damn, I wondered if she knew. I wanted to be the one to tell her. I just recently found out myself that I had a son. Wait, how did Renee find out so quickly? I just found out last night. I know that she didn't hear it from Monique," Moses said in a defeated tone.

"Well, the word on the street is…" Richard laughed.

"Man, this situation isn't funny at all. Monique has ruined my life and possibly permanently," Moses scolded Richard.

"Sorry, man, too soon, huh?" Richard apologetically said.

He waited for Moses to respond, but there was no response; Richard began explaining how Renee knew about his new parental role.

"Monique drunk called Jessica to tell her that someone was trying to blackmail her about who her baby daddy was and that it was you, my brother. She continued to tell Jessica that she pretended to be Renee when she did the DNA testing after her son, I mean your son, was born so that no one could discover the truth. Depending on your perspective, it gets better or worse, but when Jessica told Monique that she told Renee the truth, Monique went off the deep end and cursed Jessica out. Thank God.

Finally, Jessica pushed back and cursed that conniving bitch out. I never liked her lying ass. I knew in high school that she was bad news. Question for you, sir, will you request that Monique change young Christopher Harris Jr. to Byron "Moses" Banks Jr.? Then we can call him MJ!

Maybe changing his name wasn't a good idea; he is damn near forty years old," Richard quickly said. Both men chuckled, but after a while, Moses was starting to feel some anger about his situation. All the years that could have been spent raising a son made him feel empty. Moses never really thought about having children but knowing that CJ was his son made him think about his father and their relationship. What things would he have done the same way as his father, and what things would he make his own? Moses would have loved to have felt the joy of educating his son in every country he was stationed in. Instead, his son was a grown man thinking some other man was his biological father. He tried holding his emotions in without letting Richard know he was hurting. Richard was a talker, so he doubted that he had noticed that Moses was deep in thought, but somehow, Richard managed to read what he was thinking.

"Man, seriously, I can't imagine being in your shoes. First, loving a woman since high school only to destroy it by having sex with her best friend and then years later, unbeknownst to you, have a love child with the spawn of Satan. Now, you are trying to get back the love of your life. The woman that probably hates your guts, let me rephrase that, a woman who hates your fine ass. Byron "Moses Banks, the man who spread more legs than the men that the "Red Sea" drowned." Richard laughed so loud that he never heard Moses cuss him out.

"Man, fuck you. I'm over here hurting over this shit, and all your weak ass could do is joke. You're brave enough to make a stupid joke over the phone but too scared to tell your wife that you want a divorce." Moses then hung up.

Once Richard realized Moses was no longer on the phone, he wondered if he had gone too far too soon. He thought he could hear Moses talking but couldn't understand what he was saying amidst all his laughter. Richard sensed that Moses wasn't too happy with all the jokes. He warned him to stop and that it was too soon. Richard wanted to call him back but thought it would be best to allow the smoke to clear. He will text him in the morning and apologize for his lack of empathy and support.

After hanging up on Richard, Moses stepped outside to his patio with his cigar and a glass of whiskey neat. In the background, Moses could hear his music through the speakers throughout the house. As he was sitting and enjoying the smooth taste of his cigar and whiskey, an old song by Gerald LeVert, "I'd Give Anything," began to play. Moses immediately thought about Renee and how Moses searched for her through so many women and now learned that she hated him all because of Monique's lies. He poured himself another drink and felt his heartbreak over the thought of how close he was to having her back in his life. Then, as he finished his last drop of whiskey, another oldie but goodie started playing to add more pain. This was by Will Smith, in "Just the Two of Us."

As he listened to the lyrics, he thought about the movie that Will Smith and his son Jaden Smith made together, "The Pursuit of Happyness", and imagined how proud Will must have been to sit back and watch his son act. That type of pride swells deep inside your chest and grows to your face, displaying happiness through smiles and tears. Not once did he ever have the chance to know what it would feel like as a man watching his son make him the proudest man on earth. Not once did he have an opportunity to show his son the world through his eyes. Monique took all that away from him.

By the time the song ended, his face was full of tears, and he released a deep, hurtful moan that you knew came from the center of his soul. It wasn't about finding out he had a son which hurt him badly. It was the loss of a lifetime of father-and-son moments you can't get back by saying, 'I'm sorry, please forgive me.' Not that Monique offered either one of those things. Renee was right. Monique only cared for herself, not even her husband or son. He thought to himself as he knew that it was time to go inside and sleep off his night.

After waking up after passing out, as he was still wearing the same clothes from last night, he no longer wanted to be on the side waiting. He gave less than a damn who was blackmailing Monique. He wasn't going to wait for another second to clear all of this up, so he decided to contact an old Air Force buddy who went into private practice after retiring from JAG. He wanted to see if he had any rights. He knew that since CJ was now an adult he had no parental rights that he needed. Still, he also knew that Monique married into a wealthy and influential family who were also attorneys and politicians. He was meeting with him in a few hours, enough time to talk with Richard about his childish jokes and lousy timing. Now Richard had no choice but to be his wingman at the class reunion.

He pulled out his phone after feeling it vibrate in his pants pocket. He chuckled that it was Richard calling him as he answered the phone.

"I know your punk ass isn't calling me after all that shit you said last night. If I were close to your goofy ass, I'd be kicking it all over town."

He held in the laugh until he heard Richard speak, asking who he was calling a punk. They both let out a hearty laugh. Richard knew that was Moses' way of letting it go, but he still wanted to apologize to him as a man and friend.

"Man, seriously, I'm sorry about last night. It was too soon, I should have waited until I had more material after the class reunion, but then I realized I would miss everything. So, I'll wait because I like to keep whatever ass

I have left; besides, Jessica has already kicked it enough for you and my entire old neighborhood."

The two men laughed again. Moses spoke, telling him he was going to the class reunion and had no choice. He explained how Richard owed him for being insensitive about his situation. After a few minutes of back and forth, Richard agreed to attend the reunion as his wingman. Now that he had decided to go, he wondered how Jessica would feel about him joining the reunion. They were in a good space now, and Richard didn't want to mess it up again; his curiosity was getting the best of him, and Richard couldn't wait for all the drama to unfold. He knew how Jessica and Renee felt about Monique, and now add Moses' anger to the mix, and this class reunion would be more than a "Knight to Remember"; it would be epic! Maybe it was better to wait to tell Jessica about attending the class reunion.

After all, her mind wasn't going to be on why he was at the class reunion; she would focus on stopping Renee from killing Monique. After hearing Moses' plan of outing Monique at the reunion, he didn't want Moses included in a messy catfight with those three women, so he suggested that Moses should let the women fight. In the meantime, let his attorney find out what he can, and during the reunion, let Monique know how he feels about her and the damage she had caused. Moses agreed to let the women fight it out and handle the situation smartly. He wondered why the blackmailer hadn't given her their demands and why her brother-in-law's team hadn't found out about the blackmail. Maybe there wasn't anyone blackmailing her and pondered whether Monique might be doing all this herself.

Moses wanted to tell his mom that she was a grandmother, but he decided to wait until he saw her face to face to give her the disturbing, yet exciting news. He wasn't sure how she would take it, that for over thirty years, she was a grandmother and never knew. The information will kill her, and Monique will be next to be in a coffin if it does.

Two Weeks before the Reunion

After working with her trainer for six months, Renee was frustrated when she learned that she had only lost fifty pounds when her goal was seventy. Her class reunion was in two weeks, and she had desperately wanted to lose those extra twenty pounds. Carlos, her trainer gave her some tough love at her health assessment. He told Renee that losing twenty pounds in two weeks would not be a healthy goal and that she came very close to meeting her goals. Carlos walked Renee over to the floor-length mirror and smiled as he said, "Girl, you got it going on. You are a very beautiful and sexy woman. If you weren't my client and I knew that you were into younger men, I'd shoot my shot." The only thing that Renee could do was grab Carlos and hug him, thanking him for his kind words.

As Renee began to pull away from Carlos, he whispered in her ear that he was serious, he finds her to be attractive and once she was no longer his client, he wanted to take her out. Renee paused as she looked into Carlos' eyes and smiled at him to let him know that she wouldn't be opposed to seeing him. Renee decided to continue her workouts and increased her training to seven days a week for the next two weeks, but she wasn't sure if it was to lose the last twenty pounds or to flirt with Carlos and see what happens. Renee told herself that she needed to stay focused because her high school reunion was in two weeks, and it was her goal to become the belle of the ball. Renee dreaded exercising, but Carlos gave her a new motivation. On Renee's next training session, she was no longer wearing her baggy sweatpants and oversize T-shirts. Renee wore navy blue leggings with a matching bra, and when she walked inside the gym, it was as if all eyes were on her. The only eyes that she was interested in belonged to Carlos, and then it happened; it was like watching a romantic scene where the younger man looks up and his eyes meet the older woman's. But after that initially locked gaze, it was more like watching a comedy.

As Renee was walking towards Carlos, their eyes having met for what felt like hours, Renee suddenly could feel herself falling to the floor. In her mind, it was in slow motion, giving her time to jump up quickly, but instead, Renee stayed on the floor for what felt like hours. Embarrassment ensued as both young men and women ran over to her aide. As they helped her up, Renee realized that her left foot was in pain, and she could barely put her weight on it. The manager of the gym wanted to call the ambulance, but Renee refused, saying that she just needed a minute. Carlos sat with her and eventually, he offered to take her home and Uber back to the gym, and Renee agreed. Once they made it to Renee's house, Carlos helped her inside. Renee asked Carlos to close the door behind him on his way out because she was going to fill her tub with bubbles and Epson salt to see if that would help her foot. He suggested that he stick around at least until she gets out of the bathtub. Renee agreed.

Soaking in her huge tub was so therapeutic that Renee had forgotten that Carlos was still in her house. That was until she saw this chiseled, young body walking towards her, naked. Renee's mouth dropped and nervously, she giggled. Renee managed to ask Carlos what he was doing, and he just smiled as his body slowly disappeared under the suds.

"I thought that I would help take your mind off of your foot," Carlos seductively said.

After seeing what Carlos was working with, Renee was curious, but she and Gerald had an understanding, and she didn't want to cheat on him. While Renee was contemplating what to do, Carlos was pulling her towards him as he met her in the middle. Renee was lost in the excitement and decided to let the chips fall where they may and figure it out later. Carlos' touches were soft and alluring, each touch made her kitty purr, and within a few minutes, she was his. After long foreplay in what was now lukewarm water, Carlos helped Renee out of the bathtub, and she slid on top of his hardened member and they kissed. Carlos carried Renee to her bed and found his way to her treasure where he pleased her with his tongue in such a manner that Renee could only sing.

Renee forgot about the pain in her foot as Carlos flipped her to her stomach and once he put on the condom, he slid inside of her, grabbing her waist, as he thrust himself inside of her. The euphoria Renee was feeling at that moment was like the first time she had smoked a joint with Jessica as a teenager. It must have been good for Carlos because he started speaking in Spanish and spanking her buttocks. It was a different experience than what she had with Gerald, and before Renee could find her groove, Carlos had quickly finished his business. She was glad that she was at least able to experience at least one orgasm prior to him flipping her over. Once it was all over and Carlos left, Renee changed her bedding, took a shower, and then washed down a couple of Ibuprofens with a glass of wine before heading to bed. As she lay in bed, Renee thought about how she was going to tell Gerald. And before she drifted off to sleep, she decided that it was one and done, and since she used protection, Gerald didn't need to know.

The next day, Renee texted Jessica and told her what happened with her trainer Carlos, and just like a bad habit, Jessica called her. Jessica was surprised and a bit concerned because the behavior that Renee had been displaying was not that of the old Renee who had more conservative values.

"Are you going to sleep with every boy who flirts with you?" Jessica said with a concerned tone.

Renee replied, "Carlos is hardly a boy, he's a young man, and of course, I'm not going to sleep with every male that flirts with me. I'm having fun. I'm being responsible for using condoms with both guys. Besides, Carlos was a one-time thing. He's too selfish. He's nothing like Gerald who takes his time introducing his body to mine."

"Do you hear yourself, Renee? I mean, really! Are you going to become that woman who men will only see what you can do sexually and not what you bring intellectually?" Jessica responded.

"Listen, I'm not planning on dating or marrying any of them. It was a brief encounter with Carlos that will never happen again, and as for Gerald, we have an understanding. I'm 56 years old, and for most of my life, I did what was expected; now I'm doing what I want. If that makes me a slut, or a whore, then it is what it is, I'm happy because I'm finally finding my voice. I'm enjoying meeting this new me, and if you are going to be judgmental, then I won't share anything else. I'm not looking for absolution, I'm looking for satisfaction on my way to finding my happy. By the way, when did you get so judgmental?"

Jessica conceded and told Renee that she didn't mean to judge, but she had never seen this side of Renee and it concerned her. But if Renee felt like she knew what she was doing, Jessica would not question her. After they hung up, Renee could tell that it would be the last time that she confided in Jessica when it came to having sex with other men. Renee wanted to explore who she was now, which is why she had her experience with Carlos and also enjoyed the company of Gerald. It wasn't about either of them being younger men; it was more about the excitement of feeling attractive, at least that was the case for Carlos. As for Gerald, it was about how attentive he was. Renee was able to see herself through his eyes, like a mirror, and liked what she saw. She was becoming more confident; she felt sexier than ever. Renee wanted the world and was planning on getting it. Losing weight started because of her lack of confidence and not wanting to be the heaviest woman at the class reunion, but it was now about loving who she was and wanting more for herself. She deserved it. Renee raised two children alone and had the battle scars – physically and emotionally – to prove it. She hated how Jessica would tell her that she needed to love herself, regardless of her size. Of course, she was right, but it was much deeper than just loving herself irrespective of size. It was about knowing who Renee was and loving who she was as a woman.

After spending a few months with Gerald, he decided that he wanted to make it work with the mother of his children, and they ended their relationship but decided to remain friends without benefits. Renee had to admit that those few months were magical and gave her a different perspective on her womanhood. Renee's walk had more bounce in her step, and she couldn't remember the last time, if ever, that her body contorted to so many different positions, so she knew that her workouts had helped her in more than one way.

She smiled at the memories. Even though Gerald was out of the picture, when they were together, he made her feel like a younger, sexier woman who was confident, and beautiful. Her thick body no longer felt like a prison cell that held her captive, and afraid to be shown. Instead, her thickness now felt like a badge of honor. Renee and Gerald had a beautiful romance, albeit short.

On the career front, Renee wanted to be her own boss doing something that she loved, which was making jewelry, a passion she had only pursued in her spare time. She had gotten a lot of compliments from people and many of them had asked if she was selling any of her jewelry. Renee had enough in her 401k to jump-start her jewelry-making business. She had put together a business plan, and now, it was time to set up her office and workshop. AJ's old bedroom became her office and Kiana's was transformed into her workshop.

It was two weeks before the class reunion, and Moses refused to respond to Monique's calls or text messages. He would not let her know if he planned to attend the reunion. Monique thought to herself that she needed to come up with a plan. Maybe she could claim that Moses took advantage of her during a moment of weakness. But, perhaps, she could just play dumb as if she never knew that Moses was the biological father. After all, the person whose name was on the test results was Renee Morgan and not Monique Harris. "Get it together, Monique," she shouted out loud. She paced back and forth in her bedroom, trying to find a great lie – one that wouldn't make her look like a monster.

Then it hit her; she could say that she told Moses that he was the father, but he didn't want anything to do with her or their child. She was young, foolish, and scared. So, they married, soon after finding out that Monique was pregnant. In her mind, DNA only explains genetics but not who would best fit the role of being a father to her child. Yes, this would work. Moses refused to accept fatherhood, and she knew that Chris was the type of man that would be a great father. For this to work, it would mean that she would have to tell Chris and have him and Moses on the same page. Whoever was blackmailing her wouldn't stand a chance. She and Chris could get ahead of the breaking news and still come out smelling like roses. Of course, Monique knew that this would break the hearts of her husband and son to hear the truth, but eventually, they would both forgive her, and they all could move on as a family. Monique was hoping that Moses would call her back so that they could be on the same page before she broke it down to her husband. The class reunion was getting closer, and things needed to already be in place, but if she couldn't reach Moses, then plan B was to tell Chris and hope that Moses went along with it. Knowing Moses, the way she remembered, she was confident that he would go along with the plan.

Chris wouldn't have to know the entire truth because that would have chump written all over him, but with her plan, he sounded more like someone who loved his girlfriend enough to protect her and her unborn child. She was going to have to tell her husband soon. She would give Moses a few more days to return her calls, and if he didn't, she would put plan B into place and let it play out. After all, it was the devil in the details that would ultimately be the game-changer.

Today was the day, and not knowing how her husband would handle the news of their son not being his biological child was a bit scary for Monique. However, Chris was so calm and mild-tempered that she was praying those very characteristics would be her saving grace. Monique made sure that she cooked his favorite dinner and had plenty of alcohol on hand. But to be extra cautious, she made a small peach cobbler, his favorite dessert, with infused Cannabis butter. It was enough to last a few days and keep him calm. Then, she heard her husband come in and call her name.

"Nikki, where are you, girl? You have it smelling like heaven in here," Chris said. "I can't wait to dig in."

Monique smiled because Chris was freaky and frisky whenever he called her "Nikki", and it usually meant he had sex on his mind. It may be a little easier to tell him the bad news, but not before he had a few bowls of the peach cobbler, and he was good and high. Monique's anxiety was rising and could feel how nervous she was, so she ate some peach cobbler. After taking her last bite, though she was disappointed because she didn't feel anything. Her friend that gave her the cannabis-infused butter told her to be careful not to use too much, or they would be too high. She glazed the top of the cobbler with more of the butter while it was still hot so that it would soak in by the time her husband would be ready for dessert.

Finally, dinner was ready, and Monique began to set the food on the table, leaving the cobbler inside of the oven in a warm setting. Chris decided to set the tone. He told "Alexa" to play "Our playlist," a list of songs he put together to set the atmosphere of lovemaking. Before he sat down, Chris walked to Monique, gave her a sensual kiss on her neck, and whispered, "I love you, Mommy."

She instantly became wet from the softness of his lips and the warmth that she felt from his breath. She smiled and whispered back, "I love you too, Daddy."

He gave a light pat on her butt as he walked to his chair. The pat on her butt was Chris' way of letting her know that dinner would be short because he had other things on his mind. After they said grace, they began to eat; she had already put the food on their plates. Monique had spent the day preparing baked chicken with collard greens, macaroni and cheese, cornbread, and rice with her cannabis-infused peach cobbler for dessert. These were all Chris' favorite Southern comfort foods that she would cook for him when they were in college. The night was fun. They hadn't laughed and talked like this in a long time, and as they finished laughing about something that happened in college, the cannabis kicked in, and Monique was immediately high. "Oh shit!" she thought. She could feel the heaviness of her body as if she was carrying dead weight. She realized that she may have overdone it with the cannabis. She couldn't let Chris eat the peach cobbler because he would be extremely high. Monique needed to think of a way to destroy the peach cobbler so that he wouldn't eat any of it, but Monique couldn't move. He kept asking her what was wrong, and Monique couldn't explain quickly.

She saw Chris get up and assumed that he was coming over to check on her, so she put her head down to hide how high she looked. Monique knew that she was high, and things felt like they were going in slow motion, but he should have been over to her by now. Then it dawned on her that he was getting some cobbler for dessert. She quickly stood up and slowly sat right back down. Monique giggled at herself because she was high. As she composed herself to get up to remove the cobbler, Chris walked back into the dining room. He told Monique that she had put her foot in the peach cobbler. He had eaten a bowl in the kitchen and was finishing his second bowl with some vanilla ice cream. Monique's plan wasn't going the way she had anticipated. She couldn't tell him that he wasn't their son's biological father while she was high. So, she thought to herself, or at least she thought she said it in her mind. That was until she heard an angry, hurt voice screaming at her.

"What the fuck do you mean that CJ isn't my son?"

She was so high all she could do was giggle as she tried to explain. The more she laughed, the angrier Chris got. The screaming and yelling made her feel like she was going insane, and finally, she screamed back.

"Chris, I'm sorry, this isn't how I wanted to tell you. I want to discuss this but right now, I'm so high that I can't think straight. Can we talk tomorrow once the marijuana is out of our system?" With his adrenaline going, he felt the first dosage from the first bowl, and it was like he was moving and talking in slow motion. The look on his face and his slow gesture caused Monique to giggle more as she tried to explain how they both were high. All Chris heard was the peach cobbler was infused with weed. He had a confused look and asked what type of tree she put in the cobbler. Monique let out the loudest sound of laughter and laughed for several minutes, and then Chris began to laugh at her. They couldn't stop laughing, and then the second wave hit Chris, and he went from laughing to paranoid. Chris began to scream that his member was missing.

He was panicking that he needed to pee. Monique tried to explain that his member was inside his pants, but he didn't believe her. He began to ramble and then cried out, stating that without it, they couldn't have sex, and she could no longer do with her tongue that thing he had always enjoyed. Monique tried hard not to laugh, but it became overwhelmingly funny. She finally unzipped his pants and pulled out his member to show him, and before she knew it, he became aroused and kept trying to dry hump her. He was making these sexual noises like they were already engaged in sex.

"I'm going to fuck the shit out of you. Chris grabbed Monique's treasure. "Say it, Mommy, who's is this?" Before she could respond, he quickly said, "It's mine, and King Kong ain't got nothing on me."

Chris yelled, trying to sound like Denzel Washington's character from "Training Day" as he beat on his chest. He quickly went from being animated to normal, with his erect member in hand. He looked at Monique and said, "I need to seriously address two things with you. Why did you lace my food with cannabis? And were you telling the truth that CJ is not my son?" His voice cracked, and she immediately regretted the evening.

Their high went away as they both became sad with the reality of their biggest secret between them.

"I'm sorry, Chris, I didn't plan on telling you like this; I wanted to have a calm, quiet evening so that we could talk about it. Then, as I was preparing the food, I was so scared of how you would react that I put infused cannabis in the peach cobbler to help with any fallout." Monique began her lying tour to save as much of herself as possible.

She told Chris that the year they broke up, she was devastated, and Moses was around as a friend to help her through the rough patch. They only had sex once, and it wasn't until they got back together that she found out that she was pregnant. Monique explained that Moses was the first to know, but he told her to get an abortion, and when Monique refused, he told her that he wanted nothing to do with her or the baby. She began to cry the way she practiced so that it didn't look or sound fake. Monique continued to talk, telling him how scared she was and didn't know what to do. When Chris assumed that Monique was pregnant by him, it was a relief. Then he proposed, and before she knew it, his parents knew about her pregnancy, and at that point, she felt like it was too late.

Hearing the news broke Chris' heart, and it felt like he couldn't breathe. He needed some fresh air but didn't feel safe driving, so he decided to take a walk. Chris told Monique that it was too much to take in and he wanted to discuss more when their heads were clear. Their night ended sadly, but at least everything was out in the open the way Monique wanted it to be, except for her main reason for telling him, which was that she was being blackmailed and didn't know by whom.

It felt strange waking up without her husband lying next to her in bed. The events of last night were more coherent than Monique imagined they would be. They were high, but it quickly went away when Chris became angry. Finally, they discussed Chris not being the biological father of her son. She dreaded talking about it more because she knew that last night was the high Chris who led with his emotions, but the sober Chris would be representing himself as an attorney, which couldn't be good for her. She took a shower and got ready for the day, trying to prolong the inevitable as she walked down the hall to the spare bedroom that Chris had taken last night; it was empty. Monique walked downstairs, and Chris was gone. She let out a big sigh, and then she started to worry. Where was he? Was he okay? Maybe she should call him to see, but she decided to text him instead.

"Good morning: how did you sleep? I hope you aren't so mad at me that we won't be able to finish our conversation. Where are you?

Please call me."

That was odd. Where did Chris go on a Saturday morning? She knew
that he was pissed and hurt over the news, but she never thought he would
just leave without letting her know that he was leaving or where he was
going. This wasn't like him. In the pit of her stomach, she felt that her life
was at the beginning of a downward spiral, and all she could do was sit
back and watch. After a few hours, Monique still hadn't heard from her
husband, so she called him and was instantly sent to voicemail. "Shit," she
softly said. She tried to contact Moses again so they could get on the same
page with her lies, and he still wasn't answering her calls or responding to
her text. His behavior was getting on her nerves.

Monique thought he was being rude and disrespectful; she hadn't felt
this out of control in years and wasn't quite sure what to do or how to
handle it. Usually, she would call Jessica and talk things over, but Jessica
wasn't talking to her either. "Fuck them all; I don't need any of them,"
Monique angrily spouted out as she walked into her garage and got into
her jet-black Jaguar F-Pace SUV that she fondly called "Midnight". As
she rolled out of her garage, Monique received another anonymous text
message.

*"A false witness will not go unpunished, and whoever pours out lies will
perish.' Proverbs 19:9."*

The text message immediately startled Monique, and she needed to find
out who this bastard was before they ruined everything she had worked
so hard to get. She decided that since it appeared that she was out on this
island by herself, she had to resort back to her hood instincts. The trouble
was that she did need Jessica and Renee to beat this punk at their own
game. "Go to hell, Moses; you know that I'm in trouble and that I need
you," she said as tears trickled down her face. It was time to save face and
talk to Jessica. The first thing to do was to send her a text message.

"You were right about everything that you said about me. I am a bitch, and I'm so sorry for how things happened. I deserve everything that I'm getting, but my son CJ doesn't, and in the end, this will hurt him the most. I know that you and Renee hate my guts, but we promised each other that if one was ever in trouble, no matter what, the others would be there for them. I need you both. Please help me. I'm alone, and I'm scared. We are sisters for life, and I was selfish and jealous. I hurt Renee, not because I hated her but because I was jealous of the love that she and Moses had developed so quickly. I wanted that kind of love, and I thought – in my twisted mind – that I deserved it more than she did. Someone is blackmailing me, and I don't know who they are, but they are scaring me. I need you."

She felt humbled as her life was unraveling and without any way to control its outcome for the first time in her adult life. It was funny that her situation took her back to when she was a little girl attending Sunday school. The lesson was about trusting in God when you had nothing else to lean on. Her tears began to flow more, and before she knew it, she was in full ugly cry mode. During her moment, her phone rang, it was Jessica. "Shit, talking about bad timing, I have to answer, but I don't want her to hear me cry," she thought to herself as she began to wipe her face. Finally, she cleared her throat and answered her phone.

The Reckoning

Jessica had never heard Monique cry, much less an ugly cry. It was an emotional release that was difficult to explain and one that no one could ever duplicate because it was so personal. Sometimes it may sound like a train or the shrill from a tornado. At times, it was unrecognizable to the human ear. As beautiful as Monique was, her ugly cry would sound like a choir member who was tone-deaf and sang all the high notes out of tune, or a woman giving birth without drugs. It was horrible, but it was also heartbreaking.

Listening to Monique cry and trying to understand what she was conveying was difficult. Finally, Jessica understood that when Chris found out, it didn't go too well, and Monique hadn't heard from him since, and that the blackmailer went all "church" on her with a quote from the Bible. Monique asked for Jessica's forgiveness and help. After she calmed down a little, her speech was more coherent, and more of a dialog followed.

"Monique, I'm always going to be your sister, but if we are going to repair our relationship, we will have to be honest with each other. You broke your sisterhood with Renee on so many levels. You lost any trust with her, and the only reason she held on by a string to your relationship

""

was because of me. Discovering that Moses was CJ's biological father was the straw that broke the camel's back. Not only did you strain any bond between you and Renee, but you also put me in a place where I had to make a choice."

"I know, and you are right, I deserve everything I'm getting and more, but Jess, my son, your nephew, doesn't deserve any of this. You know that he is the innocent one in this mess. I know that he is now an adult and is far more capable of dealing with his emotions. But since we are being honest, I'm terrified that he will hate me, and I will lose the only thing that matters in my life." Monique said.

Jessica decided to help Monique find out who the blackmailer was. They only had two weeks before the class reunion to figure it out. Monique started to tell her the story that she told her husband when she confessed that he wasn't CJ's biological father, but she decided against it for now. She gave Jessica the only clues that she had so far. The text messages were all scripture-based and very judgmental. It was someone who knew both her and Moses, so she thought it was Renee until she found out that Renee had no clue that Moses was the father. It seemed like a lost cause because there weren't many clues.

Then she remembered the voicemail message. She thought Jessica might recognize the voice, so she asked her to listen to it through a text message she sent. After listening, Jessica called Monique back and told her that there was something familiar with the female's voice. She couldn't put her finger on it, but she was sure they both knew the blackmailer. Monique saw this as progress and finding out the blackmailer's identity could put an end to it before Chris' parents found out and made the rest of her life a living hell. She didn't want her son to find out that the man he called dad wasn't his father and that it was some stranger he had never met; that would devastate him.

Just as Monique felt good and positive about this mess she had created; she received a text message from Chris.

"Monique, we need to talk right now, where are you?"

Monique knew right away that Chris was home, and it was time for them to talk. She ended her call with Jessica, but not before telling her that Chris just texted her and wanted to talk, he was home. Monique gathered herself together as she walked back into the house and poured herself a tall glass of wine; and mumbled, "It's five o'clock somewhere, and even if it wasn't, who cares."

Monique took a big gulp of her wine and then topped it off. She walked into Chris' office; it was one of his power plays, and she knew it all too well. Whenever he needed to feel like he was in charge, his office was where they would meet to talk. It was true that she was powerless, and he held all the cards. She decided to listen and soak up all the insults that she rightfully deserved, at least that was what she said to herself. Monique sat next to Chris on his burgundy Italian leather sofa, and before she could say a word, he calmly asked her if she was telling the truth that CJ wasn't his biological son. He wasn't high anymore and needed to hear it from her mouth with a clear mind. She cleared her throat and calmly responded.

"Yes. It's true, CJ isn't your biological son, but he is your son in every way that matters." Her voice cracked, as she tried to fight back the tears. There was a long pause as the pain magnified through their silence.

"Have you always known that he wasn't my son, or was it recently discovered?" He spoke with a stern tone as he waited for her response. She didn't quite know how to answer his question. On the one hand, if she told the truth, the repercussions would be irreparable. Her marriage would be over; she would lose the family she grew to love, including the loser brother and sister-in-law who jump-started this debacle. On the other hand, if she lied, she wasn't sure how long it would last before the truth came out. Monique had so many people angry with her that any one of them could tell Chris the truth, and she still would lose him. He must have read her mind because he quickly asked her why she had to think about it. He wondered out loud if she was preparing to lie. At that point, she decided to tell the truth. As much as it would hurt them both, it was the right thing to do.

"I've known since CJ was a baby," Monique said cautiously.

"WHAT? That was over 30 years ago. Why did you let this go for so long, and what made you tell me now?" Chris spoke with a tone that Monique wasn't sure she had heard before.

"I had no plans of telling you since it's been such a long time, and I didn't see any reason for telling you now. But since your brother decided to run for governor, I've received calls and text messages about my secret with threats of going to the news outlets with an exclusive." Monique's voice began to shake as she talked.

"Does CJ know about any of this?" Chris shouted. "Does he?" he shouted louder.

"No, he doesn't know," Monique said. "But we need to tell him soon before he finds out on his own." Monique broke down in tears.

Her husband looked at her with disgust and disdain.

"We? We aren't telling him a goddamn thing. You did this all by yourself, and you will handle this on your own," Chris said in an angry tone.

"Please, baby, I know that I messed up," Monique said. "But I need you."

She stood up and walked towards her husband with her arms stretched out, only to be rejected.

In a loud cry, she spoke, "I can't do this by myself; I'm begging you to help me…please."

By this time, her arms were tightly around his neck as her tears soaked his shirt. After fighting to get Monique off him, Chris gently pushed her away. He looked into her eyes.

"I can't help you, and I want a divorce," he said, handing her a manila envelope before walking upstairs to pack his clothes.

Monique read the divorce papers and saw where she needed to sign, highlighted in yellow. There was a note attached with a list of divorce attorneys suggested for her to hire. Her heart sunk into her stomach, and she threw the papers on the desk and ran upstairs to talk to her husband. Maybe if he saw how devastated she was, he would have compassion and work things out with her.

"Chris, please don't leave me. I'm so sorry that I did any of this. I was trying to protect you and our son. I love you, baby, please don't leave me," Monique cried.

"I can't do this without you."

"You'll be fine without me," Chris responded.

He stood at the foot of their bed and asked a few more questions.

"Who is the biological father, and does he know? I'm sure you said it when you drugged me," Chris said sarcastically. "But I'd like to hear it again now that I'm no longer high."

"His name is Byron Banks," Monique said. "But he goes by his nickname from high school, Moses. We bumped into each other when I went back home after you broke up with me to be with your former girlfriend. He was there to comfort me, and before we knew it, we were back in a familiar place. We had sex, and I went back to school a few days later. I thought that we were over, and I was brokenhearted. You treated me like shit and expected me to be okay with how you treated me. You and your family made me feel like I was beneath you because I didn't come from money and prestige. I have had to prove myself ever since, and when it comes to your mom, I still must prove myself. So, no, I didn't tell you that you weren't the father of my unborn child. I loved you, and I was scared that I would lose you. I knew that Moses didn't want a child; he was moving up in the Air Force and didn't want or need a newborn child to get in his way."

When Monique first spoke, the tone was weak and timid, but as she continued to speak and thought about her past with Chris, the tone of her voice found its strength.

"Oh, you're justifying your deceit because of how I treated you in college, because my mother didn't like you? They say that mothers always know, and I dismissed it as a social difference. I knew your personality would adjust handsomely, and you, my dear, didn't disappoint. I married you because I was in love with that strong woman who pushed me to be better at whatever I wanted to do. Little did I know that the woman I fell in love with was a master-manipulating, lying bitch! Never could I have imagined that someone who I thought would always have my back would stab me the hardest, and for thirty years, slowly turn the knife until it was unrecognizable. So, no, dear, I will not stand by your side as you ruin my son's life. Yes, I said my son. He is my son in every sense of the word. But I will not stay married to someone so disgusting. Sign the goddamn papers, Monique, and be woman enough to walk away without a fight, or I'll crush you."

He walked out before Monique could see the tears streaming from his face. She could see his pain, although he was trying to mask it. She deserved every bit of the anger he threw her way, and now was frightened that her son would feel the same way and discard her the way his father did. "What a fucking mess I made," Monique cried. She may as well rip the bandage off and tell CJ the truth now, especially since he was in town for a few days. She didn't dare to call him, so she texted him instead.

"We need to talk; please come over soon."

She couldn't hold back her tears; she was a mess, and she only had herself to blame. How was she going to get through this by herself? She called Jessica to talk.

"Jessica, I can't do this anymore," Monique said. "I made such a huge mess of things, and now my world is crumbling around me. I'm waiting for CJ to come over to tell him how much of a horrible mother I am. It's good that he is only in town for a few more days so that the awkwardness won't linger on for long."

There it was, that horrible cry that Monique made. It was deafening, making it difficult for Jessica to console her old friend, her sister. So, she did the only thing that a sister would do when the other was in trouble, go to her, just like when Renee came to her during her divorce.

"I'm on my way. I'll be there by nightfall. After our last conversation, I had a feeling that you were going to need moral support, so I booked a ticket to come and see you."

Monique thanked her and told her that she loved her. After hanging up, she realized that she hadn't heard Monique tell her that she loved her for years. It was nice to hear those three words from Monique, she thought. While packing, Jessica called Renee to tell her what was happening to Monique and that she wasn't coming to see her. Throughout Renee's rants, she tried to explain that she was trying to be a good friend to someone genuinely hurting.

"A friend? Is that how you just described this heifer? The friend that slept with my boyfriend and ultimately had his baby?" Renee said. "The friend cursed you out for telling her drunken secret, although we all secretly think she told you on purpose. The same friend only just told her husband that he isn't the biological father to the son, who calls him dad. Oh, and don't forget that same friend let her son call the wrong man daddy for over thirty years; someone he doesn't share DNA with. DO YOU MEAN THAT FRIEND?" Renee shouted.

"I don't expect you to be happy about my decision," Jessica said, "but I was hoping that you would at least understand and, more importantly, respect it. We all have done things that we aren't proud of, and whether we want to admit it, we all have hurt and betrayed a friend in one way or another. Has it been to this magnitude? Probably not, but we found our way back to that friend. We loved that person like family, and when they deeply hurt us, sometimes we forgave them because they were genuinely sorry for their actions. What is that saying? Hurt people hurt people? Monique was an insecure little girl who managed to mask it by hurting others.

When we were little, others treated Monique less than us because she was the darkest-skinned of the trio. You never noticed because it's been there all your life, and it didn't affect you like Monique. It was more than being called "blackie" or "midnight". It was how society also treated her. The black teachers would compliment you by saying how pretty you looked, and Monique stood right there and never uttered a compliment her way. The boys would ask me and you out on dates, and only the ones that knew that they didn't have a chance with us, would ask her, so it was like she was getting our leftovers. Her parents called her Pepper, and not because it was endearing, but because she was the darkest of them and the feistiest.

We also played a part if we were honest. Not once did we stand up for Monique, but instead, we laughed. I get it. We were children and didn't know any better not to laugh. Now that we are adults, can you see how it affected her and what she thought about us? She didn't hate you; she was and is jealous of you. It was never about me. I'm the white girl in the group; I couldn't look black regardless of how long I tried to tan. She identified with you as her soul sister, so she always felt betrayed and looked down upon all her life. I'm not excusing her behavior; I'm just choosing to understand it," Jessica said with a maternal voice of reason. She hung up the phone, leaving her words for Renee to ponder. Her suitcase was packed, and she headed to the airport to catch her flight.

Renee was still fuming after her conversation with Jessica. Initially, she was enraged and felt betrayed that Jessica would choose Monique over her. But, after a few glasses of wine, Renee started to calm down. Renee knew that she and Monique had always put Jessica in the middle of their issues. It wasn't fair to Jessica to choose one friend over the other. At one point, they all were close friends, close like sisters. Now, neither Renee nor Monique wants to be in the same room. She didn't feel bad that she wasn't supporting Monique in her time of need. Renee thought that Monique was getting her just dessert, and no amount of tears and sad stories were going to change her mind. The only thing that she was willing to do was to be fair to Jessica. Renee knew that Jessica would be at her side had it been her going through some emotional crap. So, she decided to send her sister from another mother a text, supporting what she was doing.

"Hey, girl, I know that you are in the air by now, heading to give your support to your friend. I wanted you to know that I heard all you said, and I support your decision. Slow your roll because I can see you smiling and excited about this, but nothing has changed between Monique and me. I'm just telling you that I heard you, and I support you. I don't want to put you in the middle of our issues anymore. It's not fair to you, and for that, I apologize. BTW... when you see the bitch, please tell her that I said Karma came back

and fucked her like she fucked everyone else and today is a good day!! I'm only kidding, just a little. I had to let one more out before I left it alone. Be safe, my friend, and remember, don't get in the middle of a family argument. You will lose! Love you!”

After sending Jessica a text, she felt good about herself, and now Renee could move on from the drama of Monique Harris. “So, goodbye, and good riddance, bitch.” She raised her glass as she mumbled to herself.

"Hey, Mom, I'm here. You said that you needed to talk to me. It sounded urgent. Are you here?” CJ yelled out to his mother.

Monique could hear CJ yelling just as he did when he was a teenager. She spoke in a whisper, “He's here, but I don't think I can do this; it's too much for me." She yelled out to CJ to give her a few minutes, and she would be right down.

Monique had to pull herself together. She didn't want CJ's father to reach out to him and tell him. "He needs to hear it from me and only me," she thought to herself, pulling her hair back into a ponytail. Monique washed her face, finished her wine, and slowly headed towards the stairs. She felt like a man walking their last walk to execution as they would shout, "Dead man walking." Her legs were heavy and barely moving, and her breathing was shallow. She rarely perspired, but today, her clothes were sticking to her body, and her hair was starting to mat at the roots. She saw him smiling and staring at her, laughing, and joking around like he usually did until he saw her face and body language. She finally made it to the bottom of the stairs and slightly collapsed into his arms.

"Mom, are you all right? What's wrong? Please don't tell me that you are sick. You don't have cancer, do you?" CJ threw out so many questions that her head was beginning to spin.

"No, son, I'm not sick, but let's go into your dad's study and talk." As they walked into the study, they both were surprised that the study was empty. When did Chris come in to move out of his office?

It had to be yesterday when she was out of the house all day, she silently wondered. "Mom, where's all of Dad's stuff? Are you remodeling again?" CJ asked with a hint of hope.

"No. I'm not remodeling, son, but it's one of the reasons why I wanted to talk with you before you go back home to LA. Your father and I are getting a divorce, and it's all my fault. When your dad finished law school and I was a senior in college, we broke up briefly. While visiting my mother, I bumped into an old friend and we both were in pain and needed comforting. He was dealing with the death of his dad, and I was dealing with the devastating breakup. We ended up becoming intimate, and the next morning, we both knew that it should never have happened. Once I returned to college, your dad was there waiting for me. He apologized for his action and begged me to take him back. Of course, I immediately said yes because I was madly in love with him. He asked me to marry him, and we made love that night to celebrate our engagement. A few months later, I discovered that I was pregnant with you, and your dad was so excited that he told his parents that we were expecting, and his mother practically demanded that we have a wedding as soon as possible. It was happening so fast. I was graduating, and I wanted to wait a year to get married; however, his parents insisted that we get married before your birth. So, we got married a few months later." Monique's voice was shaky, and it cracked a few times while explaining.

CJ responded slowly, "What are you trying to tell me, Mom?"

"What I'm trying to explain," Monique said, "is that after you were born, I decided to take a paternity test to ensure that the man I married was your father. I was devastated when I got the results back saying that my old high school friend was the father. I never told your dad because I feared losing him, and I didn't want to be alone raising a child. Unfortunately, someone recently discovered my secret and is blackmailing me, which is why I'm telling you and your dad (she stutters) the truth."

CJ interrupted her.

"Are you telling me that the man I loved and called dad all my life isn't my biological father? And do you mean to tell me that had it not been for the person blackmailing you, you would have never told Dad or me the truth? Do you hear how fucked up that is, Mom? Do you? I have always heard rumors that my grandmother had some reservations that I was not biologically a Harris. So, you are saying that I'm a bastard, and my mom is a whore?" CJ angrily said.

He felt a sting on his right cheek that sent a burning sensation to his eye without notice.

"I know that I messed up, and you have every right to be angry at me, even hate me if that is what you want to do. But, I am still your mother, and I will not allow my flesh and blood to disrespect me by calling me a whore," Monique angrily shouted.

"I can't do this. "You have ruined my life, and I don't think that I want to see you for a while," CJ said.

He continued to tell Monique that the only reason she told them the truth after all these years was because of blackmail. "Why can't you see how fucked up that is and how justified I am in whatever I want to say? Yes, you are my mother, but you have deceived me in the worse way! I changed my mind; I'm leaving for L.A. tonight!" CJ yelled as he stormed out of the house.

Jessica rang the doorbell, but no one answered the door. She waited a few minutes, contemplating if she should walk inside. Finally, she was concerned about Monique, and she stepped inside; Jessica found Monique lying on her expensive chase, crying.

"Hey, hey, what's going on?" Jessica asked.

Monique managed to tell Jessica what happened in between sobs, and Jessica just held her friend until she stopped crying.

"I didn't mean for any of this to happen. I was young, and I was scared. By the time I was mature enough to understand the devastation my silence would cause, years had passed, and it was too late. I didn't want to hurt anyone, but all I've done was hurt, everyone. I have already lost my husband, and I don't know how to make it without my son. He hates me. I know that he said that he didn't, but it wasn't just his words, it was his tone, and the pain in his eyes. I can't believe how much I've hurt the ones I love. No one can hate me as much as I hate myself right now. I'm praying that everyone I hurt can find it in their heart not to hate me. I couldn't live with myself if CJ never forgives me." She cried.

Jessica hugged her friend, consoling her with tears in her eyes. She couldn't remember Monique ever being so vulnerable and allowing anyone to see it, but right now, she was the only friend Monique had, and it was about survival. Monique's marriage was over, and her relationship with CJ was on hiatus. Jessica wasn't sure where Moses stood in all this craziness, but knowing him the way she did, she could bet that he wasn't okay, and of course, her relationship with Renee was over.

My Sister's Keeper

After hearing the harsh words from her son, Monique began to unravel emotionally. It was entirely new for her; she had always been able to recover from difficult conversations. This one hit her harder than she suspected it would. No one could have prepared her for how these last two days and nights would have transpired. She was in a dangerous headspace that she tried to avoid, but hearing CJ tell her how he felt about her and dismissed her like yesterday's trash was crushing. The next day she refused to get out of bed and barely spoke with Jessica; she wouldn't eat and slept the day away. Monique realized that CJ would be angry and hurt because of the secret, but to completely dismiss her until further notice was like someone grabbing a knife and sticking it into her heart. If she was going to survive the night, two things would need to happen fast: Jessica needed to be knocking on her bedroom door for her mind not to go dark, and she needed something more potent than wine.

She knew Jessica was asleep and didn't want to wake her up. There should be enough liquor in the house to help her forget the recent events. After all, her husband was more of a hard liquor drinker, while she mostly preferred wine. Chris kept all sorts of liquor bottles in the house, and Monique was sure she could find something to drown her sorrows in for the night.

She searched downstairs, upstairs, the basement, and even the garage, and there wasn't a bottle. "Well damn, he took all the liquor?" Monique said in her annoyed voice. She grabbed a few bottles of wine from the cooler and placed them in the refrigerator, and as she was placing her wine bottles, Monique saw the peach cobbler that she had made; she never threw it out despite Chris demanding her to. It was only a few days old and still good enough to eat. Monique smiled as she remembered that she had infused it with cannabis. She grabbed the container, cut it into a nice-sized portion, and placed it in the oven. She didn't want to microwave it because she always believed that certain foods taste better when warmed up in the oven. While waiting for the cobbler to be ready, Monique finished her glass of wine and took a shower. She could have stayed in that hot, steaming shower all night. It was like all the heat from the steam removed the heaviness from her soul.

Monique put on an old pair of her favorite football team sweatpants and an extra-large T-shirt, which was an old gift from Jessica, that read, "Today, I don't give a fuck." She thought about how fitting those words were at that moment. Jessica was going to crack up laughing when she saw her wearing it. Monique giggled as she thought to herself. Her peach cobbler was good and hot, so she went to the kitchen and grabbed the vanilla ice cream from the freezer. She didn't bother removing the cobbler from the warming bowl; she placed a dish towel underneath the bowl, and voila, Monique was ready to indulge.

As Monique took her first bite, she found happiness in her soul. The cobbler was good, and she didn't realize how hungry she was until she found herself fixing another bowl, but this time she put it in a microwave. As Monique ate the last spoonful of the cobbler, Jessica walked into the kitchen and asked her what she was eating. With a mouthful, Monique managed to say peach cobbler. She then washed it down with a glass of

Chardonnay. Jessica looked at the clock and saw that it was only 7:00 at night when Monique told Jessica that she thought that she was asleep and that she didn't want to disturb her sleep. Stunned at Monique's strange behavior and her choice of clothing, she quickly assessed that she was under some sort of influence. Jessica chuckled as she spoke.

"I'll be damned. You're drunk, because the only way you would have worn that, let me think what you called it, oh yeah, that tacky hood ass t-shirt if you were out of your mind."

Monique had a look like she had a secret and was dying to tell it. Then she just blurted it out, "I'm not drunk, I'm high!" Monique told her that she laced the peach cobbler with infused cannabis. Jessica looked at her bougie friend and was pleasantly surprised by her choice of relaxation.

"I feel great! I lost my husband and my son within 48 hours. I am more alone than ever, and I have no clue what lies ahead for me." Monique screamed from the top of her lungs, "I'm that person who always has things together; even if I don't, I'll fake it until I can make it. Life, you won, and I lost. I no longer want to do this thing called life. You are a fucking bitch; you won, you won."

At that moment, the sad Monique appeared. Jessica grabbed her friend and held her, stroking her hair while Monique cried. It wasn't that horrible-sounding cry Jessica was waiting to hear, but a softer, more pain-stricken cry.

The weakness of the cry sounded like someone giving up, which worried Jessica. She only remembered hearing Monique cry like this when they were young and in Monique's bedroom. She asked why God hated her so much to make her darker than everyone else. It was a cry that a person never forgets, and soon after, Monique changed into this focus-driven person who didn't care who she stepped on.

Jessica managed to get Monique upstairs and back into her bed. She begged Jessica not to leave, and Jessica was glad that she had asked because she didn't have a good feeling about Monique's state of mind. They talked and cried while lying for hours in Monique's California King-size bed. It made Jessica feel like a small child sleeping in her parent's bed. Early the next morning, Monique and Jessica were awakened by the sound of the doorbell ringing. They slowly got out of bed and looked at each other with a puzzled look on their faces. Jessica followed Monique downstairs and to the front door. They both looked like they needed a good hot shower and some coffee.

Monique opened the door to a yard full of movers and a large moving truck. The man at the door spoke.

"Good afternoon; I'm looking for Mrs. Monique Harris."

Monique paused for a second. "I'm Mrs. Harris. Who are you? Why are you here with movers? Never mind, give me a few minutes. I think that I know what is happening."

She closed the door and looked for her cell phone, which was still sitting on the kitchen island with twenty percent battery usage left. She plugged the phone into an extra charger that was still in the kitchen after that night she had cooked dinner for Chris. She started pacing while waiting for her husband to answer her call. He sent her call straight to voicemail on the third ring, which caused her to become so furious that she didn't see Jessica and flew right by her in a rage. She opened the door and told the mover who came to the door earlier that they might as well get back into their vehicles and leave because they weren't coming in today. Before she closed the door, she told the guy to give her soon-to-be ex-husband a message from her:

"Go straight to hell and take his mama with him!

It was officially a fight, and the one thing that Monique was excellent at was fighting dirty. The Harris family may have wealth and prestige, but she knew where they buried all the bodies and every indiscretion. She had the receipts. So, if Chris and his family wanted a fight, then a fight they would get. She stopped long enough to look at Jessica and said, "Are you with me or against me?" And Jessica gave her a look that she had her back.

Their situation brought back painful memories of when Jessica and Richard fought and how ugly it had gotten. Jessica's anxiety was through the roof, and before she grabbed her suitcases and headed upstairs, she started thinking about Monique's confession regarding the peach cobbler, and how she infused it with cannabis, it made Jessica smile.

"So, you decided to indulge in your "special" peach cobbler without offering your guest a bowl?" Jessica sheepishly grinned.

"I have more of the butter; I can make us more if you like?" Monique suggested.

"I like." Jessica squalled with delight.

Monique washed her hands and prepared her now-infamous peach cobbler. She had enough ingredients for one more dish. In the meantime, Jessica found herself texting Renee and catching her up with what transpired. Renee never responded to her texts. She laid down for a few minutes to think about what her life without Richard would be like, now that she was a single woman. At first, she was excited to get back on the dating scene. At least until everyone Jessica knew told her that she should have tried to work things out because dating nowadays was a joke. It couldn't be as grim as everyone was saying, she thought to herself.

Several minutes later, Monique knocked on the door, telling her that the peach cobbler was ready. It took Jessica a few minutes to realize that someone was knocking at the door. She must have fallen asleep, she thought. Jessica got up and adjusted her eyes from blurry to clear vision. She slowly walked to the door, opening it up before Monique could knock on her bedroom door again. "Hey, sleepy head, the peach cobbler is ready, and it's better than the first one," Monique said with excitement.

Jessica smiled and gave Monique a look she hadn't given since they were children, the challenge look of who was going to beat the other to the target. Both women took off in what they thought was a sprint, only to find out they were fast walking at best to the prize. It was a tie as both women found themselves breathing heavily and needed a few minutes to catch their breath in between, laughing at themselves.

They sat in the kitchen with a half-gallon of vanilla ice cream, two bowls, and two spoons, with the peach cobbler as the centerpiece. There was silence as they indulged in this decadent treat baked in butter-infused cannabis. They laughed for what seemed like hours, reminiscing about their childhood. Jessica could sense that Monique had a lot of regrets about her behavior and losing a friendship; a sisterhood over Moses' apparent mind-blowing member that resulted in a child. The peach cobbler was beginning to hit, but it didn't give Jessica or Monique the giggles they had expected and needed. Maybe because they were already in a sad mood before the cannabis started to kick in, they both began to cry. Monique had that ugly cry that changed the course of their tear fest. Finally, Jessica couldn't take it any longer and decided to address her concerns.

"Girl, where in the hell did you get that fucked up cry? I mean, you sound crazy."

Jessica couldn't stop herself from laughing, partially because of the strange look on Monique's face. Eventually, Monique would join her friend in laughter that lasted most of the afternoon. The ladies finished off two bottles of Chardonnay and half the cannabis-infused peach cobbler. Between the wine and the cannabis, they were too out of it to make it to their perspective rooms, which they found hilarious. So, they did what every mature woman does in their state of mind; they randomly prank-called their friends. Jessica called Moses and told him that his member must be highly contagious and dipped in gold flakes to have two bitches fighting over it for over thirty freaking years. The ladies burst into laughter before Monique asked Jessica who she was calling a bitch. Monique was next, and she decided to call Chris, her soon-to-be ex-husband. It took her three times for him to stop sending her calls to voicemail and answer. Finally, she told him that if Henrietta Proud, better known as Suga Mama from "The Proud Family", and Robert Jebediah Freeman, affectionally known as Granddad from "The Boondocks", had a child, it would be his mama!

Jessica screamed out, "She called your mama ugly!"

Monique quickly hung up and burst into laughter. The ladies were enjoying themselves and promptly started again. They called everyone they could think of except for Renee and Richard. Monique dared Jessica to call Richard and tell him how much she loved him, and Jessica agreed but only if she called Renee and sincerely apologized. Monique wasn't ready, so instead, they lay on opposite ends of Monique's very large sectional in what seemed to be deep thought as they drifted off to sleep. The ladies would wake up the following day in the spot they last remembered occupying. They both suffered from an alcohol and marijuana hangover. They looked at each other and shook their heads, laughing at what they could remember from the previous day. After showering and getting dressed, the ladies decided to go out to eat instead of staying home. First, Monique changed all the locks and alarms in case Chris decided to move anything else out of the home. Next, Jessica chose to talk about their class reunion and asked Monique if she still planned on going.

"A week from today, we will be having our 35th high school reunion," Jessica said excitedly.

"About that, I'm not sure it's a good idea to go to the reunion. My soon-to-be ex-husband and my son hate me, and I'm afraid that if I leave, I'll come back to an empty house. Not to mention," Monique said sadly, "I'm just not in the mood to see old friends, enemies, and flames."

"I think you should go and get your mind off everything; have some fun and see old friends. I'm sure more people will be excited to see you than you can imagine," Jessica said.

"Do you think that Renee will be happy to see me? Considering all that I'm going through, do you think she would put behind her hatred for me and be my sister again?" Monique asked with a concerned tone.

"Do you want to reconnect with Renee, or are you trying to get enough people on your side to help you fill the void of being a soon-to-be-divorced woman? Because I'll be honest, Renee isn't ready to be your sister, I'm not going back down memory lane of the shit that you have done to her, but in all fairness, you have done some serious damage to your friendship with Renee. So, I will say this, Monique: If you are serious about mending your broken relationship with Renee, you should come to the reunion and talk with her," Jessica said.

"I don't know," Monique said. "That's a lot of anger coming my way, and I don't know if I can handle it. It would make me feel like a caged dog with no other recourse but to fight my way out of that cage."

"Let me be clear, Monique, what you are not going to do is add more fire to what a precarious relationship with Renee is already. There will be no fighting, period! If she curses you out and calls you every name but the child of God, you will take it. If she makes you feel like a hoe-ass tramp, then swallow it. Do you know why, Monique? Damn, I was trying not to walk down memory lane, but here we are. First, you slept with her boyfriend because he chose her over you, which pissed you off. Then, you saw how much she liked him, yet you spread your legs and fucked her by fucking him. Next, she tried to get over the notion that this person she loved as a sister betrayed her to hold on to a sisterhood already failing. Then, to add insult to injury, you had a baby with the man she still loves today! You lied about it for over thirty years and now want forgiveness. You gave less than a damn about her feelings this long, so yes, ma'am, you will eat, drink, and take all her shit to get it out of her system. Then and only then will you both be able to start from ground zero. I decided that you are attending the class reunion, and that settles that decision," Jessica annoyingly said.

They rode in silence back to Monique's house from a late lunch; the ladies stopped by the grocery store to buy some groceries and more wine. After they put away everything, they began to straighten up her home. Finally, Monique decided to break the ice by saying that Moses wasn't innocent in any of this mess, and why Renee forgave him so quickly and not her. Jessica kindly responded.

"She loved Moses romantically. He was a branch to her heart, but she loved you like family; you were the root of her soul. There is a big difference. Romantic love will come and go, but family love is deeply rooted, especially if it's love for someone who doesn't share the same DNA. She chooses to love you with a bond so deep that even the betrayal of sleeping with her heart only cracks the relationship but never breaks it. Having his baby and deciding to hide it from everyone is some King David and Bathsheba shit. The only difference was that you didn't put Renee on the frontline to die so that you could have Moses all to yourself."

After a brief silence, Monique looked at Jessica and said, "King David? You had to compare me to King David?" The two ladies enjoyed a good laugh. Jessica conceded that Moses wasn't innocent in any of this and confided in Monique that Renee had told her (in confidence) that she wanted nothing to do with Moses.

Monique smiled and spoke softly. "Well, if I'm going to the reunion next week, I will need a few new outfits, and while I still have his credit cards, let's do some damage." She knew that no matter how angry her husband was towards her, he wouldn't leave her high and dry financially, at least not yet. They were to meet in a few days with their attorneys to discuss the particulars of their divorce. Monique wasn't sure what she would get from the divorce, but she sure in hell would try to get as much as she felt was owed to her. She stood by his side, helping him open his first law practice, taking his side when his father and brother jumped on him for not getting into politics with them.

Monique was the one who took care of the household and sent appropriate gifts for this or that occasion. She forgave him when he cheated on her and had this emotional relationship with his now ex-office manager. Her only sin was withholding paternity DNA results, and Monique admitted that if it weren't for her blackmail issue, the secret of CJ's biological father would still be a secret. The thought of what was a good marriage ending saddened her, and she wiped a tear that dropped onto her cheek. Jessica didn't notice that Monique had checked out of their conversation because Jessica was too busy dancing over their soon-to-be shopping spree. She needed another new outfit for the reunion. Something that would be sexy and revealing, so when Richard saw the pictures, he would hate that he missed out and didn't get to see her sexiness in person. There was always a plan for getting a man's attention, even if it was to rub what he was missing in his face.

The ladies found themselves at Monique's favorite mall and store. They headed directly to the formal dress area and went their separate ways. Jessica found a few dresses that caught her eye. One dress was an emerald color with a plunging neckline, and the other dress was a basic little black halter dress. She decided to try them both on to see which one showed her features the best. She tried on the emerald dress first, which was love at first look. She knew right away that was the dress. It clung to the shape of her body, and it was clear that she wasn't the flat-chested kid from school. Next, she tried on the black dress purely out of curiosity. Although the dress was beautiful and very sexy, it didn't give her a look or feel like the emerald dress. Monique walked out of her dressing room as Jessica walked by. Monique looked stunning. She had a shimmering purple ombre off-the-shoulder dress. There was a plunging neckline with rhinestones covering the bodice and thin sleeves. The skirt of the gown hugged Monique's derriere perfectly and the long slit from her inner thigh to her hem was enough to make any man salivate. Jessica's mouth dropped as she smiled and stared in adoration.

"Girl, you look fabulous in that dress. I hope that this is the one for you," Jessica said.

"I have one more dress to try on, but I'm sure this is the dress. Jessica, the dress you have on is stunning on you. Is that the dress?" Monique responded.

"No. As beautiful as this dress is, I'm going to go with my first pick," Jessica responded with a big smile.

"Put it back on so that I can see, and then you can help me decide between this dress and the next one," Monique said, feeling the excitement.

The ladies went back into their dressing rooms and changed. Jessica stepped out first and asked the salesperson to take her picture. She wanted to send it to Renee to show her what she was wearing to the reunion. Monique stepped out wearing this sapphire dress when the salesperson gave Jessica her phone. It was cute, but it paled in comparison to the purple ombre dress. It was a form-fitting dress showing a portion of her back with a long split that looked like it would offer more than the thigh. Monique was in awe of how stunningly beautiful Jessica looked in her dress. Without saying a word, they both knew what clothing they would be showcasing at their class reunion. Now it was off to accessorize, and while the ladies were looking at the accessories, Monique's phone rang, and the caller ID showed that it was Chris calling. She decided to send it to voicemail. Vaguely, remembering the mama joke she called to tell him last night, Monique refused to let him or anyone else take her mood down.

She was finally in a good mental space despite her world crumbling. The ladies made it back to the house, exhausted from the hard labor of shopping. Jessica was ready to get back to her life tomorrow and get ready for the reunion. Renee flew in a few days ahead so that she could spend time with family and hit all her favorite food spots. On the day of the reunion, she and Renee were going to have their manicure and pedicures together, and they were each other's dates. Now that Monique was coming, Jessica told Monique they could arrive together. It would be a challenge to see if the three could get together. Jessica would wait until she could see Renee's face to break the news. "The conversation should be interesting," she thought.

While cleaning up, "Alexa" was playing "Night to Remember" by Shalamar. Renee was dancing to the beat and singing at the top of her lungs, missing every key, but she didn't care. Renee was excited. The class reunion was in another week, and she couldn't wait to see old friends and new enemies. She found the perfect dress, and after losing weight, she would walk into her reunion like the dramatic scene of a romantic movie. At first, Renee decided to wear something conservative and age-appropriate, simple yet elegant. But after looking at her new body in some of the dresses she tried on just out of curiosity, she decided that she was going to do something that she had never done, wear the sexiest dress she could find. After hours of looking and trying on dresses, Renee found herself falling in love with this sexy red gown.

The bustier was silver rhinestones accentuating her plump breasts, and her split was outlined with the same rhinestones from the top of her front leg to the hem. When she walked all anyone would see would be a very distinct thigh muscle and the rhinestones dancing in concert. Her sleeveless dress also showed off her well-toned arms as the beautiful gown slightly dragged on the floor. She wanted something sexy but age appropriate. Her new look gave her many choices, especially since fifty-five was the new thirty-five, and it'd been years since she felt so confident and sexy. Her breasts were no longer flat and sagging, looking like they belonged on the cover of the "National Geographic" magazine with large hoop earrings decorating them. Since her weight loss and body shaping transformation, she had been able to sculpt her breasts, not as firm and perky as in her twenties, but they had form and some firmness, and, in a push-up bra, her girls looked like grown-ass women standing tall and alert. She didn't have six-pack abs, but her stomach was flat. Her legs stood out, and her thighs and calves would make any thirty-year-old blush.

Renee was so proud that she stuck with her workouts and her trainer. So many mornings, she didn't want to go to the gym. Initially, Renee was apprehensive about going because of her weight insecurities and was embarrassed. Now, she walked into the gym like a boss, with her head held high and focused on her workouts. Never again would she allow her light to dim over something that she had control of changing. As she finished putting the last dish in the dishwasher, "Alexa" played Chaka Khan's "I'm Every Woman". What a perfect song to celebrate the woman I am today, Renee thought as she started singing.

A Night to Remember!

The big day had arrived. It was the who's who of Garrett Senior High School class of '83; someone from the reunion committee stood at the welcome table to greet each guest. Each person received a gift bag filled with a shot glass displaying the school colors of black and red, their mascot of a knight, a yearbook with a then-and-now photo of each classmate, and a nice ink pen with an inscription that read, "Class of '83, A Knight to Remember". In addition, each classmate and their plus one received their name tags, a knight's shield, and their name engraved on it. Trays of Hors d'oeuvres donated by a local restaurant and glasses of champagne were available throughout the meet and greet. The music playing was Shalamar's "Night to Remember". Each table had its centerpiece, highlighting all four years leading to graduation. It looked so beautiful and elegant that Jessica knew everyone would love it. She decided not to ruffle any feathers by suggesting that Renee and Monique ride with her to the reunion. Instead, she lied and told them since she was part of the committee, she had to be there early, and they didn't want anyone else to be there until it started. Both Monique and Renee arrived separately. The weather was perfect; it wasn't too hot or too cold. During mid-September in Illinois, you don't know what weather you'll end up with each day.

"Is that Byron "Moses" Banks that I see?" Jessica screamed with joy. "Damn, man, you look good. I mean catfight good."

Moses chuckled as he hugged her and whispered in her ear, "Stop being messy and stop playing on my phone. Hey, what's this nonsense that I'm hearing about, you and my boy are divorced? When I heard that, I was like, stop lying. Those two were madly in love. You guys beat the odds because your stepdad, Mr. Everett didn't play any games regarding you and the boys. I remember that night when Richard's mother caught you and him having sex at her house. Mrs. Palmer drove you home with Richard in tow and told your mom and dad, 'Ain't no white girl is going to trick my son and get pregnant.' Mr. Everett was about to go off on you, but Richard got out of the car and defended your honor. I was next door at my boy Tony Moore's house. I think that is when Mr. Everett had mad respect for Richard. He was the only dude allowed in the house."

 "Wow, I didn't know anyone knew about that situation, but don't be mistaken, he beat my ass when I got in the house. He told Richard if he ever hears about us having sex again, he was going to shoot his member off," Jessica said, laughing.

"Richard didn't tell you how we became friends?" Jessica shook her head no. "When I saw what he did, I was like; we're going to be great friends. I liked his bravery because Moms were handing out threats and insults like dollar bills at a strip club," Moses said while laughing.

Jessica began to laugh as they reminisced, but she wasn't done with him yet. "Let me ask you a question. How do you feel about my girl, Renee, between you and me? I'm only asking because I had hoped that this reunion would have brought you two back together again. That was until you impregnated her former best friend and hid it for years," she said in a judgmental tone.

"What did you just say? I just found out that I had a kid a few weeks ago when Monique called to tell me. The only reason she told me was because of some blackmail shit," Moses said, with a hint of anger.

"That bitch! Are you telling me that you didn't deny that you were the father? Because that is what Monique told her family and me about why she lied about who the father was. She said that she was scared and embarrassed." Jessica was feeling annoyed.

By this time, Moses was almost speechless, but his anger began seeping out with every word he spoke.

"Jessica, let me make myself clear. I didn't know I fathered a son until a few weeks ago. I would never deny any child of mine. That's some real bullshit, and before the night's end, I'm going to handle this shit," Moses said.

He excused himself and disappeared. He was devastated that not only had Monique kept the secret of his child away from him, but she lied to make herself look better. He could feel his emotions getting the best of him, and the last thing he needed was for Monique to see him at a weak moment and try to exploit it somehow. Moses bumped into Richard on his way out and explained what had transpired when Jessica shared more information. Richard could see the pain and the emotion laced with anger on his face, and he suggested that they go take a walk so Moses could regain his composure.

"Man, fuck Monique… Bitch! I'm glad that her world is crashing down all around her, and I hope that her husband leaves her with a penny because she is a one-cent hoe," Richard said.

"Don't talk about Monique like that. Show her a little respect," Moses spoke softly.

"Respect? What kind of respect has she shown you, her husband, her friends, and I forgot, CJ, your love child? Still too soon? So, this beast doesn't deserve respect. What she deserves is an old-fashioned ass-kicking, and if I were a woman, I'd be in that ass like a Mike Tyson fight, knocking her ass out before you can blink. Respect? Hell no, we ain't respecting her ass, what we are going to do is…"

Moses interrupted. "We aren't going to do a damn thing but get to the truth. We aren't fighting her verbally or physically. Man, I'm serious. I know how slick your tongue can be, and I need you to have my back the smart way," Moses sternly replied.

"Man, my bad. I got carried away. Only because this shit is so fucked up, and she is walking around as she got away without any consequences, but you are correct, I got you. You can count on me to be the voice of reason," Richard said apologetically. "Will he call you dad, pops, father, Byron, or Moses?"

Richard light-heartedly asked. "Richard, you're about to get your ass beat. Keep it up." Moses laughed. Both men started laughing, which was what Richard was trying to accomplish. He just wanted to end this sad conversation with a laugh so they could return to the reunion on lighter footing.

Jessica was glad that Monique walked in because she wanted to talk to her about the conversation she had had with Moses, but before she could speak, the women from the cheerleading squad grabbed her and started talking and laughing. Maybe tonight wasn't the best time to get into it with her. She'd let her enjoy herself and they could discuss the second big lie in the morning. Jessica saw someone familiar walking with Moses; low and behold, it was her ex-husband, Richard. She walked straight to him and asked why he was there and why he didn't tell her he was coming. Once he explained that he only came to give moral support to Moses, Jessica gave him a side-eye look and told him to behave tonight. Richard wanted to know if Monique lied to everyone about CJ. Jessica confirmed that it was true that Monique lied. As Richard continued his tirade of insults regarding Monique, and the last one was him calling her a troll-looking bitch, Monique was in earshot as she was walking towards the group. Monique gave Richard a quick look up and down before angrily speaking.

"Classy, Dick (she knew he hated being called that name), well done putting a woman down, especially when she is at her lowest. For the record, I never said that Moses never wanted the child; I said I didn't think he would want to get out of the Air Force to become a dad. I see why Jessica divorced your black ass, bitch."

"Whoa, whoa, wait one moment, Monique. Let's be clear, you did tell me that Moses didn't want the child, and I told you that Richard divorced me. I never wanted a divorce, and don't call my husband a bitch." Jessica furiously spoke.

"Ex," Richard interjected.

"Only I can call him a bitch," Jessica said, feeling angry as she looked at Richard and gave him a mean look.

Everyone was looking at them, wondering what was going on. Once Jessica realized they were making a spectacle of themselves, she told everyone they would talk about it later. They made their way into the reception hall and found their tables. Richard and Moses were sitting at one table on the other side of the room, while Monique and Jessica sat at another table far away from the men. Just as they were closing the door and the class president was beginning to speak, this beautiful woman who looked like she had just stepped out of every fashion magazine was standing there looking stunning. Jessica's mouth dropped as her eyes met Renee's.

Jessica smiled and mouthed the words, "You sexy ass bitch."

This one-time Renee didn't mind being called a bitch after reading Jessica's lips. Instead, she took it as a compliment. Jessica stood up and walked towards her friend Renee.

"Now where do you have me sitting? And please don't tell me I'm sitting with you and that thing over there." Renee nervously asked.

Jessica didn't get the chance to warn Renee of the small changes that she had made and presented Renee with three options: a chair next to her and Monique, a chair at Moses' and Richard's table, or she could sit with strangers. Renee smiled and rolled her eyes at Jessica as she walked towards the table of strangers. Renee greeted everyone while two of the men fussed over who would pull her chair out as their wives angrily stared at them.

Renee didn't notice Moses, but he saw her, and for the rest of the evening, he couldn't take his eyes off her. His heart was breaking, knowing that she wanted nothing to do with him, not because of the lies that Monique told everyone but because of the son they had between them. He knew his chances of having her in his life were shot. Just as he glanced in Renee's direction, after having a conversation with Richard, Moses' and Renee's eyes connected. She rolled her eyes at him as he smiled at her. After that, she never looked his way again.

Now that dinner was over, everyone was mingling, and Moses saw Renee walk toward the ladies' room. He decided he would take a chance and try to converse with her if she allowed him. While waiting for Renee,

Richard played interference with Monique, ensuring that she didn't ruin Moses' chance to have alone time with the only woman who mattered in his life other than his mother.

Richard walked up to Monique and said, "I must admit, you are a bad sistah walking in here like your shit doesn't stink. Looking around for your baby daddy after trashing his name? I never liked your monkey ass, but after what you did to my boy, I'm one level from hating you, and that's because I can't hate and get into heaven. Although I'm willing to bet that Jesus is saying right now, 'I'd still let you in, because that one right there is going where many people have told her to go, straight to hell.'" Richard burst into laughter.

"You're not funny. I'm only looking for Moses because we have a personal matter to discuss, and anyway, it's none of your business why I'm looking for him." Monique rolled her eyes as she spoke.

"Yes, it is. You don't seem to understand that Moses doesn't want you. He never wanted you. Just because you spread your legs back in high school, you thought you could keep him, but let me tell you something, sweetie; every man likes getting things for free. He messed up with Renee, and he has paid for it ever since, and thanks to you, he will pay for it for the rest of his life. He is trying to have a conversation with Renee, whom I love, and we will allow them to converse alone and uninterrupted," he said with a stern tone.

"Listen here, B-I-T-C-H," Monique said with force. "I give less than a damn why he wants to talk with Renee. We share a child, and we need to talk! Point, blank, period."

Richard chuckled. "You and Moses don't share a child," he said. "You could have shared a child, but Monique, you lied for over thirty years about the child you had with him. The child that is now a thirty-three-year-old grown-ass man who I'm pretty sure has already disowned you – that is if you told him the truth. So, do everyone a favor, take your black, ugly, and lying ass back to North Carolina, and deal with your shit!"

The tension was so thick that it was noticeable to everyone in the room, including Jessica, who stared at them with a motherly attitude that suggested 'I'm going to get deep in your ass for clowning in public' look. She then spoke after walking to where they were standing:

"Hey, what is going on over here? Everyone can hear your argument over the music."

Monique explained that he was trying to prevent her from talking with Moses because he was trying to have a conversation with Renee. She explained that what she needed to speak with Moses about was far more important than anything he and Renee could discuss. Monique continued to complain to Jessica about how rude and obnoxious her ex-husband was being. She told Jessica that no decent man should ever disrespect a woman, regardless of her behavior, past or present.

Jessica softly spoke, "You are correct, no man should ever disrespect a woman." She shot her angry eyes at Richard. "But no woman should ever disrespect a man. Too often, women love to throw a rock and hide their hands, then cry bloody murder once there is a reaction. Again, let me reiterate what I said. No man has the right to disrespect a woman, be up in her face calling her disrespectful names," she gave Richard another angry look with a deep eye roll, "however when a woman sleeps with a man who is involved with someone she considers a sister, flaunts it in her face and then spreads her legs again years later, but this time a child was the result of a 'for old time's sake' roll in the bed, that creates some issues. Then, it comes out that this same woman kept what she did a secret for over thirty years but gets busted. Yet, instead of fessing up, she throws the baby daddy under the bus to save her dirty-thirsty ass." She threw Monique a look of disgust. "Finally, to add insult to injury, her entitled ass thinks she can force herself on anyone, including interrupting time and space between a man and a woman because she said so. Leave that man alone. If this isn't some of the worst bougie privilege shit I've ever seen. And by the way, I don't want to remind you a third time of this mess you made." Jessica shook her head as she walked away.

Monique looked at Richard, who was making the gesture of a person picking their face off the floor. He said in his bass voice, as he started walking away, "Yeah, what she said, all that and then some." She stood there watching Jessica, her only friend walk away again. But Monique wasn't here to win a popularity contest; she was here to save her marriage and her family.

"Moses can have the rest of his life trying to make up with Renee; speaking with Moses is most important to me," Monique mumbled as she headed in the direction that she last saw him walk.

Monique passed a few friends reminiscing about their high school days and what they were doing now. She saw Moses, but he wasn't talking with Renee. Instead, he was talking with Diamond. The closer she got, the more that voice sounded familiar. She couldn't quite put her finger on that voice, but it triggered some strong emotions inside her. Moses' back was towards her, so he didn't see Monique coming, which was good because she didn't feel like interacting with Diamond, and their conversation seemed a bit tense.

As she turned away, she glanced over at Diamond and noticed a little smirk on her face as if she had told someone a secret. It was nice to see that a grown woman with grandkids could still entertain being messy, Monique thought sarcastically. She chuckled at her thoughts. While looking in a different direction, she accidentally bumped into Renee, the last person she wanted to see. They both stood there in silence, unsure of what to say to each other, wondering who would speak first. Monique decided that she had better say something before all she would feel would be a fist. She never knew Renee to be a physical woman, but she wasn't taking any chances after all she had put her through.

"Hi, Renee, I know I'm the last person you wanted to see, much less talk to, but I'm glad we bumped into each other. Do you mind if we talk?"

Monique was interrupted before she could continue to speak.

"No, Monique, we didn't bump into each other; you clumsily walked into me, almost spilling your drink," Renee said in an annoyed tone.

"You are right. It was my fault. Do you mind, can we go somewhere to talk? We used to be good friends before I messed all that up. I'm not asking for us to become best friends, but I'd like to explain myself," Monique said with a hint of hope in her voice.

Renee hesitated but was curious to hear what lies Monique was going to tell, so she slowly nodded her head yes. She gestured with her hand for Monique to lead the way. The ladies walked outside, where there was less noise and more privacy.

Monique humbled herself when she spoke.

"Let me start by apologizing to you for what I did in high school. I was wrong, and there isn't any excuse for my behavior. I was young, angry, and jealous of you. Renee, you were beautiful, outgoing, and everyone's friend. You could play sports, and every boy wanted to date you and Jessica. I got the boys who knew they couldn't get either of you. When I saw Moses, I wanted him for myself, and I knew that once he saw you, I didn't have a chance. Before I could tell you or Jessica that I had a crush on him, he was in your face, and you were smiling at him. I knew at that moment that I had again lost another boy to you. All my life, people have treated me as second best, and never once has anyone other than my husband felt that the darkness of my skin was beautiful. Even my nickname, Pepper, was a jab at my dark-colored skin. I know now that my family meant no harm to me, and they didn't know those mean kids in school or in the neighborhood would use what my family thought was endearing as a weapon. I wore a scar so deep inside that the only way I knew how to protect my mental and emotional state was to become the woman I am today, cold, and uncaring. I'm not saying that I'm proud of my actions. Still, I lived in survival mode so long that it became my identity." Monique humbled herself when she spoke.

Renee took a deep breath so that she could choose her words carefully. "I understand that you had low self-esteem issues growing up. I knew that you could be vicious when you felt cornered or if someone hurt you. I was never that person and I never thought that you would come for me. I protected you when I could and always stood by your side. If they made fun of you, then they made fun of me, because that was how we rolled back then. We got into so many fights at school that the principal called us into his office and gave the three of us – you, me, and Jessica – two options: suspension or that we would break up fights instead of getting into them to teach us a lesson. To his surprise, the three of us took a week's suspension, and as we explained to Principal Daniels, we were only defending ourselves from bullies who tried to come for any one of us. It was us against the bullies at school and in the neighborhood. We lost a few and won a lot; they called us the Westend Killers."

The ladies laughed at the memory as they reminisced about that life stage. Jessica walked up to the ladies as they were laughing. She was pleasantly surprised at what she witnessed and asked if they would mind if she stayed. She didn't speak then because she wanted to see where this was going and didn't want to mess up whatever they were discussing.

Renee continued talking. "The point is, Monique, I loved you like a sister, and you betrayed me like I was an enemy. You didn't come for my first boyfriend; you came after my heart. You destroyed the rest of my senior year. I was so heartbroken, not just that you slept with Moses, but you wanted the entire high school to know that you fucked him. Then to turn that knife deeper in my back, you two started dating, which was too much for me. I gave him my virginity because I was in love with him. I knew from day one that he was the only man I ever wanted. Don't get me wrong; Moses also shares the blame for my heartache. He was a boy I loved with my heart, but you were my sister whom I loved with my soul. You took the chance for me to see if he was the love of my life or just a high school love. So, for over thirty years, I wondered about the possibilities we could have had, and then when I found out that he was your baby's daddy, it destroyed my hope yet again. I know that by now I should have let it go, but I can't." Renee said, "One last thing, how do you let go of a piece of your heart that gave you hope all this time?"

Time's Up!

oth Jessica and Monique looked at Renee with a surprised look.
Neither of them thought Renee would ever let Moses go. She'd been
stuck in this fantasy time warp that seemed to only loop around them
dating. Somehow Monique managed to grab his member and insert it
inside her as if it was detachable and Moses was unaware of its use. Hearing
her tell her story of how she felt made sense to them. It wasn't that Renee
never blamed Moses for having sex with Monique because he shared the
blame, but her love for him wasn't as deep and solid as it was for Monique.
She mourned not knowing the possibilities for someone she had such a
deep and meaningful connection with, and a piece of her died when it was
her sister who took those possibilities away, not once but twice, solidifying
her and Moses' chances would be gone forever.

The mood was a little scary for Jessica. She got nervous whenever it
got too quiet; that was when her anxiety started to surface. She decided
to speak up. Since everyone was pouring out their hearts, she wanted to
do the same. She mentioned that when she was 17, she got pregnant and
had an abortion. Richard begged Jessica not to have the procedure done;
he didn't believe in them, but he thought it was her body and would
support her decision. Jessica knew if she told her stepfather that she was

pregnant, he would most likely make her keep it, and she wouldn't have been able to go to college. She and Richard broke up for a short time because it was too painful for him, and she was a reminder that she had killed his child. Eventually, his love was more profound than his pain, and they reunited. After they married, she tried getting pregnant, but all the doctors said it would be difficult because whoever performed the abortion left a lot of scar tissue from a somewhat botched abortion. They never said that she couldn't get pregnant. But the doctor only projected her chances of getting pregnant at just five percent. Jessica accepted that and for the next five years, she put her body, Richard, and their marriage through challenging times. She began to sob a little, and the women embraced her, but she wanted to continue her story. After a while, Jessica conceded that trying to get pregnant and having a baby was no longer an option.

She wanted to try adoption, but Richard put his foot down, telling her he didn't want to have a baby at his age. She remembered a discussion they had about his reasoning for why he didn't want to adopt, and what he said was that they were forty-five years old. He was preparing for his golden years to travel and not change diapers. He didn't want to be the old guy at the daycare or graduation, correcting other parents that he wasn't the grandfather; he was the father. He didn't want to see the embarrassing looks he would get and maybe a few questions about why he waited so long. He said he didn't want to find himself hanging around listening to younger fathers discussing why their wives weren't giving them the necessary sex they needed while he gets tired of just pulling it out to urinate. He still couldn't believe how demanding Jessica was before the divorce.

She was like a horny teenage boy, and he was like someone's grandmother who lost interest after menopause twenty years ago. Men's sex drive after forty goes down considerably, unlike women whose hormones are raging at age forty and all they want is sex. They seem to have grown beards, mustaches, and sideburns on their faces, some of which are thicker than their men's, and all they want is to fuck all day. It's like these women have sucked the testosterone right out of the member of their men, allowing the sperm to migrate into their bodies, creating a sex drive in women like they had bionic powers through their treasure. She explained how he rambled for almost a half-hour in a rant that had nothing to do with adopting a baby. Jessica paused as she wondered why she was carrying on, and just then, she looked at Renee and Monique who looked at her like she was crazy. They all looked at each other again and burst into laughter while simultaneously screaming, "Only that damn Richard!" Both Renee and Monique knew that it bothered Jessica not to have any children of her own, which was why she had become so close to Renee's twins.

"Why didn't you say something to us? You know that we would have been there for you," Renee spoke softly.

"I know, but you must understand, the only ones who knew were Richard and me. Oh, I forgot, and Moses," Jessica hesitantly said.

"Moses, who?" Renee blurted out in disbelief.

Jessica gave Renee the look of 'quit playing'. Monique, who had been quiet for a while, cleared her throat and mentioned that she knew Moses and Richard were best friends and that she wasn't shocked that he would be in on their secret.

"So, I'm the only one in this group who didn't know how close Richard and Moses were back then?" Renee said with a hint of annoyance and hurt.

"Moses was a touchy subject where you were concerned," Jessica said. "You weren't ready to receive any form of information if it was attached to his name. Remember when we had our high school graduation, and Moses gave you a graduation card with money in it? You didn't just throw away the card, you burned it up, but not before taking that One-hundred-dollar gift out; and then you cried as if you just caught him cheating. As years passed and if Richard brought up Moses' name, you'd scream never to speak his name in your presence, and if we are going, to be honest, you were in love then, but you hated him. You were all over the place, and no one knew when it was safe to bring up his name. Eventually, we got the memo and stopped telling you anything about Moses. So don't be upset or even hurt thinking of betrayal once again. You did this one all by yourself. You aren't always the victim; shit just happens to people," Jessica said with a matter-of-fact tone. Monique giggled, amused by how much of a sister they were to each other even after all these years. She looked at Renee and co-signed with what Jessica said.

"Fix your face, Renee; out of the three of us, you hold on to that victim role and wear it like the purple heart of heartbreak," Monique said as she giggled.

Jessica didn't laugh because she wasn't sure how Renee would respond, and then Monique looked at Renee and spoke. "Too soon?" Now the three ladies burst into a gut-busting laugh that lasted so long that no one noticed Richard and Moses walking toward them.

The laughter stopped once the ladies saw the two men, and Jessica looked at Richard angrily. She knew that the beautiful moment that they had just shared was still very fresh and tender. But unfortunately, the wrong words or gestures had the potential to blow everything back up. Being the dick that he was, Richard shrugged his shoulders and asked Jessica what was up with the attitude. She pulled him away from everyone to explain the breakthrough between Renee and Monique and how fragile the moment was at that time.

In the meantime, Moses decided to test the waters with Renee. He grabbed her arm and asked if they could go somewhere to talk. She pulled her arm away from him, slapped his face, and in her best "Miss Sophia" voice, from the "Color Purple" said, "Hell no." She gave the same snarl and walked away. The slap was so loud that Jessica and Richard stopped talking, and Richard asked with amusement, "Did she just slap you? Man, I know your face hurts because I felt the vibration over here." He laughed.

Suddenly, he felt a punch in his chest that turned his laughter into coughing. "Damnit, Jessica, it ain't going to be too much more of you hitting me. It's a man's right to punch the shit out of their ex-wife," Richard said while rubbing his chest. He then went to chase after Jessica, which left Monique and Moses alone. There was an awkward silence, and as Moses turned to leave, still massaging the right side of his face, Monique grabbed his hand and softly said, "Can we talk? I know I hurt you by keeping this secret for so long, but when I realized how it would affect you, my husband, and my son, I thought it was too late for me to speak up. If I told you, there was no way that you would have kept my secret, and I couldn't let you tell my son or my husband. I was stuck hoping and praying every day that no one would ever learn my terrible secret. Not that you were my son's biological father but that I never told you. Each year that passed, the guilt dug deeper in my soul; honestly, if it hadn't been for the blackmailer, I may have never spoken up."

"I don't want to get into this right now," Moses said, "but I am curious about one thing, did you tell Renee everything? I mean everything and be honest," Moses curiously asked.

Monique paused as she searched her brain for any indication that she missed telling Renee anything. "I told Renee everything. I don't think that we resolved our decades-long issues with each other, but I think that we made a few baby steps today. I must admit that it felt good to laugh and joke like in old times. Renee explained why she was more offended by me than you and how our sisterhood had such a strong bond, and if I'm being completely honest, I felt that strong bond as well," Monique replied.

"How did she handle you telling her that you used her name and information as an alias on a paternity test proving that her so-called son was also my son? Go ahead, tell me what she said?"

Moses' face was now burning with anger as he waited for an answer. Another pause and Monique could feel the heat of anger rising within her, and just like any live volcano, she erupted without notice.

"No, you're right; I didn't tell her, not because I didn't want to, but because Jessica had interrupted our conversation while we were talking. Please don't think I wasn't sincere about my apologies to Renee. I meant every word of it. I had planned on telling her before the three of us went back inside the reunion, but then you guys came over and interrupted us. Then you, thinking that you still had such an influence over Renee that all you had to do was touch her, and she would melt like butter, and then you present that infamous panty-dropping smile along with those sexy eyes, and she was going to do whatever you asked? Even Superman has a bad day, and by the way, how's the jaw? That was a powerful slap that she planted on you. Whether you like it or not, we still need to talk about your fatherhood and what are your expectations for both our son and me." She chuckled. As she started walking away, he shouted to her that this was far from being over.

"I see why people hate you. It's hard to like someone who never liked themselves, but I don't hate you, I pity you; I always have felt sorry for you. The sex we had was what every boy wanted, free! I knew you liked me; otherwise, why would a girl spread her legs for her best friend's man?"

Before he knew it, she had walked back to him, and as their eyes met and he saw the pain he had just inflicted on her, she slapped the left side of his face sternly, telling him to go to hell. They both walked away with tears in their eyes but for different reasons. Her tears were for her emotional pain and his from the sting of his second slap of the night.

While Richard tried to catch up with Jessica, he saw Renee walking. "Hold up, young lady; I need to holler at you for a minute," Richard said in a flat tone.

Renee stopped and looked at Richard. "What? Please don't try to defend him; he was and has been wrong for far too long," Renee said in a huff.

"Oh, you best believe I'm going to defend my friend. I know he hurt you, and there is no excuse for what he had done, but damit, Renee, it was over three decades ago. You had ample time to slap the shit out of Moses the rest of the school year, but no, you waited until your black ass was good and grown. Seriously, you owe that man an apology. How would you feel if he slapped you?"

"He better not slap me," Renee quickly responded as she huffed at Richard; she shook her head as she looked at him. Richard was always saying things he knew he would never harm a woman, much less allow another man in his presence to do. He was notorious for stirring up the mess, and what a pain Richard could be most of the time, but she loved him like a brother and wouldn't change anything about his messy ass.

"Listen to me, sis, you are better than that; I've been telling you to let that past shit go. That's why you don't have a man now, and I'm not talking about that young man that got your guts all twisted up having your old ass doing young freaky shit. Let what happened in high school go, girl; no man wants to compete with a ghost from your past that still carries a love/hate relationship in your head. I love you, though." He sensed that he may have gone too far with his tough brother talk.

Renee was quiet as if she wasn't sure how to respond. At first, he thought that she was going to render that famous slap on his face, so he braced for it, but no, she sobbed a little before speaking.

"You are right, I was wrong for waiting so long to slap him, and I've held in this pain far too long. What you are not going to do, though, is talk to me about what I am doing with my friend, sexually speaking. I'm pissed that Jessica even told you about it. How embarrassing that you know about my sex life." Renee shook her head.

"Don't be upset with Jessica. She was excited that your drought was finally over and that maybe it would make you a happier person. When a woman doesn't have sex for a long time, she becomes mean and bitter over the slightest things like an old boyfriend who broke her heart decades ago."

He looked at her with a smirk on his face. They both laughed because who could stay angry at the stupidity of Richard Palmer? The class clown and nerd who thought that he was cool brother extraordinaire.

"I know you do have the best intentions for my well-being. You have been looking out not just for me but my twins, your godchildren, for a long time. So, I appreciate you; I'll apologize to Moses for the slap but not for my feelings, and if you ever discuss my sex life again, I'm going to unfriend you."

"Wait, I'm not on social media," Richard said. "That doesn't mean I won't unfriend you, fool." She winked, and they both laughed as they hugged each other. Richard said they better head back in before missing all the fun. They walked back into the reception hall to hear one of their favorite rap songs, "La Di Da Di" by Doug E. Fresh and Slick Rick. Everyone was on the dance floor, dancing to the 80s classics. Richard grabbed Renee's hands as they made their way to the dance floor (they had been dancing partners throughout high school because Jessica and Moses didn't have any rhythm) and started to dance. Richard immediately started doing "The Prep" and Renee joined him. They went from dancing "The Prep" to "The Alf" and ended with "The Roger Rabbit". By the song's end, they were cracking up and out of breath.

Renee glanced over and saw Moses talking with Jessica and figured she needed to let go of her pain and apologize to him. She walked towards them, and just when she got the nerve up to tap him to get his attention, her foot slipped, as she touched him while in his blind spot, his reflex of being in combat came into play, and he ended up accidentally pushing her on to the floor. She fell hard and realized she was in a lot of pain, thinking she had broken her leg. He apologized profusely, explaining that he never meant any harm and that it was a knee-jerk reaction. He tried to help her, but she was in a lot of pain. Jessica checked her out and told her that she wasn't a doctor but based on her experience, it looked like Renee had broken her leg. Jessica said she would take her to the emergency room, but Moses insisted that he take her since it was his fault that she was injured. Moses scooped Renee and carried her to his car, maneuvers that resembled a romantic movie scene.

Monique was in the bathroom drying her eyes and fixing her face when all this mayhem occurred. One of the women from her old cheerleading squad gave her a blow-by-blow play of what happened and mentioned how Moses and Renee looked like the black version of "An Officer and a Gentleman". At first, Monique was concerned, but then she was happy that she missed out on the trip to the emergency room. She wanted to go to her hotel room and try to talk with CJ. Monique hoped that enough time had gone by that he wanted to speak. She was glad Renee and the gang would be detained for a couple of hours so that if her call went well, she could have a decent conversation without any interruptions, but if it went wrong, she could cry herself to sleep. Her phone buzzed, and she hoped that it was CJ responding to her text, but it wasn't him. It was Jessica letting her know what transpired and where they all were heading. She replied that someone from the reunion told her what happened, that she hoped Renee would be all right, and that she would use this alone time to try to talk to her son.

Monique asked Jessica to keep that part to herself because if it went wrong, she didn't want Moses asking questions, Richard rubbing it in, and Renee being in her feelings. Jessica understood and promised to keep it to herself. Besides, everyone was focusing on the queen of being a victim. "Renee is so dramatic, Jessica, lol," in her text message. Monique responded with a "lol" emoji.

Monique was now in her hotel room and decided to wait to call her son. She was hoping that he would call her or maybe just send a text so that she knew there was still life in their relationship. After her shower, Monique decided to text Jessica to check on Renee. There was a text from her son, and she froze, afraid to read what he had to say.

"Mom, I know you aren't a bad person, but what you did or didn't do was terrible. The aftermath of pain that you left in your path of lies has destroyed a family. A husband who wants nothing to do with you, his wife. Not because he doesn't love you, because he does, but

your betrayal destroyed his trust in you and your relationship. As for me, I'm lost and questioning my own identity because now I don't know who I am as a man. You will always be my mom, but I need space. I know that it's difficult for you to stay away from me. I know that you want to erase the past and do things differently, but you can't, and here we are at the beginning of our new normal. Please respect my request for space; I'm sorry, I can't be your person now. I know you are in pain but imagine how sad I feel. So, for now, let me reach out to you. I promise that I won't take this long again. I know that you are out of your mind with worry, and you can respond to my text but don't overdo it. Remember, we are taking baby steps. I love you, Mom. CJ."

After reading her son's text, it left her with mixed emotions. Monique was happy that at least CJ was communicating with her, but he was still very distant. She prayed that she could repair their relationship, and at this point, nothing and no one else mattered but him. Monique had come to terms with her marriage ending. She understood the unforgivable lines she crossed, as well as the hurt and betrayal her family was feeling. Monique met with an attorney before she went to the class reunion. She wasn't asking for much, but her attorney, Stephanie Bayfield, Esq., wasn't having any part of her throwing herself on her sword because she screwed up. Her attorney conceded that it was an irreparable screw-up regarding saving her marriage, but that doesn't negate the fact that she deserves more than deuce signs and a date to prepare for moving out of the family home. Monique liked her attorney. She had the tenacity of a young person protesting their civil rights amid smoke bombs and rubber bullets. Stephanie Bayfield was a beautiful young woman with a dark skin complexion, big beautiful eyes, long hair, and a cute shape. If it weren't for the fact that she was the attorney helping in her divorce, she would introduce her to CJ, Monique thought. It would be awkward now if she introduced them. Maybe after the divorce and if CJ had forgiven her, she would set them up.

Monique hadn't heard anything back from Jessica regarding Renee's injury, but she figured no news was good news. She had a few gummy edibles that one of the ladies at their women's club gave her and decided it was a long day and that she wanted to relax. Before everyone went home from the class reunion, there was a luncheon where they wanted to give out gifts for participation. At first, she wasn't going to attend, but she wanted to talk with Diamond before leaving. Something about how she smirked at her tonight didn't sit quite well with her, and she intended to get to the bottom of it. Monique chewed her green apple Jolly Rancher edible and sat up to read a book for the night until her body powered down, and she could no longer focus on what she was reading. She fell asleep wearing her eyeglasses and sitting up. Monique kept her phone on in case CJ ever wanted or needed her; she could hear his calls or texts. No one else called her except him and Chris, especially at night. When she woke up, she noticed she had two missed calls and four texts – two texts from Jessica and two from her son.

What the Heart Wants

Moses was following Richard and Jessica to the emergency room. Since he was alone with Renee, it was the perfect time to say his peace. Of course, this wasn't luck because as Jessica and Renee were talking, Moses and Richard were scheming to ensure that Renee and Jessica didn't end up in the same vehicle. Moses wanted some alone time with Renee. Being the friend that he is, Richard gladly assisted. Unbeknownst to Jessica and Renee, Moses had a plan, and no one was going to ruin it, Renee had no choice but to listen.

"Are you comfortable back there?" Moses asked. Renee reluctantly responded.

"I'm about as comfortable as I will be riding in the back seat as you hit every pothole, causing my leg to painfully vibrate." It was killing Renee to be kind to him, Moses thought.

"May I ask what it was that you wanted to say to me before you were injured?" He spoke cautiously.

"Oh. Well. I was trying to apologize for slapping you earlier, but now I think we are even." She let out a giggle.

They both laughed as he tried to explain that he never meant to hurt her, and it was just a reaction that one could say was developed while in the military. They both laughed, and she jokingly said he needed to check his PTSD because he was too touchy. As she continued to laugh, he did not. Moses explained that, unfortunately, he still carried a little bit of PTSD, which he would have to deal with for the rest of his life. He saw more than he wanted and did too much of what he didn't want to do. He said it changed the man that he was, he explained. He found that running and doing yoga helped him get through his anxiety; he had been doing these exercises for over 15 years, which changed his life.

While talking, Renee realized he was no longer laughing with her and had his serious voice.

PTSD! She slapped a man who had PTSD. Was he going to kill me now? Renee thought to herself. She began to look for Richard and Jessica and realized that they were in the front, and it would be too late if he were going to kill her. "What in the hell were you thinking, fool?" She silently fussed at herself.

"I'm sorry that you have PTSD. I hear it's no joke, and before I forget, I'm sorry for slapping you. Had I known you suffered from that, it would have been hugs and kisses all night," she said jokingly but being serious at the same time.

'She is afraid of me,' he thought. Well, he may as well have a little fun. "I'm better now. Just if I continue to take my drugs and do my exercises, I won't attack anyone else. I've calmed down since my last encounter."

Moses began to tell this story about how this man barely bumped him one day, and before he knew it, he had broken his arm in three places. It took six police officers to calm him down.

"So, I'm glad that you apologized to me. It may have been worse than a possible broken leg," he said as he smirked. There was silence in the car, and he couldn't take it any longer and burst into laughter.

"Girl, I know damn well your ass wasn't afraid of me," Moses questioned as he laughed.

Renee paused because, in her mind, she was thinking, "Hell yeah, the thought had crossed my mind!" Then, she answered his question. "I'm not afraid, but I don't know you anymore, Moses, and honestly, I don't know what you can do to me. I'd like to believe that you are a gentle giant with a heart of gold. I can still see parts of the young man I fell deeply and madly in love with, who made my heart smile every time I heard his voice," she softly said.

'We are doing this now,' he thought. "I want to apologize for how I treated you back then. I cannot justify my behavior, but that was the worst thing I had ever done to someone I loved. I was deeply and madly in love with you, too, and unfortunately, back then I let the other head make decisions based on lust. You know that what happened between Monique and me was just sex, and I know it was a double betrayal for you. I guess," he said softly, "because I knew how much you loved me, that no matter what I had done, it would never be enough for you to leave me."

They both sat for a few minutes and listened to the radio, unsure of what to say next. Finally, Moses decided to continue speaking; he came this far to tell her how he felt and may as well continue since she couldn't walk away. He looked at her in the rearview mirror, observing her beautiful face.

Her eyes were sad, and it was as if he felt her pain, and before he knew it, it just came out of his mouth. "I never stopped loving you. I came close to marrying a few times, but I couldn't. They were great women, but not for me. It sounds ridiculous because we haven't been together in decades, but I knew that you were my heart from the moment I saw you—my bone.

I have regretted messing up all those years and, most of all, not fighting for you. Now that I'm at a place where I hope we can start all over, I find myself in yet another one of Monique's dramas. I'm playing the starring role of the missing baby daddy," Moses said, with disdain in his voice.

As Renee listened intently, she understood what Moses was trying to say, because she felt the same way. She resented Jessica and Monique for questioning her undying love for Moses because now everyone would know that he feels the same way. Moses and Monique will always be connected, though Renee wasn't sure how to feel about that. She just didn't know how comfortable she would be seeing them together with their son.

"Renee, I'm not a weak man, but I'm weak for you, and I'm still in love with you. I know after all these years, that it's not infatuation, because it hasn't faded away, in fact, after seeing you, one may say that it intensified. You are the love of my life, and now that you are this close to me, baby, I'm not ready or willing to walk away from you. So please tell me what I can do to earn your trust." He stole a look in the rearview mirror, even as he spoke, and could see her smile.

She caught him staring at her while she was smiling. Then she spoke.

"I know that it's not infatuation because I'm in love with you too," she said shyly.

Moses paused, carefully choosing his words, before responding out loud.

It felt immature to say because it's been so long since we've seen each other," he said, "but the minute I laid eyes on you, my life changed. I don't want to be without you ever again. So many years wasted searching for what we had, regretting not looking for you, and begging your forgiveness for breaking your heart. I only came to this reunion hoping you would be here and that it would bring us back together again."

Though on her way to the emergency room, Renee forgot about her injury and the pain during the last 10 minutes. Once they arrived at the hospital, Moses spotted Jessica waiting with Richard and a wheelchair, Moses dropped Renee at the entrance and went to park the car.

Once inside, Jessica took over explaining to the people at the registration who she was and that she worked there, hoping that would help her friend be seen more quickly. After Renee answered a few questions, the nurse ushered her into the examination room, where they quickly took her vitals. Jessica was right there and never missed a beat. The young black nurse asked Renee if she wanted Jessica to stay, and Renee nodded yes. She could barely speak due to the intense pain that she was now feeling. Jessica couldn't contain herself because of her excitement about what she had witnessed earlier, she watched Moses pick Renee up from his rear passenger side and how Renee hugged Moses like two people madly in love as he gently placed her in the wheelchair Richard had gotten for her.

"Girl, what were you and Moses talking about on the way here? From where I'm standing, it looks like you guys seemed to have buried the hatchet and rekindled some things." She smirked.

Renee was glad that they were ready to send her to the examination room. She wasn't ready to explain their ride to the ER to Jessica. Jessica was impressed with the speedy service but thought to herself that Renee wasn't that important. Later, Jessica would find out that one of her favorite doctors was there to perform emergency surgery. Luckily, he saw her rushing in and inquired about her visit. Renee was seen faster because of him. While Renee was getting her leg x-rayed, Jessica decided to go to the waiting room to give the guys an update. Richard was fast asleep, but Moses was just sitting with a concerned look on his face. She sat next to him to give an update, and she could tell he was relieved. However, she was curious about his feelings for Renee and vice versa.

"I'm not trying to get into your business," Jessica said, although Moses looked at her as if he didn't believe her. "Okay, I am trying to get into your business, but only because I care about the two of you. You have been like a brother to me since I and big head over there met, and you know Renee has always been like my sister. So, what's going on? I can feel the connection between the two of you that weren't there an hour ago. I'm glad you guys are talking things out, but don't rush into anything. Be easy," Jessica said with a smile.

"I'm in love with her, Jess, plain and simple. I've been all over the world, met some gorgeous women, and almost married a few. But they don't do for me what Renee does. She's the most beautiful woman I have ever met. Not just on the outside, but on the inside. When we were together, she always championed my side; right, wrong, or indifferent. She stood there with me. Now, don't get me wrong; she got in my ass when we were alone," he chuckled, but that was between us. Being inside of her making love, was like feeding my soul. It's difficult to explain, but we spoke a language only our souls could speak. I know that it sounds like some hippy crap, but I knew for certain that Renee would be my wife, and as I sit here with you, I'm going to do everything in my power to marry her. When she forgave me, it gave me the hope that I needed."

"You both are crazy and need to slow your old asses down,' Jessica said. "Marriage is hard and can also be hurtful, lonely, angry, loving, kind, and beautiful, but never perfect."

"I get it," Moses said. "Believe me, I do. But I honestly don't care what anyone says other than Renee. So, no disrespect, but I'm not letting any time slip past us if I can help it."

"I thought Renee was crazy and stuck in the past with her undying declaration of true love for you," Jessica said. "I see you are just as crazy and deserve each other." She chuckled while walking back to Renee. The doctor was in Renee's examining room to discuss her injury. It was her doctor's friend. They spoke to each other, and he explained that his patient couldn't have surgery so before he headed home, he had the nurse bring Renee into the examination room for him to examine. Before he could continue, Renee blurted out about her broken leg, and that she had to wear a cast.

"I knew it was possible, but I didn't think he pushed you that hard," Jessica said.

"Wait," the doctor said. "Are you saying that a man did this to you? Is this a direct result of domestic violence? If it was, Jessica, you know I must report this to the police," the doctor said.

"NO! You have misunderstood," she quickly responded. "We were at our high school reunion, and Renee came up on our friend's blindside, and when she gently touched him, it startled him, and he reacted on reflex, which caused her to fall."

The doctor looked at Renee for confirmation, and she nodded in agreement. He was satisfied with their story and told Renee that someone would be in to take her to have her cast put on her leg. Thanks to the narcotics they gave her, Renee wasn't feeling any pain. Jessica stayed in the examination room, catching up with her doctor friend as they wheeled Renee away. Renee could hear Jessica's flirty laugh as she rolled down the hall. Eventually, Jessica returned to the waiting room to give the guys the latest update.

"I see sleeping beauty is awake," she jokingly said. Jessica told them Renee's leg was broken and would be out of commission for a while. She told Moses that she had enough room for them both at her home if he wanted to extend his time and spend with Renee. Richard lovingly looked at his ex-wife playing matchmaker, and he approved. He always hoped that those two would find their way back to each other.

With a cast on her leg, Renee held her crutches across the wheelchair arms, leaving the ER. She looked at her exhausted friends and thanked them for being there and waiting. Richard and Jessica were more than friends, they were family, and Moses, well, time will tell, she thought to herself. Being a gentleman, Moses carried Renee from the wheelchair to the front seat of his SUV. He volunteered to take her back to her hotel room and Renee politely accepted. She didn't know if it was the drugs or their conversation, but she thought it would be great to feel him lying beside her in bed. Once they arrived at the hotel, Moses went to park his SUV after he helped Renee into the lobby. The drugs dug deeper into her system while she waited for his return. It was like she could barely keep her eyes open, and as Moses helped her inside her hotel room, she could feel her body powering down and lights out before she knew it.

***

Monique had one of the best rests that she had in days. She needed that, and thanks to a few glasses of wine and a few edibles taking the edge off, she slept like a baby. She was at peace with her conversation with CJ, and in time, they would find their way back to being mother and son. She checked her phone to see if Jessica had any updates about Renee. Monique had a few messages; one read that Renee broke her leg and was wearing a cast and would have to stay off it for a few days. The other text read that she thinks that Moses and Renee were getting reacquainted.

Monique took in all the information from last night's events and decided it was time to be happy for them, but it left her sad, not knowing where that left her with either of them. Will she and Moses be able to come together for the sake of their son? Can they be friends? Will Renee distance herself more knowing that she and Moses shared a son? She saw the last text and the time it was sent, which meant they had just gone to bed not too long ago. Monique decided to go to the bruncheon with the rest of the former cheerleaders and pom-pom squad from school. That would keep her mind occupied and give the others time to sleep before their last class outing, bowling. Renee couldn't bowl, so Monique wondered if she and Moses would sit this last event out. She texted Moses to see if he would be open to talking to her about their son.

"Good morning. I know things got a little ugly between us last night, and I was hoping we could start over and talk. Jessica told me that Renee had broken her leg. I hope that she's okay. I wanted to know if maybe we can discuss CJ. I know what I did was wrong, and I am deeply sorry. Can we please talk later today before bowling? Please say yes. I promise that I will come in peace. I want us to be on the same page, and I'm sure you must have many questions for me."

Monique felt so disconnected from the rest of the crew. While she was rubbing elbows with the black elites in Charlotte, North Carolina, they were bonding with each other. It took her life to implode to see how much of life she had missed with her friends. Of course, she loved her husband and his family, but it was about the image for them. This weekend she could see that her childhood friends loved each other for who they were, and it didn't matter how crazy, angry, or delusional they became. They loved and accepted one another authentically.

To find true lifelong friends who love all of you is rare. Friendships are typically torn apart because of jealousy, miscommunication, and betrayal. Monique shed a few tears when she thought about how she would do anything to have that type of friendship again, but she was the black sheep. How could she show them how genuine and sorry she was for causing so much pain? Maybe the bridge to her being a part of the crew again was through Renee.

Jessica left the door open for them to have a fresh start, and she thought that she saw a small window with Renee, but time will tell. Monique wondered how she was going to get Moses to talk to her about CJ when he refused to speak to her now. Before leaving for the cheerleader and pom-pom brunch, Monique thought it would be a good idea to write Renee and Moses each a letter. A letter apologizing for how she ruined their relationship and how she hoped that they could find a way back to each other.

Renee,

You were one of my oldest and once my dearest friends. You and I shared a lifetime of friendship and a sisterhood full of love. I know what I did to you back in high school was unforgivable, yet you did everything you could to forgive me. I know that I broke your trust and shattered my loyalty when I deliberately had sex with Moses. I won't insult your intelligence by giving you excuses because, in the grand scheme of things, a friend/sister wouldn't allow her deepest insecurities to destroy a friendship with a friend who was more of a sister. I mourned our dying relationship, and because Jessica was the glue that held up our fragile relationship, it prolonged its inevitable death. After the truth about my son and his biological father, Moses, came out, I felt the door to our friendship was closed. I was pleasantly surprised by how open you were during our conversation last night, and I'm praying that this was a sliver of a sign that we may have a chance at some level of friendship. I understand that you owe me nothing, and I owe you everything. I learned a life lesson, and I pray it isn't too late to make amends for those willing to give me another chance. I miss our talks and our girl trips. I miss you, my friend, and, in my heart, you will forever be my sister. Please allow me the opportunity to prove to you my loyalty.

Monique

After completing her letter, she felt emotional thinking back to their childhood and how they saw each other. They would spend nights in each other's homes, and when Jessica came into the picture, it was the three of them – thick as thieves. She wiped the tears from her eyes and started on Moses' letter.

Byron,

This is one of the most challenging letters I have ever written. I don't know how I will put into words my most profound regret, which is not telling you about our son of thirty-three years. I robbed you and CJ of an opportunity to bond as father and son. I'm sorry for lying all these years and throwing you under the bus when I got caught in my web of lies when I told my husband and son that you never wanted to be a part of CJ's life, which is why I never told anyone the truth. But, once I'm home, I'm telling the truth to everyone that matters; that you only found out a few weeks ago, right around the same time that everyone else did. I want you to get to know CJ, and I know that I can't replace a lifetime of memories and experiences, but I'm going to do my best to try. Moses, I see so much of you in him that sometimes I have to take a step back and catch my breath. You will love the man he's become; he is kind, intelligent, soft-spoken, caring, and so much more. I've enclosed a few photos of CJ as a baby and a teenager for you to keep. I hope you will find it in your heart to forgive me one day. Please allow me to be the bridge between you and your son.

Monique

Reunited

It felt good to feel him inside of her last night. The way he looked into her eyes and held her as they made love was like they were in love again. They were in sync, and when she moaned, he groaned, and as she reached her climax, she whispered, asking if he still loved her. It'd been so long since she had sex, and regardless of what Renee said, a real dick always outweighs a fake one. She lay in bed pretending to be still asleep as she basked in the memory of such an explosive night. "Jessica, are you awake?" Richard asked.

Jessica slowly rolled over with a smile and responded with a "Yes."

"We need to talk about last night and what happened between us. I don't want what happened to be misconstrued as us getting back together. We were getting to a place where we were enjoying our friendship, and I didn't want to complicate things with sex. I'm not saying this was a mistake, but it should never have happened, and I take full responsibility for it."

She could feel her face getting red, and fast. Before she could keep her alter ego, "Natasha Romanoff" aka Black Widow from Marvel Comics, from taking over, she found herself speaking a slew of profanity words rolled from her tongue as if she were singing in an opera. "Natasha Romanoff" had arrived. Richard couldn't understand how he had hurt her by stating the obvious. He knew the only time "Natasha" came out was because someone hurt her feelings, leaving her vulnerable. He thought, 'She couldn't still be in love with me, could she?' This time he decided not to run away from the issue and instead put into practice what he learned through their marriage.

Their marriage lasted five more years before Richard decided it was time to end what had already died. So, this time they were going to talk about how they felt. But to be honest with himself, what transpired last night was more than feeding a need if truth be told.

They both showered and were getting dressed when there was a knock at the door. Jessica saw on her phone who the person was ringing her doorbell frequently. After Richard moved out, she decided to put in a security system where she could see who was at her door at a moment's notice. This time, it was Monique, and as Jessica walked downstairs to answer the door, Richard asked her if she was expecting company. Jessica shook her head "No" and replied that it was Monique at the door.

Richard found himself immediately annoyed at the interruption. He didn't want anything or anyone to prevent them from discussing what happened last night and, more importantly, her response this morning. Perhaps Richard could have been gentler with his words and timing, but he didn't want to lose what they were creating. He could hear the greetings between the two women and decided that he would remain upstairs, focusing on softening his tone and the content of what he wanted to discuss. It was difficult for him to focus once Richard heard Moses' name and the word son. He decided to join the ladies downstairs to ensure that Monique wasn't trying to do something crazy. As Richard descended the stairs, he could only see the back of Monique's head walking out of the door. Richard looked at Jessica with a confused look, wondering what was going on. Jessica suggested that they go into the kitchen so that she could grab some breakfast. Jessica pulled out the skillet, holding some bacon and ingredients for pancakes. She prepared the skillet and allowed it to get to the right temperature before adding the bacon. While waiting, Jessica prepared the pancake batter and, during all this, told him about the conversation with Monique. While talking, Richard noticed she didn't make enough for him.

"I'm sorry, I don't mean to interrupt you, but that doesn't look like it's enough for the both of us," he said slowly.

Jessica smiled at him and said, "Boy, I'm not cooking your ass anything. Since last night meant nothing, I'm going to treat your ass like nothing."

In his mind, he saw this playing out differently. Jessica sat beside him to add more torture to his growling stomach and began eating. Renee called Jessica during her breakfast, and she began to tell her about her night after leaving the emergency room. She walked away from her food, but not before telling Richard not to touch her breakfast. Before Jessica was entirely out of eyesight, Richard grabbed the extra fork, dug into the pancakes, poured more syrup, and devoured the entire plate within seconds. He had swallowed the last drop of orange juice and knew, after wiping his mouth and releasing a few burps, that his ex-wife would have a fit. Richard washed his hands and fired up the stove for the bacon, and while the pan was getting hot, Richard poured more pancake mix into the bowl but added a little cinnamon and vanilla extract for a little flavor. He had just plated the food, placed it back in the spot where Jessica sat, and poured a glass of orange juice; she walked in and saw the fresh and still hot food and glass of orange juice waiting for her.

"You ate my breakfast when I left, didn't you?" She smirked.

"Yes, I did," he said. "I could feel my stomach hitting my back, saying, 'your punk ass better eat those pancakes,' and I couldn't let my stomach call me out like that, so I had to man up and kill it." He cracked up laughing.

"You are stupid," Jessica said, as she joined in with laughter.

After a few minutes of laughing, she dug into the pancakes and noticed the flavor difference. She complimented Richard on his pancake-making skills and, while eating, continued to fill him in on the noticeably short visit from Monique and what happened between Renee and Moses. She started with the less scintillating news as she showed him the two letters Monique asked her to give to Moses and Renee. Jessica answered Richard's question before he could ask; she informed Richard that Monique wouldn't tell her what the letters contained. Unfortunately, the envelopes made it impossible for them to peek inside to read the notes. It was time for some tea, and Jessica told Richard he might want to sit down for the Renee and Moses news. He looked at her with a smirk on his face. Richard loved hearing good tea if it involved someone other than him. Richard then asked how Renee was feeling and if she was up for the last night of the reunion. Jessica mentioned that she was still in pain and that Moses had just left her room to shower and change into fresh clothes.

Richard paused what he was doing and looked at Jessica with a huge grin. She smiled back and continued to tell him that Moses was bringing back some breakfast, and while he was out, Renee had asked Jessica to come over to help her shower. She didn't feel comfortable asking Moses. They were getting to know each other again, and it was too soon. Richard chimed in by saying she was comfortable enough for him to sleep in her bed. They giggled as they left the house; Jessica was heading to Renee, and Richard went looking for Moses. Richard told Jessica to text him if there was more to the story and that he would do the same thing. The two were like children who just saw something they shouldn't have, and were eager to see more. Richard called Moses to see what was up and if he wanted to hang out while Jessica helped Renee get dressed. They met up at Richard's place, and as he stepped into Moses' rented Cadillac SUV, he asked a straightforward question as he handed him the letter from Monique.

"Did you sleep well last night, bro?" Richard smirked.

Moses looked at him.

"Man, how in the hell… I'm going to assume that Renee told Jessica that I spent the night," Moses responded.

"Not in the way that you think. She called to ask her to come over and help her shower and get dressed. She mentioned that you just left to freshen up and grab breakfast," Richard responded.

"In other words, yes! Women are calculating and good at sending messages that men always miss," Moses said with a smile.

They both burst into a hearty laugh as Richard agreed with Moses' accurate assessment of the situation. Moses explained that although they slept in the same bed, nothing happened. She was too high from taking the pain medication to do anything but sleep. He helped her remove her gown and slipped her pajama top on as she tried to cover her breast with one arm and then the other. But not before he could see her voluptuous breasts calling his name. He continued by explaining how sexy and beautiful she was to him, even in a drugged state of mind. He said that after he helped her get into bed, she invited him to join her so they could continue their conversation. By the time they started talking, the heaviness of the evening had finally taken its toll, and before he knew it, it was morning, and he had overstayed his welcome, or so he thought. He apologized for falling asleep in her bed and explained that it wasn't his intention to invade her bed and her privacy. To his surprise, Renee smiled and said she was glad he was there; she felt cared for and protected.

"Man, you didn't, you know… have sex? I mean, you are right there in the same bed where you already saw her tits. You may as well have slid your hand down and tested the waters." Richard smiled.

"I'm not going to dignify that with a response, you pervert," Moses said, notably irritated. "I wasn't going to take advantage of an injured woman heavily on narcotics."

"I forgot about that," Richard said. "I wasn't suggesting that you 'Cosby' her, I mean allegedly 'Cosby' her… (too soon?). Moses interrupted with a chuckle.

Richard continued, "I sometimes put my foot right in my mouth, my bad."

Moses looked at his friend and shook his head as he chuckled.

"Between you and me, and tell the truth," Richard said. "If she wasn't on pain pills and knocked out, you could have created the 'Moses' effects like old times and spread those legs. I mean if she wasn't high." Richard laughed.

Moses confessed that seeing her breasts stirred up some old feelings sexually, but he refused to continue this conversation with Richard. He wanted to respect Renee because he didn't see her as a piece of meat or an opportunity to have sex, as Richard had said. Moses wanted her – but not for a good time; Moses wanted her for a lifetime. Richard began to search his pockets as if he was looking for something, and when Moses asked him what was going on. He confessed that he thought he lost the letter from Monique that Jessica asked him to hand-deliver to him.

"You already gave me that letter. I'm not going to read it right now. I'm not in a headspace to entertain Monique. I'll read it once I'm home, but my full attention is now on that beautiful woman I left lying in bed this morning," Moses said.

"Yeah, fuck Monique!" Richard said in an animated voice. They both looked at each other and once again burst into laughter.

Jessica finally made it to Renee's hotel room. Renee called the front desk after she hung up with Jessica, asking for a keycard for her upon arrival. Once Jessica arrived and headed to the front desk, she let herself into the room, where she saw Renee lying on the bed with her hand held out. Jessica giggled and handed her a chicken biscuit and hash browns. Renee was on carbohydrate overload, and she was in heaven. Jessica figured it would be lunch or maybe dinner by the time Moses and Richard arrived.

Renee told Jessica that she had stayed away from those establishments when she was in full workout mode to lose weight. However, now that she was ninety percent at her goal, she was ready for some tasty carbs. Jessica also stopped at the nearest drugstore and purchased a few plastic covers for Renee's cast to prevent it from getting wet in the shower. After Renee had eaten, Jessica gave her the letter from Monique.

"What is this?" Renee asked.

"It's a letter from Monique that she asked me to give you. She wasn't sure if she would see you because of your injury, with tonight being the last night for our class reunion weekend," Jessica responded.

Renee looked at the envelope, deciding whether to open it now or wait until later.

"If you don't open the envelope and read that letter, I'm going to scream," Jessica said anxiously.

Renee looked at Jessica's face and quickly opened the letter. Then, she started reading the letter silently until Jessica screamed. "Read the letter out loud, please, read that damn letter out loud." Renee didn't skip a beat, she kept reading the letter silently, and once she finished, she laid it on the bed.

"Jessica don't be so rude. The letter wasn't for you. If Monique wanted you to read it, she wouldn't have sealed the envelope." She laughed.

"What?" Jessica responded in a confused tone.

"Now, can you help prep me for the shower?" Renee asked. Jessica looked at Renee and rolled her eyes; she stood up, snatched the letter off the bed, and started reading it.

"Can you at least help me put on this plastic thing on my leg before you read my letter, ma'am?" Renee asked.

There was a pause, and Jessica responded that the letter wasn't long, and she only had a few lines left to read. After reading the letter, she helped prepare Renee's leg.

"So now that you have read my letter, what are your thoughts on what Monique wrote?" Renee asked.

"Well, to be honest, it sounds like this weekend, along with her situation, has caused her to take a deep look into her life. She sounds like she misses the relationship that the two of you once shared and you being her oldest friend. She wants to fix it. How do you feel about this? Are you willing to let go of the past?" Jessica asked.

"It's too soon for me to let bygones be bygones. There's too much hurt, and I can't forget how deeply Monique betrayed me. Especially now that there is a living and breathing reminder for the rest of my life," Renee sadly responded.

Renee made her way to the shower with Jessica's assistance. Usually, she would have waited for the water to get nice and hot, but she didn't want to slip, so she turned the water on after climbing into the tub-shower combo. While in the shower, she had a few minutes to gather her thoughts about Monique's letter.

Although she appreciated her realization of the pain and carnage of emotions left in her path, she wasn't ready to do kumbaya with her dear old friend. She felt a chill and realized that she had stayed in the shower too long and the water was running cold. She had to rinse off in cold water and heard men's voices talking when she dried off.

She shouted out to Jessica to see who was in her room. Jessica walked in and said, "I wasn't sure what was going on in that shower. You took so long that I told Richard that you must be masturbating since you didn't get the chance to unleash all that pent-up sexual frustration that you had towards Moses last night." Jessica smiled and winked at Renee. "Richard rushed Moses over so the two of you could rekindle what transpired those years ago," Jessica smirked. She watched Renee struggle to put on her sundress. She finally walked over to help her girl out.

Renee looked at Jessica and asked if Moses was out there as a girlish smile covered her face. Jessica walked off without answering her question, shaking her head as Renee overheard her tell the men in the room that she was dressing, and that they could all leave in a minute. Renee decided to go bowling since it was the last day of the class reunion events, and she wanted to say goodbye to some of her classmates. Renee heard the door to her room open and Jessica's voice saying goodbye. 'They aren't going to wait for me,' she thought. She tried rushing, but one of her crutches fell. "Shit," she angrily uttered. Then, she heard this voice that was deep and smooth.

She smiled because she recognized that voice. It was Moses. He asked if she was okay, and Renee responded that she was, but she was having a difficult time picking up her fallen crutch from the floor. He asked if she was decent. When she responded with a yes, he walked into the bathroom with his swag walk and sexy smile as he complimented how breathtakingly beautiful she looked. She blushed and thanked him. As he bent down to pick up the fallen crutch, she had a perfect view of his well-shaped ass. It was more mature than what she had remembered in high school, and as old habits were hard to break, she was biting her lips as her eyes captured the lovely view with nothing but pure lust. He stood up with the crutch in his hand, and as he looked at her, he smiled, chuckled, and said, "Looking at my ass, huh? I hope you liked what you saw because I love what I see!"

Renee pretended to look confused.

"I'm not sure what you mean. I was putting the finishing touches on my make-up."

"I'm sure that you were putting the finishing touches on your makeup, but the way you are biting your bottom lip tells me that you saw something that you like, and the only thing you saw was my ass," he said, smiling.

She blushed because she wasn't aware that she still bit her bottom lip and that after all these years, he remembered. Moses had a firm grip around her waist, and when their eyes met, they embraced in a kiss; a kiss that had his member hardening and her panties dampening. Before they realized it, they were in full contact mode. His shirt was off, and her dress was around her feet. He picked her up and carried her to bed. Her mind was saying no too soon, way too soon, but her treasure was screaming YAASSS BITCH, WE'RE FUCKING TODAY!" As he lay on her mattress, he slowly took off his pants and boxers; she could see his member purging itself out.

She lay there in awe of perfection. Never had she ever seen such a beautiful member. It had a nice dark brown sugar color with a streak of blackness highlighting his veins, and it was smooth and perfectly shaped as if God designed it with her in mind. He held his member in his hand, slowly stroking it, and it was all she could do not to grab it with her mouth and inhale.

Finally, Moses asked her if she was sure she was ready because there was no rush.

He said. "I've waited this long. I can wait longer."

She smiled and shook her head yes as she spoke. "I'm sure. I don't want to wait.

He helped her remove her panties, and they began to kiss. Her hands found themselves massaging his member, and his hand found its way to her treasure; as they massaged each other, their moans became deeper and louder. Finally, he reached her breasts; her nipples were hard and tender to the touch. The more he licked and sucked, the wetter she seemed to get.

He started kissing her stomach, then her thighs, and when he got to her inner thighs, her moan changed, and her breathing was going into a rhythm of heavy and then light. His lips and then his tongue touched one of the jewels of her treasure, and as he kissed, she moaned.

He went from kissing to lightly licking and tasting her juices. After what seemed like hours of pure ecstasy, Moses opened into full combat mode, and he took all of Renee in. He knew that she'd be singing and, just like that, she was in full opera mode. Her voice released this beautiful note as she released her juices flowing like a stream after the snow had melted. He unwrapped a condom and placed it on his hard member as he watched her swollen jewel vibrate from the power of her release. He quickly moved his way up to her lips as he kissed her stomach and nibbled on her breast. They were kissing, and after the third tongue movement, he slid inside, causing her to inhale and then exhale with a purring alto voice. They quickly found their groove, and as he pushed in, she moved her hips up and forward, and the slow dance became a quick salsa dance. After a while, they fell into a silence of pure lovemaking. She could feel his member inside her touching her walls, and he felt her warm juices quickly multiplying; as his eyes rolled into his head, he whispered, "I'm going to fuck the shit out of you!"

 She replied, "You promise?" And they were like two teenagers falling in love. After an hour and a half, they knew they would miss the last class reunion event. Renee and Moses decided to take in the moment without Richard or Jessica trying to push them together.

Sorry

J essica reminded Richard to be on his best behavior regarding Monique. She made him promise that if he couldn't be nice, to be quiet. The night was going well, but Jessica was wondering what had happened to Renee and Moses. She hoped nothing went wrong. Jessica tried calling and texting them both, but neither one was responding. Finally, she told Richard that something must have happened, and they needed to go. Richard looked at Jessica as if she was crazy. "You better leave them alone. I'm surprised you haven't realized that those two are in the hotel enjoying an entanglement. Moses, oh Moses," he animatedly joked.

"Spread my sea and stick your magical staff inside of me."

Jessica looked at him and laughed, calling him stupid, but she knew he was probably right. She'll get the tea from Renee later. Monique was in tears as they turned around to walk, then she spoke.

"Did I hear you correctly? Are Moses and Renee in her hotel room having sex? I don't care, but I need to talk with him before we all return to our homes. Didn't you give Moses and Renee my letters?" Monique tearfully asked.

"Yeah, about that," Richard said with an annoyed tone. "Moses wasn't interested in reading your letter at this time. He said that he would wait until he got home because his focus was on Renee and trying to build a future together."

Jessica cleared her throat and responded, "Renee read the letter, but right now, she isn't ready to rekindle you all's friendship. She said that it was too much pain to change overnight." Monique looked defeated. "Look, Monique, you must understand that to forgive and forget the pain you caused them both is going to take time. You aren't alone. You have Richard and me, and we will help to be the bridge between you guys."

"Um." Richard sighed and then quickly agreed after Jessica shot him a look that reminded him of his mother's expression of disapproval. "Yeah, Monique, we'll be that bridge," he spoke slowly.

Jessica walked over to hug Monique and gestured for Richard to follow; he reluctantly followed her actions.

"Thank you, Jessica, for your support. You too – Richard. Listen, Richard, I know that you are only supporting me because you love Jessica; but I'll take whatever support that I can get."

Diamond walked in, speaking to everyone as she made her way to the three of them; she looked at Monique and said, "Where's your baby daddy? Did he leave without saying goodbye" Diamond didn't give Monique a second to respond; as she was walking away, Monique and Jessica recognized her voice as being on Monique's voicemail. As Monique and Jessica locked eyes, they both understood their next move and based on Jessica's body language, Richard knew that something was about to go down.

"Bitch, I know that you are the one trying to blackmail me…but what I don't understand is, why?" Monique scowled.

Diamond smiled, which enraged Monique even more, causing her to take Diamond's bait.

"Oh, I see we want to play games. Well, this is my life that you are playing with, and there is nothing funny about this shit, Diamond," Monique angrily responded.

Diamond smiled again.

Monique agitatedly responded, "I'm sure if your mother were still alive, she wouldn't be proud of what you are doing."

"She died living in disgrace because of a lie by a jealous woman who thought that her husband had been cheating on her with my mom and that my mom was pregnant with her husband's love child. And because the woman's husband was the pastor, every Christian woman in the community turned against my mom. These so-called saints treated my mom like she was wearing the scarlet letter, and the only person who knew the truth would never speak up. You should ask your mother what she knows about that; after all, Monique, you have more in common with your mother than you realize," Diamond replied.

"Please don't tell me that you are blaming my mother for the actions of the town whore." Monique smirked.

"Go to hell!" Diamond yelled.

"If I go, anything you want me to say to your mom?" Monique quickly responded.

Without hesitation, Diamond punched Monique in the face with such force that Monique stumbled backward, and as Monique regained her composure, she quickly grabbed Diamond's lace front. Diamond outweighed Monique significantly, and from the looks of things, it wouldn't be long before this fight was over. Monique found herself in a headlock, as Diamond continued to punch her in the face. Jessica jumped in and pulled Diamond's weave off, exposing her balding head. Diamond flung Jessica across the floor, calling her a stank bitch, causing Diamond to loosen her grip, allowing Monique to get out of the headlock and land a solid shot to the bridge of Diamond's nose. Blood gushed out, and Richard was videotaping as he shouted, "World Star." Most everyone else was trying to stop the fight, and then the police came.

The first officer to arrive was old high school alumni and friends of Richard and Jessica, Officer Michaels. He asked Richard what happened, and Richard began to explain what transpired and how the fight ensued.

"Now, I know that all of you ladies know better than fighting; you all are too old for this mess," he scolded. He told everyone that, unfortunately, they would all be under arrest. Because of the late hour, they would have to spend the night in jail but would be able to post bail in the morning. In concert, the three ladies pleaded with the officer to give them another chance and that they won't press charges against each other. The officer told them that since there were significant injuries, it was out of his hands.

He had no choice but to arrest and take them to jail. Monique said that Diamond was blackmailing her, which was why they were fighting. Officer Michaels explained to Diamond that she could be in a lot of trouble if Monique could successfully prove her accusations. The officer looked at Diamond and then the other women and told them they were doing too much. As the paramedics checked out the women, Officer Michaels gave them their Miranda rights. The women cried as Richard tried to convince the officer to let the women go. They had been drinking and that played into how they were trying to deal with unresolved issues from their childhood. He was trying to appeal to the officer's compassion.

But the officer was adamant; it was still out of his hands. Once the paramedics cleared the ladies, they would head to the jail. Other cruisers arrived as the paramedics explained that it looks like Diamond had a broken nose, Monique had a fractured hand, and Jessica had bruised ribs, and x-rays should confirm it. They all needed to go to the emergency room, but Jessica refused help. She explained that she was an RN and that if it got worse, she would go. Two cruisers took Monique and Diamond to the emergency room while Officer Michaels took Jessica to jail. None of the ladies had handcuffs because the officers felt sorry for them and found a little humor in the battle. One officer commented that they were some tough-ass ladies, as he gestures his hands saying, "Westend for Life!"

Hours later, all three ladies were sharing a cell, and although Jessica wasn't feeling the best, she was trying to fight it. Finally, she lasted long enough to hear Diamond's confession.

"My hate for Monique started when I accidentally learned how the "Christian" women of Morning Baptist Church ostracized my mother over a lie that Monique's mother created to keep the truth of her affair from coming to light. My father died in a car accident when my mother was very early in her pregnancy with me, which is why my mother moved back to her hometown to be closer to her mom. My grandmother and Monique's mother were best friends, which is how our mothers knew each other.

There was a rumor brewing within the church that the pastor was having an affair with someone, and that woman was carrying his child. Somehow Monique's mother convinced the first lady that it was my mom who was having the affair, and back then, DNA wasn't available. The pastor denied the accusations that he was carrying on with my mom, but Monique's mother lied and said that she saw them coming out of a hotel parking lot as she was driving by one day. Once my mom began to show her pregnancy, everyone in town thought that she was some whore of a woman who had gotten pregnant by not only a married man but a man of the cloth.

I've watched Monique hurt so many people throughout the years and knew one day Karma would set up camp in her evil ass and it did. After my mom died, I moved to Charlotte, North Carolina. I wanted to become more involved in politics, so I began volunteering for this up-and-coming politician, Mark Harris. I heard about his horrible sister-in-law and how everyone was nervous because there was something in her past that seemed a little shady but unproven. At first, I didn't pay too much attention until I overheard someone say that the sister-in-law was from Rockford, Illinois. You can imagine my surprise, and I asked what her name was. Someone said the sister-in-law's name was Monique, and I told myself it couldn't be that same hateful bitch that I knew."

She continued, "The more I investigated, the more I realized that it was Monique's thirsty ass. Since some of the people on Mark's team knew that I was from Rockford; they asked if I also knew Renee Morgan and Byron Banks. During their vetting investigation, they probed into the background of Monique's close friends and family. They found where Renee Morgan requested DNA for her male child proving that Byron "Moses" Banks was the biological father, but then the trail stopped in Charleston and picked back up in Atlanta, Georgia years later with Renee having twins. As the investigation continued, they couldn't find out anything else about Renee's oldest child, her son. I acknowledged that we all grew up together, and so they asked me if I could give more insight into the relationship between Renee, Moses, and their child. I confessed that I hadn't seen anyone from high school. But as fate would have it, I went back home to see the headstone I had purchased for my mom's grave. I bumped into this white Polly at the mall and asked if she remembered me after introducing myself. She tried to act like she didn't remember me, but her body language said it all, and how could she forget that ass whipping I had given her in grade school? After a few minutes of awkward small talk, I asked when Moses and Renee had a baby, and Jessica responded that they didn't have a child together. Jessica's response had me thinking, so I dug a little more and realized that Monique's son, CJ, would be the same age. That's when I realized that this dusty-ass bitch used her best friend's identity to hide her own while trying to find out who her baby's daddy was. The last piece of the puzzle came from my memory of Moses' dad's funeral, and I also saw Monique there. At the time, it looked innocent, and neither one was married. So, I did the math and realized that it was true, and I was right; Moses was the biological father of Monique's son. I couldn't figure out how you, Monique, managed to get Moses' DNA without him knowing. Had you requested it from the military, they would have notified Moses. I knew that your actions were nefarious, so I decided to mess with your head. I realized no one knew your secret, Monique, not your husband, son, friends, and certainly not Moses.

So, let's talk about mothers. It was your mother who was having an affair with the pastor. She hid who your real father was and only my mom knew the truth. Unlike your mother, my mom kept your mom's secret and took it to her grave. I only found out because of the journals my mom had, and after reading them, I found out the truth. I guess the apple didn't fall far from the tree either. After I calmed down, I decided to be creative. When I called and left you that voicemail, I knew that your dumb ass wouldn't have figured out that it was me. I never blackmailed you. I never asked for anything; I only judged your action. The only way to get my revenge on you and your mother was to expose the truth and destroy your family because your mom destroyed mine. Once everyone knew your secret, and I knew that your social circle, not to mention your in-laws, would disown you, leaving you alone and miserable. Then you would know how it felt to be rejected, isolated, and not wanted. And the cherry on the top," Diamond gloated, "was revealing that your DNA wasn't what you thought that it was!"

Monique looked devastated; she wasn't sure if she could believe the news about her mom, so she would have to put that on the back burner for later. But now, Diamond had exposed everything, including the part she still held on to about using Renee's identity. She admitted that when she was with Moses for their brief encounter, she had accidentally taken his hairbrush when she grabbed the shirt that she had been wearing the previous night. Monique wanted to keep it for old times' sake and after Chris' proposal, she placed the shirt and hairbrush in a plastic bag to preserve his memory. When she realized that she was pregnant, she used the brush to recover his DNA.

"I'm confused, Monique; I thought you were sincere with your apology tour. Instead, you wrote Renee a fucking letter spilling your guts out pleading for a second chance while holding on to this nugget," Jessica, barely breathing, said.

"You read the letter that I gave to Renee, that was private, and you had no business reading it," Monique shot back.

"Bitch, is that all that you got from this? And when I tell Renee this shit, our mild manner friend is going to be livid, and I wouldn't blame her if she wanted to beat your ass," Jessica responded as she slowly walked towards Monique and collapsed in her arms.

The ladies yelled for help, and two of the guards came over to investigate the commotion. One of them looked at Jessica and knew that she was in distress. The officers called for assistance and an ambulance. They handcuffed Diamond and Monique as they watched Jessica turn blue. The officers placed Jessica on a gurney and one of the officers climbed on top of Jessica, trying to save her life as they whisked her away.

Richard had no clue what was happening because he was outside the jail trying to find out about their bail and to see if it was possible to have it set that night. He overheard one of the officers say that the inmate who came in with possible bruised ribs had to be taken to the hospital because she couldn't breathe, and they suspected one of her ribs had punctured her lung.

Richard had to stay in the waiting room. He called Moses to inform him what happened, but his call went straight to voicemail, so he tried Renee's cell phone and got the same response. Richard was trying not to get frustrated because they deserved some alone time, but things had drastically changed, and he needed to contact them. Richard decided to look up the hotel's phone number and talk with someone at the front desk. He asked the manager to go to Renee's room and tell them to call him because Jessica was heading to the hospital.

It felt good to be in his arms and feel his body. Renee was still smiling after the mind-blowing sex they had just experienced. It was worth missing the last class reunion event. She was tired, and her right leg was throbbing. She wasn't sure how she managed to get into some of those positions with her broken leg. She smiled as she kissed Moses, and he then helped her into the shower. As he contemplated joining her, there was a knock at the door. He threw on his pants and answered the door. After receiving the news from the hotel's manager, he turned his phone on and called Richard.

"Hey, man, I just spoke with the hotel manager. What in the hell happened?" Moses asked.

Richard told him about Diamond and how she was the blackmailer. Monique and Diamond started fist fighting if you can call it that. Since Diamond was getting the best of Monique, Jessica jumped in, and Diamond beat both of their asses. Diamond had a scar that needed stitches from Monique's ring and a broken nose from when Monique punched her in the face. Monique had a fractured hand from that punch, and after Diamond threw Jessica, she landed on something hard and broke a few of her ribs, which punctured one of her lungs. He also mentioned that Monique had used Renee's name as an alias for a paternity test to find out who was the biological father of her son CJ.

Everyone was going to be okay. Jessica had it the worst and will have to stay in the hospital for a few days. Moses told Richard before he hung up that they were getting dressed to come to the hospital. Moses heard Renee calling out for him from the shower.

He helped her get out of her shower while explaining the recent events, starting with the hotel manager, the fight, and Jessica in the hospital. Renee couldn't believe what she was hearing. "Diamond from high school was the one blackmailing Monique," Renee repeated.

"Who started the fight?" she asked.

Moses explained that he didn't know, but they needed to go. He had to run to his hotel to shower and change. They left the hotel after Renee quickly dressed. Renee was in a wheelchair holding her crutches while Moses pushed. Once they got to the hospital, Moses would let Renee out at the front where Richard planned to meet them. It was like De ja vu but this time she wasn't the patient. She still couldn't believe that they were all fighting with Diamond, someone she hadn't seen since high school. Before Renee got out of the SUV, Moses grabbed her arm and explained the one thing that he dreaded telling her, that Monique used her name as an alias to find out if Moses was the father of her newborn baby.

"I knew that I couldn't trust that bitch! She had ample time to tell me the truth, but no, she decided what pieces of the truth she wanted to tell. She can hang up any hope of the two of us ever becoming friends again. It would be best for Jessica to leave this relationship broken." As she spoke, her calmness grew into anger.

Richard approached the car with a wheelchair and looked at Moses, asking him if he had just told her about the stolen identity shit Monique pulled because he could hear Renee's loud banter as Richard walked towards them. Richard opened Renee's door and helped her out. Moses grabbed her crutches from the backseat and gave them to Richard before leaving to find a parking space. Once Moses found Renee and Richard in the lobby, Richard asked if they wanted to see the recorded fight. They both looked at him in awe at such a stupid question. He chuckled after looking at their expressions and pulled out his phone. He had to narrate what led to the fight, and as the conflict began, he sounded like Howard Cosell giving a blow-by-blow play of any of Muhammad Ali's fights. He was so dramatic with his storytelling that they felt like they were there watching it in person. Moses asked Richard why he didn't stop the fight, and he responded that he was recording. Both Moses and Renee shook their heads and laughed as Moses said, "Typical Richard."

They reached the waiting room on the floor where Jessica's room was, and they let Renee go in first while they talked about Moses' night with Renee; they knew that they both were eager to talk about it but were playing it cool. Besides, they figured that the women would talk about it, and Richard would bet money that Jessica would bring it up. Renee smiled as she walked into the room of her friend, who was asleep. She turned around to leave because she didn't want to wake her up.

"Bitch, where are you going? You just got here," Jessica said in a groggy voice.

"Bitch? We talked about you calling me that word, but I'll let it slide since you are injured. I thought you were asleep; I was leaving so that you could rest. Did you know? Did you know that Monique used my name as an alias to find out if Moses was his son?" Renee responded.

"Yes. Moses wanted to tell you when the time was right. I'm so angry with Monique. Jessica softly screamed. She had ample time to tell you.

"What in the hell is wrong with her? She isn't happy unless she has destroyed everyone in her path," Renee spoke firmly.

"Last night was crazy," Jessica said. "Be glad you weren't there to witness…"

"Yeah," Renee said, interrupting Jessica. "I'm happy that I wasn't around." Jessica could sense the tension and changed the subject to a lighter, more welcoming note.

Once the Dust Settles

I see you are still letting Moses use his staff to spread your sea?" Jessica grinned.

"I see that you are still letting Diamond beat that ass." Renee chuckled.

The ladies let out a hearty laugh, well, Jessica tried, but she coughed instead. Renee grabbed a chair and sat next to her dear friend. Renee asked Jessica how she was feeling and if it was hard to breathe. Jessica told her that she felt better, but the news of the day wasn't about her health; it was Renee's and Moses' sexual reconnection. Renee rolled her eyes and gushed like a schoolgirl as she began to spill the tea. Renee started with, "It was like we never skipped a beat!" The sex was far more mature than Renee had remembered. She continued to share the details with her longtime girlfriend about such a beautiful night with the man she always said was the love of her life. Then, Renee dropped a little bomb by telling her that Moses lives not far from where she lived in Tampa. Renee explained that she and Moses decided that he would temporarily move in with her to help as she recuperated. Jessica was stunned by the news and excited at the same time.

"Girl, are you serious? You don't think that you are going too fast?"

she asked in a concerned tone.

"We aren't getting married, and we both thought that since we lived in the same city, what a wonderful way of getting to know each other while he helped me out," Renee said. "Let's face it, you aren't in any shape to help me in and out of the shower these days."

"First, let me remind you that you have a beautiful marble walk-in shower, and second, I want to make sure that you aren't allowing your sexual feelings to get mixed up with the fact that you don't know this man," Jessica said. "Sex may not be the best way to get to know each other. Girl, you know I love you both, and I'm all for you getting back together. I'm there cheering, but be easy, slow it down. What is the rush?" Jessica asked.

"Listen, Jessica; I appreciate the concern, I do, but we both are in our fifties, and we have more time behind us than we do in front of us," Renee said. "We are taking it in stride that we both are comfortable with walking to our beat. We understand that we don't know each other, and Moses isn't moving in with me permanently. He is only staying until I can walk on this foot without crutches."

Renee was grateful for such a friend who cared enough to ask the difficult questions, knowing that it may cause some friction. Renee asked whether she had heard from Monique because there were a few things she wanted to get off her chest. Jessica said that Monique stopped by earlier to say her goodbyes. Monique figured Renee wouldn't want anything from her, not even an apology. Jessica mentioned that Monique said she was too old and tired to fight anyone else in her lifetime.

"Everyone is too old to be fighting," Renee said. "I'm shaking my head at your old asses fighting and going to jail; this ain't old bitches gone wild." She laughed.

Richard couldn't wait for Renee to leave so that he could find out some of the juicy details from Moses. He knew how private Moses was and getting any information would be tough. However, he could see the love between those two, and as much as it didn't make sense to people, he understood. Sometimes if you are fortunate, you find that one person who is your soulmate. Love is almost instantaneous, impossible to understand or explain. That was what Richard saw when he looked at Renee and Moses. Although they both went their separate ways after graduating from high school, their deep love for each other never faded. Moses couldn't go through with any marriages, and Renee never got married.

When Richard asked Moses about Renee and their night of lust, Moses' eyes sparkled as he smiled. Although the two men were having the same conversation, they were on different pages. While Richard homed in on the physical need and satisfaction, Moses focused on his emotions and how being with Renee felt comfortable. He was tired of Richard's high school mentality and how he seemed satisfied with just scraping the physical layers of a relationship but never digging deep into its core. Maybe it was the divorce, and he felt like sowing his wild oats again at fifty-six. But from where he stood, it looked like Richard was still very much in love with Jessica. This sex talk was just Richard's way of hiding his true feelings for Jessica. Perhaps he regretted the divorce and wished that he had tried harder to fix their marriage. Moses mentioned to Richard that he did reach out to Monique after reading her letter.

When Richard asked what they talked about, Moses explained that the conversation was short. "I asked her to please tell me about my son, so Monique started by telling me that he was thirty-three years old. He dropped out of college to pursue his acting career and lives in Los Angeles.

CJ has been on a few television shows and commercials and is now in a few movies. She proudly announced that he's an up-and-coming actor and currently dating an actress named Mia Goodloe." Moses looked at Richard, and said, "Man, I think I may know who my son might be. Remember when I consulted on this military movie in LA and met this young man? He was a movie star, so he and I spent time together. He mentioned that his mom was from a town in Illinois, but he couldn't remember the city's name. He said he never visited it whenever his mom would go; she would never take him.

One day I walked into his trailer and saw these incredible drawings. This young man could draw, and I remember telling him that my mom was a retired art teacher, and she was still good. I didn't make a connection to Monique or me because of his name, Harris Jesse. We had a connection. He was playing the lead role of an Air Force pilot. We had lunch together, reviewing some of the scripts to make them more believable. His girlfriend, Mia Goodloe, stopped by, and he introduced us to each other. She's more beautiful in person. He made an impression on me as a good man. I asked Monique for several pictures of him as a baby, growing up as a child, and now. I can't believe it; I have a son," Moses said with pride.

"Damn, man, you have a son," Richard said, with a smile.

"I have a son," Moses shouted out loudly.

Everyone in the waiting room stared and then slowly clapped because he was clearly of the age of men who were celebrating being a grandfather and not a new father. After watching everyone's confused reactions, Richard burst into laughter and said, "It's a rough crowd." Renee was walking toward them, and Moses stood up, kissed her on the lips, and asked for Jessica's room number. It was Renee's turn to be grilled by him, and he knew that this nut would crack easily. Richard cracked his knuckles and smiled at Renee. She knew that Richard wanted to discuss last night with Moses, but first, she asked him why everyone was looking at her so strangely. After Richard stopped laughing, he told her that Moses shouted from the top of his lungs that he was a father, and Richard assumed that when Renee came down, and Moses kissed her, everyone thought she was the baby's mama. He began to laugh again. They both had a good laugh at their reactions.

"Now that we got the pleasantries out the way, I have a few questions for you. First, did you all start with Marvin Gaye's 'Let's Get it on', and before you knew it, and with the help of the Isley's Brothers, you slid 'Between the Sheets' with Moses?" Richard chuckled as he spoke in code.

An older black lady was sitting next to Renee and overheard their conversation. She high-fived Renee and said, "Yes, they made some good love-making songs." Renee and Richard looked at each other and burst into laughter, and of course, Richard decided to take it a little further. "They are good at singing love songs that put you in the mood for making love, but they ain't got nothing on Al Green, The Temptations, Smokey Robinson; you know, groups that created love songs back in your day, the kind that a man could get a good nut… Ouch!" Richard yelled as he rubbed the back of his arm where Renee pinched him. The older woman asked if he was okay, and he told her that he must have gotten bitten by a bug. He gave Renee a smirk to say he wouldn't quit, at least not right now.

The older woman told him that she couldn't get into secular music when she was younger because her father was a Baptist preacher. It was forbidden to listen to music that wasn't godly. She continued that since she became an adult, she learned by studying the Bible that the music back in the day was okay to listen to; it was respectful. But the music today, well, let's say that her father would be rolling in his grave if it was the music of yesterday. Could you imagine how the saints back then would have reacted to "WAP" once they understood what it meant?

She laughed a contagious, hearty laugh, causing them both to do the same.

"So, you are telling us that you know what 'WAP' means, and you listened to it as well?" Richard was intrigued.

The woman told him that she was old, not dead. She had a boyfriend, and they got down at least once weekly to keep the body fine-tuned. Richard grimaced at the visual of two older adults having sex as Renee chuckled, whispering to him that's what he gets for being messy.

After things got quiet, Richard couldn't let go of the conversation earlier about sex and decided that he needed more information.

"Excuse me, ma'am, I'm not trying to be rude, but one day, I'm going to be old, and I'd like to think that I would still be hitting, I mean having sex well into my 70s and 80s. How?"

He spoke with a confused look on his face. She explained that once you reach a certain age, you know that every day is precious, so you live every second as if it's your last second here on earth. "Having a little blue pill and lubricant handy also helps; if you get my drift," she said as she winked.

They all had a good laugh.

She said, "I know that y'all too young for this, but when my man played Al Green, I knew that we were going to make some beautiful love, and when he played Barry White, well," she laughed, "I knew that he was ready for the get down." She laughed.

She had the entire row laughing. She was describing today's music and comparing it to the past. She said men knew how to chase a woman back in the day. They respected women, and women respected themselves. Back then, you couldn't call women bitches and hoes in songs, but now, the women will sing right along with them. Hell, some of the words are so catchy I even find me saying bitch or hoe." Richard mumbled to Renee, saying that Moses needed to hurry up so they could leave because the images of older adults having sex were killing him.

They embraced each other with a gentle hug and a kiss. "Eventful night, huh?" Moses said with a smile as he pointed at the marks the handcuffs made. Jessica smiled as she acknowledged and said they had to do her court appearance earlier by video conference. The prosecutor decided to drop all charges and not waste taxpayers' money, each woman paid fines before being released along with a promise to set a better example for the youth of this town. Jessica had to wait for her attorney to arrive, which was why she was so hungry. Moses was happy that they didn't have to go to jail. In his opinion, the fight was stupid, and he hoped Richard wouldn't post the video on social media. He had always known that "Westend" women knew how to battle. He chuckled to himself.

"I don't want to talk about me; I want to talk about what is going on with the two most important people in my life right now. What am I hearing about you moving in with Renee for a few weeks to help her out? You guys don't think that you are moving too fast"? Jessica asked.

"Of course, we are moving fast. I won't deny that, but each step feels right," Moses said. "We aren't children. We know that there are going to be some things we don't know about each other that may give us some pause. We aren't getting married, nor will we live together long; it's the best solution to a temporary problem. We have a lot to catch up on, and neither of us wants to miss anything else in the other's life. Just be happy for us, and if down the road we figured out that we are better off as friends, then at least we tried." He smiled.

She nodded in approval, and he could tell she needed her rest, but he had to ask before leaving. "What's up with you and my boy? You guys have been thick as thieves, and when he called me to tell me what happened, I could tell he was concerned. For the first time since I arrived, his ass didn't try to crack a joke or act like an asshole. I think that he regrets the divorce."

He paused, waiting for a reaction, knowing they still loved each other deep inside. He wanted to test the waters to see if he was right, and he was. They still loved each other. He knew that he and Renee were leaving in a few days, and before Moses left Jessica's room, he wanted to make sure that they at least acknowledged that they both still loved each other. Finally, it was Jessica's turn to confess. He looked at her to coach her to speak, and she finally broke down.

"Richard will always be in my life, but I'm not as sure as a husband."

Moses was surprised to hear what Jessica had just confessed, partly because he knew that Richard was still in love with her and wished they were back together. He had to understand why she felt like this, so he asked.

"Why aren't you sure? You guys hung out all weekend, and he was in a panic when you got your ass beat, then went to jail, and now, here lying in the hospital." He laughed.

"Oh, we got jokes. Well, if I'm going, to be honest," she said, "I think I want what Renee has; it looks good on her."

"What? Me?" he confusingly asked.

Jessica stared at him for a few seconds before responding.

"You have been hanging around Richard too long this weekend; his stupidity has rubbed off on you." They both chuckled. "Maybe you don't know, but Renee took time for herself. She decided that she needed to know the new woman who no longer had small children and needed her every second of the day – a woman who has decided to retire and focus on her next chapter in life. A woman who wanted to live her way without any apologies for who she has become," she replied.

Moses was rubbing his face and stroking his salt-and-pepper beard. She had to admit that the older he got, the more distinguished he became. Monique should have waited for the grown Moses because Jessica was sure he was worth the steal. She laughed at herself while still admiring his good looks.

"Are you finished?" He smirked.

"Finished what, talking? Yes," she said while turning a shade of red.

"I was talking about staring at me, but if you want to save face, we can say talking." He chuckled.

"Again, you've been around my ex far too long. Not only are you not funny, but you also have asshole tendencies," Jessica said while laughing.

After they stopped laughing, he looked at her, grabbed her hand, and told Jessica to do whatever made her happy. Everyone's happiness is different, so find what made her happy. During her journey, if she and Richard only remained friends, he would respect her decision. It was time for him to go. Moses said, "I know Richard wants to eat dinner with you, and yes, he ordered your favorite burger and fries. They should be here by now." He kissed her and gave her a gentle hug. While making his way to Renee and Richard, he received a text from Monique, photo attachments of their son when he was about five or six years old. As he stopped and looked at the photos, he could see himself as a child in the pictures. He now understood why she never took her son to Rockford; she feared someone like Jessica would recognize this child as belonging to Moses.

His heart swelled up with pride and joy, but the loss of not being a father hurt. He saw Renee looking around by the entrance, and Richard was walking inside with a bag in his hand. Moses was ready to spend the rest of the evening with his lady, and he knew that Richard wanted time with Jessica. Richard hugged them both and thanked them for hanging out with him and being there for him and Jessica. They told them that tomorrow was their last day in town, and they were leaving before sunrise the next day. As Richard and Moses hugged, Moses whispered to him, "If you are still in love with her and want her back, you must swallow your pride and fight for her."

He told Richard that life is far too short to be bullshitting over shallow-ass things that hold no weight in life, and now that he had Renee in his life, he was throwing caution to the wind and putting everything into this relationship. Moses didn't care how short of a time they were together or how much they did or didn't know about each other. He knew in his heart that she was and always had been the missing rhythm of his heartbeat. Ever since the night they spent together, his irregular heartbeat had now found its rhythm. It was up to him to repair their relationship.

On the way back to their rooms, Moses proposed that he cancel his last night and stay with her for their stay. She thought that he would never ask; she smiled and agreed. Renee reached for his hand as he drove to his hotel, which only took a few minutes. As Moses quickly walked out with bags in tow, she looked at him, and before she could ask him how he packed so quickly, Moses smiled at Renee and explained. He decided to pack up everything just in case she agreed with his idea. She pulled him close to her and gave him a passionate kiss.

He pulled his car up to valet when they arrived at her hotel. The guy opened Renee's door and helped her out of the car and into the wheelchair. While assisting Renee, the guy took out Moses' luggage and placed it inside the hotel lobby.

The concierge assisted by having someone from the front desk take his luggage to their room while he pushed Renee. By the time they made it inside the room, they were tired and wanted to shower and eat. She suggested they kill two birds with one stone by taking a shower together and ordering some food to be delivered. Just like that, he was on the floor placing her leg in a plastic foot cover. She hooked her iPhone to her charger and selected her favorite playlist from Pandora. He helped her take off her clothes, and then he removed his clothing. He caught her staring and smiling at his member, and she saw him smiling and staring at her girls. He helped her get into the shower, and as he closed the shower curtain, one of the songs from Eric Benet, "Real Love", began to play.

He grabbed a fresh washcloth, poured her liquid soap, and started with her back. As the washcloth touched her back, he slid it up and down. He repeated the same motion to her front, after helping her turn around. He took his time holding her breasts, ensuring that he washed every inch of it, and then he and the towel traveled from neck to her treasure. She was clean-shaven, and the smoothness of her skin was turning him on. Once she was completely clean, it was his turn, and she took a fresh washcloth and made sure that it had plenty of soap. She did things differently. She started with his member.

She grabbed this long, thick, and perfect member, and as she began to wash, he started to kiss her – first her neck and then her breast. She pulled herself away so that she could finish bathing him. Once she completed the front, he turned around to repeat the washing process on his back. He took over the washing because as much as he appreciated how sensual she was trying to be, Moses was ready to wash quickly, rinse, and maybe dry off as he couldn't wait to feel her warm juices surrounding his aroused member. After they cleaned up, he turned to face her and slowly kissed her. As he kissed her, he grabbed one of her breasts and started massaging it, and before she knew it, he was sucking her nipples. The water hit Renee right at the collarbone as it ran down her chest and the top of his head. He alternated sucking between the two breasts until he heard her soft falsetto whimpers grow into a deep alto voice.

 He knew that his sucking and licking her nipples as he placed his two fingers between her legs were going to give her pure satisfaction, but when he turned her around and bent her slightly over, she could feel the now warm water on her back and down her buttocks as he entered inside of her. It was all she could do to hold on, but he had a tight grip on her, and there was no way she would fall. They began kissing again as his hand made its way between her legs, and it stayed there for what felt like hours of foreplay. She was on her way to her second solo when they felt the water cool a bit, but he didn't skip a beat when he slid inside of her. They found themselves heading towards the bed.

Amore

Renee didn't have time to dry off before Moses picked her up and carried her to the bed. She was soaking wet from inside and out. It was her turn, and she grabbed his hand and placed him in front of her as she was sitting up. She grabbed his member with her hand and began to massage it as he closed his eyes and exhaled. His baritone song was warming up, but she wasn't ready for him to explode; this was, after all, foreplay. They began kissing, which became more intense with a little more force. He started with her toes, sending sensations all through her body. Then he kissed her legs until he got to her inner thighs. Moses could feel more of the wetness between her legs which excited him even more. He kissed her gently, taking it all in, and he could feel her jewel expanding in size from his kissing.

 Moses smiled as he heard her sing. It was a beautiful sound, and it was so full of power as it released her nectar, and he swallowed every drop. Moses made his way back to her breast while kissing her body with every movement. He reached for her nipples, caressing one breast with his left hand as he engulfed the other breast with his mouth. Moses could sense the sensitivity with every stroke and gentle nibble. Finally, he made his way to Renee's lips, and they kissed, as he gently slid inside this warm treasure of love. At first, he was doing all the work, thinking that he had zapped all her energy. Finally, Renee regained her composure and met him stride for stride. Their lovemaking continued for what seemed like hours – until he began to warm up for his song. Moses kept hitting her spot, and before Renee knew it, her eyes rolled in her head as she reached ecstasy; he joined her, and they both hit a note of satisfaction. They worked themselves into quite an appetite.

While Moses showered, Renee called housekeeping for more towels and a set of fresh sheets. She also ordered dinner for them to enjoy. He finished his shower just as housekeeping arrived. Renee showered next while Moses made up the bed and tidied up a bit, waiting for the food delivery.

While still in the shower, Renee started to assess her journey. She was finally finding her new self– one where motherhood took on a different perspective and being– an encompassing parent wasn't necessary, nor warranted by either adult child. Renee was finding her own footing, shifting her passion for making custom jewelry from just a hobby into a business. Renee was stronger than she had realized and understood that she allowed fear to paralyze her dreams. Not being sexually active for those many years hadn't given Renee much experience, but what she lacked in knowledge was quickly overshadowed by her creativity and imagination. Renee smiled as she rinsed off, acknowledging that in her bed, lay this strong, sexy, handsome man who so far was walking at the same beat as her drum, and it felt good. Was it possible to have both her newfound freedom and this man? Maybe it depended on how she defined freedom. Moses felt good; never had anyone swept Renee off her feet with so much swag and girth. Renee couldn't explain it, but she loved him.

During their conversation, Moses explained that he could never find any woman who filled his heart the way she had in the past. He knew in high school that she was the one when he slept with Monique after Renee broke up with him and he stayed with Monique for the rest of their senior year in high school. Moses never imagined that his reckless behavior would have ended his relationship with the one person he ever really loved. He didn't want to show how hurt he was because of his mistake, so he dealt with the consequences of his actions. He didn't like that he and Monique shared a son, and he didn't want that to be the reason why his and Renee's relationship didn't work. Between the incredible sex and dinner, Renee was beyond tired and as Moses continued to talk, Renee found herself drifting off to sleep.

Moses was feeling anxious, knowing that CJ may not want anything to do with him, especially once he realized they had already met. The anticipation was killing him, so he texted CJ asking if they could meet up soon; he had something important to discuss with him. CJ responded, telling him he was in Charlotte, North Carolina, dealing with family matters and will be leaving early next week. Moses desperately wanted to talk with CJ; he was hoping to get this out without Monique being in the picture. He no longer cared how anyone felt. Moses had a son and had every right to see him and acknowledge their father-and-son connection. Moses thought long and hard about how he would respond to CJ's text. He preferred to do this face-to-face, but he didn't want to show up out of the blue; he asked if he had a few minutes to talk. At that moment, Moses decided to tell CJ the truth over the phone, and they could work out everything else later. CJ called him a few minutes later. Moses found himself fumbling over his words and, at times, not knowing how to approach the subject. Thankfully, CJ broke the ice.

"I think you are trying to tell me that you are my biological father."

"How did you find out?" Moses stuttered.

CJ nervously chuckled, and then he said that if Moses knew anything about his mother, he knew that no one would ever upstage her if she could help it.

"I want us to meet. I know that it may be too soon after finding out that I'm your father, but I really want to talk," Moses blurted out.

There was a long pause before anyone spoke, and just when Moses was beginning to feel defeated, CJ spoke softly.

"I'd like to meet as well."

Although it may have seemed like there should be some sort of celebration, both men knew that for CJ it was more complicated than meeting his biological father. Moses understood and didn't want to add more to the family drama by mentioning that Richard would be coming as well. It was better to ask for forgiveness than to ask for permission. Besides, as much as Richard and Monique hated each other, there was no way he would give Monique a reason to back out now.

The next morning Moses decided to tell Renee about his conversation with CJ last night.

"I was talking with CJ, and we decided that we should meet soon to talk," Moses said with pride in his voice.

"That's nice, I'm glad that you both were able to connect. Where are you meeting?" Renee asked in a curious tone.

Without missing a step, Moses quickly said, "CJ is staying at his moms for a few more days and she had agreed to allow us to meet at her home."

"I see; you are just going to pretend that I didn't know that CJ's mom is Monique?" Renee replied with annoyance.

This was going to be their first fight; it was like watching an accident happening right before your eyes and feeling helpless to prevent it.

"Of course, Monique is CJ's mother. I never tried to hide that fact, but I was trying to be sensitive toward your insecurities," Moses said cautiously.

"And yet you agreed to meet at Monique's without thinking about how I may feel uncomfortable being in that woman's house!" Renee responded.

"Of course, I thought about it, which is why I decided to take Richard and not you. I'll meet you back in Tampa after I spend time with my son." Moses spoke with authority.

Just as Renee was gearing up to say something, there was a knock at the door. Moses looked at his watch and realized that Richard and Jessica were scheduled to meet them at the hotel so they could ride together for breakfast, and it was probably them knocking at the door. Moses opened the door to see two puzzled faces staring at him.

"What is going on in here?" Jessica asked "Yeah, we can hear you two arguing down the hall," Richard said. "And please tell me it's not about Monique."

An awkward silence fell over the room, which was making Richard and Jessica regret knocking on the door. Renee apologized and suggested that they go to breakfast. The drive to the restaurant was uncomfortably quiet, at least until Moses asked Richard to take a quick trip to Charlotte, N.C. with him when he goes to spend time with CJ.

Richard being Richard, jokingly responded, "I'll be happy to attend the family reunion." Without warning, Richard felt a poke in his side, a sign from Jessica to cut out the jokes, because this subject was sensitive.

Before the couple exited the car, Moses explained the argument and looked at Renee to tell her that he was trying to protect her and what they were developing. His visit was to see and talk with CJ, not to spend time with Monique. He continued to say that Richard was going to be that buffer between him and Monique so that she wouldn't interrupt his visit with his son. Before Renee could speak, both Jessica and Richard agreed with Moses and felt that it was thoughtful of Moses to try and protect Renee. Renee felt like everyone was against her, and her best friend could sense her anger rising.

"Wait one damn minute; I'm not going to sit here and let you all gang up on me and make me feel like an insecure teenage girl again. I'm not insecure at all. I can't stop Moses from sleeping with Monique now no more than I could over thirty years ago. I'm upset that you didn't respect me enough to want to discuss your plans with me. Moses, you made plans for yourself and me without any thought about what I wanted or how I felt. Go enjoy your time with CJ and I hope that it works out for you both, I'm leaving tomorrow to go back to Tampa." Moses refused to leave their conversation in the car alone.

"How are you going to get back to Tampa alone, Renee?" Moses asked.

"I'll manage, you may not know this about me, but I'm resourceful. I don't need a…"

"Nope, we are not going down this road," Jessica interrupted Renee's soon-to-be 'I'm an independent woman, hear me roar' speech. "Gentle-men, can you give us a few minutes alone while I speak to my best friend?" Jessica asked.

The men left the table and stepped outside, heading to the cigar store next door. While they were walking, Richard decided to joke with Moses.

"I was going to ask your advice on how to get my wife back, but it looks like you may need to figure out how you plan on holding on to Renee," Richard said grinning.

Moses looked at Richard like he wanted to hit him and then burst into a chuckle shaking his head in agreement. The two men laughed as they walked into the store. While the men were gone, Jessica reminded Renee that her mantra of 'I am independent' and 'hear me roar' shouldn't be her go-to when she was feeling defensive. Jessica explained why she understood both sides and suggested that Renee give Moses some grace. They were still getting to know each other, and Moses had the best intentions, although his delivery was a miss.

Renee knew in her heart that Jessica was right. She was feeding off her fears from the past. Either she and Moses go their separate ways because she can't trust him and Monique to be alone, or she trusts him. But trust in a man that you no longer know? The reality of her weekend love affair with the only man she ever loved was rearing its scary head. She needed time to think clearly, and with Moses and Richard away, it would give her time to do so. Renee looked at Jessica and agreed. She told Jessica that it was better to find out now if she couldn't trust Moses.

A New Day

Monique couldn't believe that she got into a fight with Diamond. Maybe her mother-in-law was right about her; perhaps everyone was right. She can speak refined with the best of them, walk with grace, and present herself as a well-polished educated woman. Monique knew she had cleaned up well after leaving the hood. But she allowed a hood rat like Diamond to get under her skin, causing her to act out of character. Because of Diamond, Monique ruined her life, and her secret was out. Monique intended to bury her secret, and now she found herself on an island all by herself. Her soon-to-be ex-husband Chris wanted nothing to do with her. He won't talk to her, other than to communicate through a divorce attorney. His family had already disowned her, and she was no longer allowed onto any family property. Once she and Chris were divorced, she had ninety days to move out of her home, which her husband owned. Monique would be given an undisclosed amount of money if she signed a "Non-Disclosure Agreement (NDA) agreeing to never tell anyone that Chris isn't CJ's father. She could keep her car, clothes, and jewelry. All this was in the legal divorce documents that her husband's attorney sent over to her attorney, Stephanie Bayfield, to discuss and make any changes or requests. Her attorney told her to take out any emotions and consider this a hostile takeover. For example, although her husband Chris owned their home, (it was a wedding gift from his parents), she had lived in that house for over thirty years, and if they wanted her out, they would have to pay for it. Chris' family and her attorney didn't know that Chris added a post-pre-nuptial clause after their 25th anniversary. The addendum said that if they were still married after thirty years, the pre-nuptial agreement would be null and void and that she would get half of his inheritance. This act of love was his gift to her. He never filed it because he knew that someone in his family would find out and make him change it. His best friend Kevin Thornberry, who happens to be a judge, and two witnesses watched as they signed the addendum. After the document was notarized, both Chris and Monique kept a separate copy for safekeeping. He didn't want his family to know because of how they felt about her.

Since his family wanted to play hardball, that's what they shall do, and this little gem will be her golden ticket. Monique wasn't going to do anything with it because of the mess she had created. But now they wanted to disown her son, the young man who still saw them as family. He was also a victim in this, so why punish him? Because he didn't have a speck of their DNA inside of him? She was meeting with her attorney later in the day, which would be a game-changer when she shared this little nugget with her attorney. The amount they were willing to settle on was an insult, to say the least, and unacceptable.

She will not live struggling. They could have the house because it was now too big and filled with too many memories that would be painful. She knew their family's wealth was several hundreds of millions of dollars that grew from generation to generation. She knew her husband and what was happening wasn't his own doing. It's that mother-in-law who didn't like her because of her background. When Chris married Monique and because they both were so young, Mrs. Cora Jean took pride in meddling and controlling their lives. What Mrs. Cora Jean didn't bet on was Monique slowly distancing her and Chris from the family. Taking back control over their lives. Chris wouldn't admit it, but he was relieved that Monique changed the course of their life; it allowed him to breathe and focus on what was important to him. Mrs. Cora Jean tried every trick in the book, but Monique was always three steps ahead of her, and eventually Mrs. Cora Jean conceded and silently stepped aside. Monique was a different young bride. She knew because, after all, games recognize games. In the beginning, Monique toed the line just like the rest, but she had plans for her life and marriage.

She was waiting for the right opportunity because she understood that her mother-in-law was a force to be reckoned with, and Mrs. Cora Jean was an OG of mothers-in-law, a woman who played the part of a doting and submissive wife and mother, but behind the curtain stood the family's puppet master. Monique had seen the best; if she was honest, she had admired Cora Jean Harris. In addition, Monique had picked up a few things here and there herself that the woman had mastered. Her mother-in-law ran the family from afar like the Wizard of Oz, Chris' father was loud and intimidating, but Ole' Mrs. Cora Jean, well… she was ruthless. Without her input, no one in the Harris family dared make significant moves.

She put her two cents into all her grown children's lives. She told the wives what committee they were to become a part of and how they should dress and behave. She had her say in the schools their children would attend and would even send over the nannies that she had interviewed and deemed acceptable to be caretakers of her grandchildren. Monique fell into place for most of her mother-in-law's commandments because this was the life she had always wanted. If it meant some sacrifices, then so be it, which was why the news of the post-nuptial would send her bougie ass spinning in every direction when she'd learn what her son had done.

Chris and Monique would go to church every Sunday and return to her in-law's home for Sunday dinner. For more than fifteen years, she had never eaten Sunday dinners at home until they started to break away from the family. Major holidays like Thanksgiving and Christmas were at Chris' parent's home enduring the same routine as the years before, the holidays were important to Mrs. Cora Jean, and every holiday 'Judge' and Mark would ruin it. Chris felt sorry for his mother, and we accepted that Thanksgiving and Christmas would be spent with the Harris clan. Their family was supreme, and everyone else was inconsequential. Christmas was the biggest holiday of them all, and they not only had to spend the night, but also had to wear the same color pajamas with those holiday words written all over them, and year after year, she would pick the same green color.

On Christmas Eve, everyone had to be at the family home by six o'clock in the evening to have dinner. The only problem was neither her father nor brother-in-law would ever make it until after everyone had gone to bed. Christmas breakfast would always feel tense as neither her mother nor her sister-in-law would be in a festive mood and quickly excuse themselves from breakfast, stating how exhausted they were from preparing the food. There had always been a rumor that both Harris men had wandering eyes and hands. The gossip for years had been that Judge not only has a sidepiece but another family as well. Mrs. Cora Jean knew all about it but dealt with it because of how much she would lose.

Looking back over her life, Monique realized that she gave up a lot of her identity to become a "Harris". Now that she would soon no longer be a part of the family dynasty, Monique wasn't sure who she was anymore. She thought long and hard about her demands from this family as she wrote her counteroffer to give to her attorney. Monique would give up the house in Charlotte, North Carolina. However, she wanted half of the money for what it would have cost if they had sold it. Monique wanted spousal support of thirty thousand dollars a month until death or marriage. She would give up the burial plot next to Chris in exchange for them purchasing her a burial plot of her choosing, and to piss the entire family off, she wanted to keep her last name. Monique earned the right to carry the family name; if they wanted it that badly, they would have to make her an offer.

She wasn't sure what the price would be, but there was time to think about it. Now that she had made her counteroffer, she was going to get ready to meet with her attorney and she was excited about her meeting. Why should she live like a poor woman because she lied and held a secret for so long? They needed to think about how much of a sacrifice she made to help her husband become an attorney and how she had to put up with Mrs. Cora Jean's bullshit all these years. Perhaps she was shortchanging herself.

Monique would give up everything if she could have her son back. If CJ could only see her as he used to, instead of as a conniving bitch of a mother who destroyed his life. She badly wanted to talk to him, hold him in her arms, and hear his infectious laugh. Instead, he had put her in time out, but at least he texted her once weekly so that she knew he was alive. When CJ discovered that his family disowned him, he was heartbroken, but when the only father he knew distanced himself, that was devastating. He refused to speak to CJ or even text him to see how he was doing.

Monique was on her way to see her attorney, and she was feeling good about where she was going to stand financially. Since the Harris family wanted to treat CJ like a red-headed stepson, she would treat them like the enemy. She walked into the restaurant looking fabulous, wearing an above-the-knee black dress with an embellished puff sleeve. She wore her diamond stud earrings with a simple single diamond necklace and her black Christian Louboutin Marlenarock leather heels. Monique was making a statement, and when her attorney looked up and saw her walking toward her, she couldn't help but smile and nod with approval. Monique gestured to her attorney not to get up, and she bent down to give her an air kiss. Once she sat down and settled in her chair, her attorney softly chuckled and said, "Well, damn; they have no clue what beast they have awakened." It was a nice compliment coming from someone whose livelihood is to tear apart the opposition and leave very little on the table.

The waitress approached to take Monique's drink order. She requested a glass of Merlot as she placed her diamond-quilted Chanel handbag on the chair next to her. Monique kept the manila envelope she brought in her hand and slid it across the table to her attorney as if she didn't want any prying eyes to see what she was doing. Her attorney grabbed it and then looked at her for permission to open it. Monique gestured her approval. She slowly took out the document that Monique had given to her and read it. Her attorney couldn't believe what Monique had handed her. She smiled like the cat that just swallowed the canary. Stephanie took a sip of her wine, Cabernet Sauvignon, and then asked Monique why this information hadn't been given to her.

Stephanie expressed how much of a game-changer this would be when presented as their new counteroffer. Monique said that the only reason she decided to go after them was how they treated her son, their grandson, nephew, cousin, and great-grandson, whom they all knew and said they loved. In her wildest dreams, Monique never thought they would treat CJ like the plague. When CJ's girlfriend Mia told her how heartbroken he was, it broke her heart, so this was no longer about getting what she deserved. It was about destroying them to hurt her son. Of course, Monique knew she had a hand in all of this, but CJ was innocent. He had no idea that Chris wasn't his father, and after all these years, did it matter? He was the only father her son knew, and he taught him how to be a man.

Monique was now in full mother-bear mode, and she was going to protect CJ by any means necessary, and she meant any means. After her explanation, everything made sense to her attorney. Monique had drawn a line in the sand. She was dressing for a mind-fucking battle, and was ready for every bit of it, Stephanie Bayfield Esq. thought to herself. After their successful meeting, Monique saw a few women from her social club. She hesitated to go over there to say hello for fear of rejection. Still, Monique reminded herself that she was a boss, and she got this. Monique gracefully walked to the ladies sitting and greeted them with a hello and a smile. There was this awkward pause before one of them decided to speak.

"Hello, Monique. We didn't expect to run into you here. We figured that you'd be hiding somewhere, but if you're going to do the walk of shame, you may as well do it dining at 'Palais Sophistique s', French for 'sophisticated palates'. No one ever said that you didn't have balls or two baby daddies," Lauren Elizabeth Stalls said with a smirk.

Lauren Stalls was Monique's nemesis ever since Monique out-hosted her on the "Belle of the Ball" five years straight; Lauren had been out for blood. Now she had the ammunition to fire at Monique, but Lauren wasn't aware that the bear was already poked, and it wasn't a great idea to keep poking. Monique slightly leaned in as she smiled and whispered,

"Does Thomas still wear your panties when he is in surgery?"

It was a known secret that Dr. Thomas Stalls was into wearing women's panties, especially when operating. When Monique dropped that little nugget of information, it was her way of telling every woman sitting there that they would not be coming for her anytime soon because the gloves were off as far as she was concerned. Monique left the women sitting there embarrassed, shocked, and angry. As she turned the corner to head out the door, she heard one woman loudly say, "Low-class bitch," which was followed by laughter. None of that bothered Monique, because she knew she would be the last person standing once the dust settled. Each woman had forgotten that she knew everyone's secret in their small circle. After all, her soon-to-be ex-husband was friends with their spouses, and as their hypothetical attorney they all would ask hypothetical questions because he wasn't trying to climb the social circle like his family; he was considered a trusted friend. He would give them off-the-record advice as a friend and not their attorney. These so-called friends didn't know when Chris and Monique had pillow talk it would be about them.

Chris told Monique who was doing what and with whom, who was in financial disarray, and what child was getting kicked out of school, couldn't get into the best college, was pregnant, or got some girl pregnant. She knew all the actors and their skeletons and refused to allow them to thumb their noses at her as if she was less than shit. If the statement that you can take the girl out of the hood but can't take the hood out of the girl were ever a person, it would show Monique's face. Growing up in the west end of Rockford, Illinois, gave Monique some handy tools; they were her survival skills, and it was time to blow the dust off them bad boys and put them to use. She felt a hint of sadness that her two friends wouldn't be there to help her out, and she knew deep in her heart that she had to do everything in her power to regain their trust and friendship. Her revenge on this entitled group of women would be much sweeter with her friends.

Despite Chris' recent actions towards CJ, Monique knew deep inside that Chris was still a good father. He loved this boy with every fiber of his being, which was why she was so confused as to why he was letting Mrs. Cora Jean run his life, especially at his age. He was a grown man with wealth who didn't need to depend on getting an inheritance from his parents. Now that they knew CJ didn't have the Harris blood running through his veins, they had already disinherited him from the family's fortune. Her soon-to-be ex-husband was a coward regarding his parents, especially his mother. Mrs. Cora Jean Harris, the matriarch, had her heavy foot on everyone's throat, controlling what they did, said, and thought. If they wanted any of the inheritance, she dangled that will in front of them like a carrot. The only exception was Judge.

He came and went as he pleased without apologies or reasons for his behavior. The Harris' had three sons. Theodore Jr. was the eldest of the three boys and the smartest. He was his father's favorite and could never do anything wrong. When he was a senior in high school, right before graduation, he and a few of his friends were having a pool party. Teddy, Theodore's nickname from his mother, had been drinking and slipped into the pool while everyone else was watching the fireworks. The Judge found him lying facing down in the deep end. After a week of being on life support, the family decided to turn it off and allow Teddy to pass away.

At the time, Mark was a sophomore at the same high school, Noble Academy, and Chris was two years behind Mark and in the eighth grade. Teddy's death was hard on everyone but tougher on The Judge. For nearly five years, he had forbidden anyone to swim in the pool or be anywhere near that area. He created a shrine for his dead son so his other two sons understood that he would never love them as deeply as he had loved Teddy. Chris had always been his mother's favorite, and she never let a moment go by from telling the world her true feelings. Mark was always the odd child out. When Teddy was alive, Mark was that middle child who was blamed for everything. He grew thick skin like his father and was ruthless like his mother, which made him a great litigator. His weakness was feeling inadequate because he wasn't the favorite of either parent. What Mark lacked was the nurturing a mother gives to her children.

His mother wasn't the hugging and kissing type. She showed her affection by rewarding her sons by challenging them to be better than the others. Chris, on the other hand, has always been independent – a trait that his father always admired. Studying was effortless for Chris, who never struggled with law school and passed the bar on the first attempt. But he never wanted to become an attorney. His heart was in architecture; he loved designing and building things.

He once told Monique that he struck a deal with his father and that he would carry on the family tradition and become an attorney. Still, he would never get into politics. But in return, the Judge would allow him to marry whomever he wanted to, preventing Mrs. Cora Jean from interfering. Chris had allowed his mother to influence him because he wanted her to approve of him all his life; she was his Achilles heel. When he broke it off with Monique, the love of his life, it was to reconnect with his ex-girlfriend, Stephanie Marie Hollis's daughter, the child of his mother's best friend at the bequest of his mother. She was a beautiful girl who was proper and blended well in their society and the best friend of her nemesis, Lauren Elizabeth Stalls. The world seemed to get smaller and smaller.

What he loved about Monique was also what he later hated about her. He loved her tenacity and street smarts with a swag. She was a woman who walked with confidence. She had this sexy vibe without trying and was unaware of her beauty because her focus wasn't on how she looked but on what she was doing in life. She could roll up her sleeves and get into the trenches with the best of them, helping wherever needed without wearing make-up or exposing her body to prove that she had what everyone could see. She was that one sexy hood chick who focused on getting out of the hood instead of embracing the hood environment. She was intelligent, independent, and sexy, all wrapped up in a beautiful body. That was a woman who had swag.

Family Reunion

The couples resumed eating breakfast, and throughout the course, Jessica and Richard could see Moses and Renee slowly making up and smiling at each other like love-struck teenagers. In their discussion, Moses and Renee decided to stay an extra two days in town to ensure that Jessica was cleared of her injuries from the infamous fight to travel. Then Richard and Moses will travel to Charlotte, North Carolina, hoping for a happy union between Moses and his son. Richard would be his buffer in case Monique decided to clown. The women, Renee, and Jessica would return to Renee's home in Tampa, Florida.

A few days later, it was time for everyone to head to their perspective designations. But for their last night together before they headed to Charlotte, Moses wanted it to be perfect for him and Renee. He wanted to talk about their future. He asked Richard if he was sure that he wanted to get back together with Jessica, and if so, said tonight was the night. Moses explained to Richard that life was too short to second guess; he should go for it. Although Jessica had confessed that she didn't want to get back together with Richard, Moses couldn't imagine how Jessica didn't feel the same way as Richard. Maybe what Jessica needed was to hear Richard's declaration of his undying love.

When you think about soulmates, you think about two adult people who met and decided to date, marry, and stay committed until one of them died. You don't think about two teenagers who meet, have sex, and proclaim their undying love for each other, especially when the guy sleeps with the girl's best friend. You chalk it up as puppy love and virgin disorder. In Richard's mind, a virgin disorder was when a virgin had sex for the first time causing a euphoria of untapped pleasure that caused the virgin to fall deeply in love with the person who took their virginity. He thought Renee was dramatic until Moses also expressed his love for her. Maybe he needed to pay more attention to Moses and what he was doing for Renee and do the same to win Jessica back.

"I know you said that you didn't think you wanted to get back with Richard," Renee said, "but I wouldn't be a good friend if I didn't ask why you felt this way."

"It's simple," Jessica explained. "Richard is the only man I've ever been with, and I want to explore my options. I know that he loves me and regrets the divorce, but I want us both to explore and if we find our way back, we can think about a future together."

"You better stay with that man you will be disappointed when you enter the single life and want to date because you will meet all kinds of boys pretending to be men. I met this guy through an online dating service, and things started nicely after the first week, but he quickly wanted to talk about sex. He wanted me to help him get his rocks off by talking dirty to him. When I told him I wasn't looking for that type of relationship, he apologized and never called me again. Another guy I also met online said hello, and that he liked my profile, and if I was interested, please respond. I responded by saying 'Hello, my name is Renee.' He said in a passive-aggressive tone that he hoped I wasn't the type of woman who expected him to carry on the conversation. When I responded that I was greeting him back since he initiated the conversation, I assumed that he had something to say, but he deleted me. Last, but certainly not least, there was the guy online who ghosted me. He was my favorite, which is why my heart is open today. Ironic, huh?" Renee sighed.

"I'm not planning on getting on any online dating sites," Jessica said. "I hear enough horror stories about them that I know better than to invest my time or money into finding anyone. So, instead, I'm looking to meet someone from a friend who has a friend, or by chance." Jessica smiled.

"You don't know how bad it is out there; let me school you a little," Renee said. "Now, let's take out gay and undercover men, married men, men living with their girlfriends, men in prison, men on drugs, men who don't want to work, and men who only date a specific type of woman, non-black. Whatever is left, you are going to have to break down more, men who are only looking for sex, liars who say they are looking for a serious relationship but aren't, men who are down on their luck, who lack a place to call their own or don't own a car, these are all, hashtag scrubs. Then, you compete with other women for the rest of the catches because of the high ratio." Renee rolled her eyes.

Jessica's confidence started to wither, but then she said whoever God had for her would be for her. Renee agreed but with a smirk on her face. She acknowledged that whomever God had for her was for her, but what if you already have the person God had for you? You may not get another chance at what you already have in a mate. Renee just wanted her friend to slow her roll and not think that the grass was greener on the other side, because on the other side, there was no grass. Jessica wasn't letting it go, she wanted to see what different types of men were out there, and if it meant losing Richard for good, she was willing to take that chance. Renee asked

Jessica a question, "Why is it that some married women are trying to go back to being single? They want to hit the clubs dressed like they are in their 20s, dating all types of men, living the single life, and then one day, they realize that being single isn't all that it's cracked up to be. You can release yourself with a toy, but it can't kiss or cuddle with you. A couple's outing with friends is not an option. If you are the only single person, you get fewer and fewer invitations, and eventually, they stop coming at all. You're tired of killing spiders, and other insects, cutting your lawn, or fixing anything in the home that your man would normally do. Some married women think that single women have it made because of the freedom to come and go as they, please. No one to answer to, a different member whenever she wants, no more expectation of cooking, and she can look however she likes when alone. But eventually, it gets old, and you become lonely." Renee told Jessica that at this point, a man missing most of his teeth, with an eighth-grade education but who adored the hell out of you, now seemed like he had potential. Renee could tell that Jessica was annoyed with her, but she was trying to say to her best friend that she was making the biggest mistake in her life. Based on her body language and the scowl on her face, Renee realized that it was a mistake that her friend wanted to explore on her own. And as her friend, she would be there to comfort her and silently in her head said I told you so.

The men walked into what felt like a little chill in the air. They look at each other, wondering which one would bring it up, or do they just ignore it silently? They both decided to ignore it. Moses walked up to Renee and kissed her on the lips. Richard kissed Jessica on her cheek. She smiled. Knowing his ex-wife as he did, he asked if anything was wrong. She shook her head to gesture that there wasn't anything wrong as she pulled away. The men looked at each other with confusion and walked back out of the room. Finally, Moses suggested that they let sleeping dogs lie so that they all could enjoy their last night together. Richard knew he wouldn't sleep with Jessica but wanted to have a meaningful conversation alone. It was time for dinner, and everyone was now at the dining table. Suddenly, Moses asked who had cooked dinner. Jessica smirked, telling him that it shouldn't matter who cooked. He said the last time she cooked that he ate was the last time he would eat her non-seasoned food.

Moses and Richard chuckled because they both knew of the story about how she wanted to cook Thanksgiving dinner for Richard's mother; in fact, she insisted that she cook. It was her kitchen, and she knew her way around it. Richard looked at Moses and told him that her cooking had improved since the infamous Thanksgiving dinner. Renee looked confused and asked what happened at Thanksgiving dinner. Jessica covered her face and started laughing. Then Richard looked at Renee, smiled, and began telling her the story. He started with how Jessica had it in her mind to cook Thanksgiving dinner for him and his mom. Richard tried to discourage her from cooking. He told her that black folks don't play when it comes to Thanksgiving dinner. If you are going to cook, you better come correct, and his mother wasn't sure that she had it in her to cook soul food. Jessica interrupted and told Renee that his mother said to her that she is white, and white people don't season their food. Being the supportive husband, Richard reassured his mother that she was up for the challenge. He continued with his story.

Jessica gave Richard the menu for Thanksgiving. Collard greens with smoked turkey wings, cornbread dressing with giblet gravy, macaroni and cheese, potato salad, turkey, cranberry sauce, candied yams, and for dessert, sweet potato pies, chocolate cake, and banana pudding. Instead, she cooked Turkey and stuffing, jiffy cornbread, boxed macaroni and cheese, green bean casserole, store-bought potato salad, canned cranberry sauce, canned candied yams, and for dessert, pumpkin pies, chocolate cake, and banana pudding. He knew their kitchen didn't smell like his mother's kitchen when she cooked Thanksgiving dinner. Jessica explained that she had changed her mind about something she had perfected. Jessica assured him that her food was full of flavor and that his mom would love it. He continued with the story, explaining that he was trying to think of how he could avoid lying to his mother about dinner.

As he walked into his mother's home, the aroma of Thanksgiving waffled throughout the house. That was when he knew that his mother wasn't taking anything by chance, and as she turned off the fire from the burners on the stove and oven, their eyes locked, and without any words, they understood each other. He hugged and kissed her and said thank you for being you. They both laughed. He said his mother told him he better teach his wife how to cook southern soul food if he expects her to be at their dinner table.

They went back to his home, where his mother pretended to like her food, and then right after dinner, she made up an excuse that her blood pressure was too high, and she needed to go home to lie down. Richard told Jessica that he would run his mother back home and stay a little while to ensure she was okay. Jessica interrupted again to explain that they knew she was a nurse, and she was pretty sure his mother was faking. Jessica couldn't figure out why Richard was going along with the fakery. Finally, Jessica realized that he wasn't eating like he usually ate. Jessica offered to ride with them, and when they tried to talk her out of it, she knew that her mother-in-law had cooked, and they were going back to eat at her house. She insisted on riding along; after all, she was the medical professional in the family and could help if necessary. Richard continued to say that he and his mother were like, 'Okay, you can come but don't get mad.

Once they all made it inside his mother's house, they both looked at Jessica as she realized she wasn't ready. After they all washed up and his mother warmed the food, Jessica took one fork full of her food and then another and another, and after a while, she said, 'Mom, please teach me to cook like you.' It was the first time Jessica had eaten his mother's cooking. His mother was from the South and didn't think it was good for black men to date, much less marry white women. She feared that Richard and Jessica would have threats, or worse, lynched; after all, Black men die for lesser things. That day, Richard's mother and Jessica formed a friendship that lasted until she died a few years ago. Richard got quiet, remembering his mother and how much he missed her. Finally, Jessica broke the silence, "So, to set the record straight, Moses, not only can I cook, but I learned from the best cook on this side of the Mississippi." They all laughed as Richard shook his head in agreement.

After dinner, the women put the food away and washed dishes while the men went outside to smoke their cigars and sip on some whiskey. It was a bit awkward between them because of their previous conversation about dating. Renee broke the awkward silence first.

"Hey, I want to clear the air between us. Of course, I will support whatever decision you make. My only intention was to express how difficult it is in the single world. People make it look great, but the truth is, most of us are trying to get where most married people already are in relationships. We don't walk around sad; we will make the best of what we have, but we would rather switch places. That is all that I was trying to say, our grass isn't greener, hell there is very little grass to nurture, but if this is what you want, I got you because I love you," Renee said. Jessica walked toward her best friend, and they embraced. It was a moment that the two women needed to receive from each other. The men came back in while the women were heading to bed. They had an early flight and wanted to get some rest. Richard quickly intervened and grabbed Jessica's hand.

"Can we talk for a few minutes?" he asked.

"Now? What is so important that it couldn't wait until they return from their trip?" Jessica wondered.

Finally, she gave in, and they walked into the kitchen but not before he stopped and poured himself a glass of whiskey for a little liquid courage. He cleared his throat and took a long sip. She knew they could use something to relax them, so she joined him in a nightcap.

"Jessica, it's been great how we have been able to redevelop our friendship, and I realized that I want more; I always wanted more toward our relationship. I fucked up; there, I said it. I never wanted a divorce. I knew that you blamed me for not becoming a mother, and we waited too late toward the end. I didn't want to be known as the old man with a young child. Now we're without children. I couldn't stand the pain in your eyes. I didn't want to be like these old ass actors who were still having babies at the age of seventy. I knew it would break you when I told you I didn't want to adopt. We were halfway through our forties, and I wanted to spend the rest of my life with you, traveling and doing whatever we wanted to do. I didn't want to be so tired that I couldn't do our family justice. Our child deserved better; so did we, and I'm sorry for what I put you through; it was not the best part of me," Richard softly spoke.

Jessica looked at him, finished her drink, and responded. "Richard, you know that you are the love of my life, but I'm not ready for marriage. I want to stay and live a single life for a while. I'm not saying I never want to rekindle things between us, but not right now. I hope that you understand. I'm not trying to hurt you, but I need some time to breathe."

"How much time do you think you need? A day? Because I can handle a day." Jessica gave him a look. "You need more than a day? A week, month, maybe a year?" Richard shouted.

"I don't know how much time I need. You want me to answer you, but I can't. It may be forever; I just don't know. I'm not asking you to wait on me, but if you are going to wait, then you will have to be patient," Jessica huffed.

Richard ran his fingers over his short grayish hair and rubbed his face. Finally, he kissed her on the forehead and said goodnight.

She knew that he was hurt. The time they spent together over the weekend felt good, but it was too soon after the divorce to want to get back together. She felt a tear fall on her cheek, quickly wiping her face as she said goodnight.

Renee waited for Moses to get out of the shower. She changed her mind about wanting to discuss his trip to meet his son. Renee was feeling anxious and needed reassurance that Monique wouldn't accidentally fall on his member for the third time. She knew that her insecurities were getting the best of her, but then again, the two had a history together, like it or not, and she would have to figure out a way to get over it. Tonight wasn't going to be that night, so she made sure that her girls looked lovely and plump, and she knew Moses would want to engage in nipple-to-lip conversations.

After his shower, he dried off, feeling good about how he would address his trip with Renee. Moses didn't want to do or say anything that would cause her to feel any anxiety over his absence. Moses had no intention of doing anything with Monique. Those days were way behind him, and he never wanted to do anything to lose Renee again. Moses walked to the bed with his boxers on, and Renee lost focus on what she was doing.

Of course, Moses couldn't focus when he saw her breast sitting up high, friendly, and round. He quickly dismissed the conversation that he worked himself up to have and climbed into bed as they began to kiss. Renee came back to her senses and pulled away from him. He had a look of confusion on his face. Finally, she smiled and said, "What if they hear us?"

He smiled back as he tilted his head and said, "Then they will hear us!"

They begin kissing and touching each other, but they can't fully commit, finally, Moses says, "We need to clear the air about Monique, don't we?" Renee sat up and began to express her concerns, and Moses was able to address them one by one, reassuring her that he only had eyes and his heart for her. Then, they set their alarm on their iPhones and turned the lights off, and during their kissing, he mumbled the words, "Marry me."

She Said Yes

Renee responded with a "yes" as she smiled and closed her eyes. She knew that he didn't mean he wanted to get married tomorrow or the next day, but eventually. She and Moses had agreed to ride together to O'Hare airport with Jessica and Richard. Both Richard and Jessica regretted their decision to ride together after their conversation last night. The ride to the airport was silently awkward for Moses and Renee. While the two love birds were bursting at the seams, they read the temperature in the car, looked at each other, and without saying a word, knew it was best to keep their enthusiasm to themselves.

The ride to the airport was long and quiet. The conversation finally started when Jessica asked Moses what hotel they were staying at and for how long. After Moses replied to Jessica, Richard asked Renee when she could manage independently without crutches. She responded it should be in a few weeks. The awkwardness still circled in the air, but Richard didn't care. Suddenly he blurted out a question to Renee that caught her off guard, and she quickly understood why Richard and Jessica were acting weird.

"Renee, tell me what you think. I approached Jessica last night, pouring

"

out my undying love for her, wanting to reconnect and be a couple again. She shot me down. She gave me some bullshit excuse that she wanted to live a single life because she never experienced it on her own. Before Moses and you got together, was living a single life something you would prefer?" There was that awkward silence again.

Then, suddenly, Jessica yelled, "How dare you try to bring my friend into this, Richard… I swear sometimes you can be such a jerk!"

Renee was about to speak when Moses gently grabbed her arm, he slowly shook his head no, and she held his hand and gave it a soft squeeze and smile. It was her way of letting him know she wouldn't respond to Richard's question. The argument between Richard and Jessica continued until they arrived at the airport. They all walked together in silence. Moses and Renee held hands while Richard and Jessica were shooting daggers at each other with their eyes. They finally made it inside the airport, where they would separate and go to their designated airlines. Moses grabbed Renee. While kissing her goodbye, he whispered to her that he loved her, and then she whispered that she loved him back. In the meantime, Jessica and Richard rolled their eyes at the public display of affection they had to witness.

Once out of earshot, Moses and Renee separately asked their friends what was happening and when the fight began. From that moment on, neither Moses nor Renee could get a word in edgewise, at least not until they reached the security checkpoint. Jessica told her that what Richard said in the car was true. He poured his heart out, and she knew he was fighting for their relationship, but when she told him that she wanted to stay single for a while, he exploded. She realized Richard was beyond hurt, putting everything into their relationship.

She told Renee that since the night that they had sex, he had been acting differently – more like her husband instead of her ex-husband, especially after Renee and Moses reunited. Jessica continued her rant until they boarded the plane. It was clear that she loved Richard. Maybe she just needed to be single for a while before she settled back with him. Renee finally understood. It wasn't that Jessica thought a single life was greener. She never experienced being alone, dating other men, or even having sex with different men. Her heart belonged to Richard, but now that they were divorced, Jessica wanted a moment to walk on the other side. Renee was dying to tell Jessica that Moses asked her to marry him, but while listening to Jessica's rant about Richard, she realized that she wanted to bask in the moment a bit longer by herself.

Renee and Moses spoke briefly about what he had asked her the night before. They knew no one else would understand their shared love and getting to know each other again was just par for the course. It wasn't like they were teenagers allowing their emotions to spark sexual intimacy. They had something real during high school; had it not been for Monique and his boyish stupidity, their lives would have been very different. They would have been married with children. Life had a sense of humor, though, because they weren't mature enough back then to see the kind of love they had for each other. Had Renee and Moses stayed together after high school, they would probably be like Jessica and Richard, divorced, holding on to regrets, or like other couples who once were deeply in love, but who now hated each other, or they could be like Monique; well, maybe not Monique. Renee and Jessica would be landing soon, and she was glad that needing a wheelchair would allow her to leave first. Renee was ready to get back to her home and soon to Moses. Her heart smiled as she thought about the two of them and so braced for the plane to land.

Moses could see Richard's hurt and couldn't remember the last time he saw his friend like this. Moses felt terrible for him, knowing how much Richard wanted to reconnect with Jessica. While waiting to board their plane, Richard talked about how Jessica was his heart and how much he loved her. Richard couldn't understand why she loved him as much as she said but didn't want to reconnect. He didn't buy that Jessica wanted to live a single life. Maybe she met someone else and didn't want to tell him. He had so many questions he wanted to ask her, but, of course, she was heading to Tampa to hang out with Renee while Moses tried to play daddy, he thought. Moses attempted to approach the subject carefully and suggested he take a page out of Jessica's book and enjoy the single life but don't throw away their friendship. He may discover that the decision to divorce was the right choice, and to hold on to old memories of happier times. He told Richard that things happen for a reason, and maybe this was his chance to know who he was as a man so that he could become a better man and a better friend.

"What are you saying, Moses? Do I need to become one with my inner self? I know who I am, and I'm fine just the way I am. Jessica must find her inner woman, especially how she fought and carried on over the weekend," Richard said, in a raised pitch.

Moses looked at him and calmly offered a suggestion. "Man, use your inside voice. Everybody doesn't need to know that your ex-wife would rather be single than date you again," he said with a smirk.

Richard beamed like a proud father because that would have been some shit that he would have said to Moses. He was proud of his friend for sticking one to him.

"Man, fuck you!" Richard said loudly.

The men laughed as people lined up to board the plane. Moses wanted to tell Richard that he had asked Renee to marry him last night, but it wasn't the right time. He wasn't like Richard, who would throw salt in your wound and then ask if it hurt. He must admit that when he heard her say yes, she would marry him, it made him the happiest man ever. He got why their friends were saying it was too soon, and if it were anyone else, he would agree. But he loved her for so many years that he didn't want to wait to date and get to know each other before they said Idido. They will deal with any red flags along the way. They boarded the plane and found their seats. After getting comfortable, he looked out the window, feeling the sun's heat on his face, and immediately turned the air on above him as he closed the shade. Moses was a big man. He wasn't fat but he had a thick frame and needed room for comfort. Richard had a thinner frame with long legs, he sat in an aisle seat. Both men were relieved that no one sat in the middle chair, giving them the space and the freedom to continue to talk. But once the plane was in the air, both men found themselves drifting off to sleep; they slept until they felt the plane's wheels hit the ground. Neither one had gotten much sleep the night before and felt the heaviness from lack of sleep. They both looked at each other and were glad they made it without incident. They hated flying but found it necessary to get to their destination promptly. As they headed off the plane, Richard picked up where he started with Jessica, but all Moses could do was think about seeing CJ. He abruptly interrupted Richard's sad song of his undying love because this trip was not about him. Moses wanted to convey what he needed from him, making sure that if somehow Monique happened to worm her way into their time, he was to be the buffer. Once they picked up their luggage and rented an SUV, Moses called CJ to let him know they were in town and to see if the meeting was still on. Moses asked if it was okay if his best friend Richard tagged along for dinner. CJ paused as he hesitated to speak. CJ told Moses that if it were his house, it wouldn't be a problem, but since this was something his mom had prepared, perhaps it could just be the three of them. Besides, his mother told him if a man named Richard was with Moses, they both could turn around and leave. Moses understood, but he didn't want to leave without his protection.

Richard had a way of getting under Monique's skin and shutting her up; Moses needed his interference. CJ could sense Moses' uneasiness and changed his mind. He told him that Richard could come over as well. He knew that his mom was still trying to get on his good side, so as much as she would hate to see Richard, she would be on her best behavior. No one knew his mom better than him. CJ was curious to see what else his mother might be hiding. Dinner was set for 8:00 p.m., giving him and Richard time to go to the hotel, relax, and refresh. Moses ended his call with CJ as he drove to the valet parking at the hotel.

Moses gave his keys to a valet to park the SUV as they grabbed their luggage. Upon entering the hotel to register and grab the keycard to their rooms, Moses received a text from Renee telling him good luck and that she hoped everything was going well with him and his son.

Jessica had made the reservations for them, and he was impressed with her excellent taste. The men walked through the lobby to their separate rooms. As the men entered their rooms, Richard was glad to have a moment to himself to gather his thoughts; he had time to cool off and get out of his feelings. Richard knew that Moses was right; it didn't matter how much Richard loved Jessica, she had to be on the same page, and if she wanted to stay single for a while, Richard honestly had no say in it. He knew he didn't want to lose her completely, even if it meant only being friends. If that was all she could give him right now, he would accept it. He wasn't sure if he would be ready to move on to date other women, but Richard also knew that he didn't want to be alone. There was something sad to him when he saw anyone being alone.

He didn't want to end up a lonely man, hitting on young women who only viewed him as a sugar daddy. He wasn't ready to speak to Jessica on the phone, so he texted her instead to let her know that he understood and respected her decision. In his text, he explained that he loved her enough to let her go, and if a friendship was all that remained out of their marriage, then he was still a lucky man.

It was time for Richard to get dressed so he could deal with Medusa, also known as Monique. He would rather get beat up by Diamond than see her again. But he was here for his best friend. Speaking of Diamond, he still had the video of the fight; he watched it after taking a shower and getting dressed. Moses was knocking at his door right when Diamond flung Jessica as if she were a shotput ball, and Diamond was at the Olympics, giving it her all to win the gold. He turned the video off and answered the door.

"Richard, are you ready?" Moses asked. Richard grabbed his keycard, wallet, and keys as he headed out the door. Richard was shorter than Moses but could dress his ass off. He had a flair for colors and style. He wore a pair of white jeans with a taupe vest; the cut of the vest had three buttons down the front, right above the navel, leaving the rest of his chest exposed. But Richard decided to wear a white button-down shirt underneath his vest and cocoa brown leather loafers at the last minute. In addition, he wore Tom Ford's Oud Wood Eau De Parfum cologne, a diamond stud in both of his earlobes, a gold herringbone chain, and on his right arm was a Gold Movado Sapphire Watch. The grey in his short-cut salt and pepper hair sparkled like diamonds glistening under the lights.

Richard commented on Moses' attire as he walked out of his room. Moses' outfit consisted of a pair of blue jeans and a silver short-sleeved button-down shirt (allowing him to exhibit his tattooed sleeve on his right arm). He complimented the look with a pair of black boots and a black straw fedora hat. His diamond accent Movado Face watch sparkled, and his diamond studs twinkled with each movement. He donned a silver diamond cut chain that hung around his neck, showing off his masculine chest, and the cologne he wore was Christian Dior's Sauvage Eau De Parfum. Moses' salt and pepper beard twinkled like stars on a clear summer night.

"Awe shit! Man, what are you trying to do? Once Medusa, I mean Monique sees your fine black ass, she will want to walk down memory lane trying to capture that moment that made her betrayal of her best friend well worth it. I'm not talking about high school dick Moses, but Mandingo grown-ass man Moses. Moses with the golden staff that even when it went from hard to soft was a big ass snake." Richard laughed so hard that he couldn't hear Moses respond as he joined him in laughter.

"I know that I look good for an old man," Moses said, smiling as he pretended to brush something off his shoulders. "But dude, look at you! Who are you trying to impress? Jessica isn't here. Oh! I forgot – she friend-zoned you. Too soon?" Moses laughed.

"Hell yeah, it's too soon! You know my heart is still in its sensitive state, but I get it; it was your immature way of getting me back. Besides, I know that I look good, I was always the better dresser between the two of us, but I must say, you clean up well, my friend." Richard chuckled. "Maybe I'll find a few single women while we are out. A freak, preferably one who wants to take a ride on Big Daddy. Someone who can take me on an "Exorcist" ride, make my damn eyes roll up in my head, and make it spin around as I scream profanity at her. Someone young enough to handle the stamina yet experienced enough to show daddy what she wants." He began to slap himself on his butt.

Moses shook his head and gestured for them to leave. On their ride to Monique's home, Richard suggested to Moses that he better not take any pictures with Monique. He warned him that she had nothing to lose and everything to gain. "What's perfect than having Mommy and his real daddy back together again? And you can finally be a family," Richard explained. Moses looked at Richard for a second and asked him to be serious, and Richard replied that he was serious. He just wanted his friend to be aware.

"I'll bet that Monique will come out wearing a tight-fitting dress showing the shape of her big juicy ass, and all her breasts except her areolas will be out. Her face is going to be drag queen beat (he snaps his fingers), flawless, and her weave will be flowing down her back like she's Elsa from the Disney picture 'Frozen', Richard said.

Moses had a surprised look when he turned to his friend with a question. "Wait… what do you know about 'Elsa' or 'Frozen'? You don't have any children, or do you?" Moses curiously asked.

"Hell, no, I don't have any children," Richard said, "but I watch television, and sometimes when I'm flipping through the channels, I come across one of Disney's movies. Watching these movies keeps you feeling like a kid at heart." Richard smiled as he pointed to his heart.

Moses quickly changed the subject. "We are close to the house, and for the first time, I'll meet CJ as his father. So, I need you to be there for me if Monique tries anything, and I mean anything. You know I love you like a brother," Moses said.

"Yeah, I love you too, bro," Richard replied.

They made it to Monique's house and sat composing themselves in the car for a few minutes. It was going to be a big night for Moses, and his wingman, Richard, was determined that Monique wouldn't ruin it for the father and son. Before they opened their doors, Renee called Moses to wish him good luck and tell him that she loved him. He didn't know how she knew, but she gave him just what he needed from the woman he loved; without a doubt, he would marry her, and Monique didn't stand a chance. Nevertheless, he was here for his son and to bond with him as much as possible for the short time they would be together.

"Wait, I almost forgot, this will help calm your nerves," Richard said.

"What are you giving me? Edibles?" Moses said.

"Yes, edibles, I have four left, two for you and two for me. Eating a few edibles will help us both relax," Richard responded. "Edibles like the gummy candy that you buy at the grocery store or that you buy at a marijuana dispensary?" Moses asked in disbelief.

"The latter, man, now chew up so that we can get through this as painlessly as possible," Richard quickly responded.

"I'm not eating those, and you shouldn't either," Moses said, annoyed. Richard placed the gummies back into his pocket as the men got out of the car and slowly walked toward the front door. Richard grabbed Moses before reaching the door and called him by his birth name.

"Byron, I'm proud of you, man, and I got you."

Moses shook his head, acknowledging that he knew. They hugged, and then Moses rang the doorbell. The front door flung open, Monique wore a tight red dress showing her breasts with a low-cut front, and just as Richard predicted, the dress accentuated her derriere. The men stood still as Monique smiled and said, "Moses, I'm so glad that you made it." She hugged him tightly and gently kissed him. She gave Richard a stern look and dryly spoke, "Richard."

"Elsa, I mean Monique," Richard quickly corrected himself. "What did you call me? Elsa? Why did you call me that name? Are you trying to say that I'm cold as ice?" Monique scowled. Moses found himself chuckling as his mind processed their conversation on the way here. He shook his head and thought to himself, 'That Damn Richard!' Richard explained to Monique that he was telling Moses about the Disney movie "Frozen". She looked at him and shook her head. They all walked inside, and she asked the men if they would like a drink. Richard was the first to speak and asked what she had, and she quickly responded, "For you, water." Then she turned her attention to Moses and asked him what his poison was, and at that moment, Richard hummed the song "Let it Go". Moses chuckled and pretended that he was coughing to prevent Monique from getting upset with him early in their visit. Monique noticed Moses looking around, and she realized that he was looking for CJ. She looked at Moses and told him that he was on a call with the movie producer of his next film and that he would be down shortly. Monique guided them into the parlor, where they all would sit down to talk. She asked about Jessica and Renee, and then Richard told her that Jessica went to Tampa to help Renee until Moses could get there to take over. Monique looked a bit surprised to hear they were so close so soon. She was hoping to rekindle the romance between her and Moses now that it was clear that her marriage and her friendship with Renee were both over. She smiled and thought letting a perfectly good man go to waste didn't make sense.

Oh Richard!

Monique left the room to see what was taking CJ so long, and as she was leaving, Richard quickly turned to Moses and asked if he wanted those two gummies. He pulled out the package, grabbed two, and placed them into his mouth. Moses quickly held out his hand, put the two gummies in his mouth, and chewed. Richard assured him that the gummies were mild. At least that is what the young black man at the hotel told him when he asked where to get some gummies. Richard looked at Moses and reminded him to be on his "P's" and "Q's" because Medusa was out for blood. At that point, he understood what Richard had been trying to warn him about all along. He looked at Richard and told him it was time to lock in, "Am I my brother's keeper's oath." Richard agreed, and they recited the oath.

"As a brother, I vow to hold my brother accountable for his actions, but never will I allow him to go alone in a situation that will cause him physical, mental, emotional, or financial harm. Am I my brother's keeper? Yes. If he loses his mind and goes against the morals of our manhood for love or lust, he permits his brother to knock the fuck out of him and bring him back to his senses." They grunted as a grizzly bear and man hug.

They sat down, and Monique and CJ walked into the parlor as they got comfortable. Moses didn't realize the massive grin that emerged so naturally as he stood up to greet CJ for the first time as his son. The father and son embraced each other, their faces lit up with a smile, and for a quick second, there was a little emotion showing, but not from the men or Monique, but from Richard. He mentioned that the moment that they shared was beautiful. Moses and CJ sat next to each other as Monique disappeared into the kitchen for a few minutes. He introduced CJ to Richard, telling him that Richard was his best friend and his brother from another mother. Richard smiled at his friend's acknowledgment of their closeness, not that Moses hadn't done it before, but this time it was more noteworthy because Moses said it to his son. The two men greeted each other with a hug, and Richard smiled and told CJ he could call him Uncle Richard. He paused and then said,

"Since your ass is old, how about you call me Richard, and later if you feel comfortable, call me "unc", (short for uncle).

All three men burst into laughter, needing to remove the nervous energy they all could feel in the room. Monique announced dinner was ready, so Richard and Moses followed CJ into the dining room. Monique set the table for four people, and CJ and Moses sat next to each other. Richard sat in one of the two remaining chairs across from Moses, which meant that Monique would sit next to her nemesis, Richard.

As she walked in with the last dish, she suggested CJ sit across from his father. That way, they would have a better view of each other while continuing their conversation. Moving would leave an empty seat next to Moses and away from Richard. After growing up with only women, Richard learned a few things from them. He quickly responded by suggesting that Moses move to the empty chair next to him, leaving Monique to sit next to their son. Before Monique could object, Moses quickly stood up and moved into the empty chair. Richard smiled at

Monique and thanked her for her suggestion because it was a perfect move. But, of course, he wanted her to understand that game recognizes the game. She forced a smile as she responded to Richard, acknowledging his approval.

'I see you,' she thought to herself as she raised her wine glass to toast the occasion. At that very second, Richard and Moses started to feel the effects of the gummies they had eaten. Each of the men had a different reaction. Moses was talking slower than usual, emphasizing every word, while Richard couldn't stop laughing.

Finally, Monique looked at the two men and asked them if they were okay, and that was when CJ realized what was happening and ran interference.

He laughed to himself because he, too, had partaken in a few gummies. The table became quiet as everyone enjoyed the soulful food that Monique cooked. She wasn't sure if she still knew how to cook. It had been a long time since she cooked after marrying Chris. Moses complimented Monique on a great meal. She blushed, telling him that her mother always told her that the best way to a man's heart was to feed him a good Southern meal. Everyone chuckled, and then Richard spoke.

"Well, shit, maybe you should have cooked for Moses instead of spreading your legs."

Moses gave him a swift sidekick. Richard was just warming up. He also told Monique that being a great cook is fantastic, but when you find your soulmate like Moses had with Renee, nothing and no one else matters. CJ unwittingly agreed with Richard, which felt like a dagger in Monique's back. He spoke about Mia Goodloe, the woman he loved. Monique was tired of Richard's games; she knew she only had a short time to make her move, and she would take it when CJ excused himself to leave for the airport. He had to leave earlier than he had anticipated for his new movie.

She planned to drink too much to drive and ask Richard to take him in her car, the new black-on-black Mercedes-Benz GLC Coupe she had just purchased. She would phrase it as a way of burying the hatch between the two of them. Proud of her plan, Monique devilishly grinned as she took a sip of her wine.

The two men continued their conversation, and just as Monique snapped out of her daydream, she heard Moses ask CJ about Mia, stating that it had been a while since he had seen her. Moses asked CJ to give her his love. Monique couldn't believe what she was hearing. How did Moses know Mia? Was it possible that Moses was a part of Diamond's bribe after all? She asked Moses if he and Mia were friends. As Moses began to respond, CJ jumped in and told his mom that Moses was the consultant in the previous movie he starred in before he retired from the military. CJ could tell that Moses had a difficult time focusing.

He also knew that look his mother gave when she didn't believe someone and thought they were trying to make her feel stupid. He quickly changed the subject and asked Moses about Renee and if he planned on marrying her. By this time, Richard had put the pieces together and could see the old Monique rearing her jealous head. He knew that her son knew nothing about her childhood and who his mother was, but he was about to get a front-row seat. Richard decided to play puppet master to his Medusa. He jumped into the conversation, telling CJ how much Moses and Renee were in love and how it went back to high school.

"Just think; you'll be able to witness the marriage of one of your parents and," Richard added, "you'd love your new stepmother, Renee." Richard burst into laughter, causing Monique to fight the urge to cuss him out. She felt hurt that CJ would agree, pushing the dagger deeper into her back; Moses, without hesitation, slowly spoke, telling everyone that he asked Renee to marry him last night. CJ congratulated Moses as Richard shouted,

"Oh! When were you going to tell your boy?"

Monique exploded with "OMG… what in the hell? Moses, are you serious? Did you ask Renee to marry you? Did she say yes?"

"Who is being stupid now, Monique?" Richard interjected. "Do you think this man would tell his son, brother, and his random childhood side-chick that he asked the love of his life since high school to marry him if she said no?" Richard chuckled, shaking his head at Monique.

Monique slowly looked at Richard; everything else was a blur from then on. Finally, she stood up, grabbed a glass of water, and walked next to Richard. He looked at her and told her to sit down and stop acting like he was Diamond. That was when Monique threw the water in Richard's face, and then she threw the glass at him, hitting him in the left eye, giving him a deep cut right along his eyebrow, as she told him to go to hell, calling him a bitch ass nigga. Moses and CJ jumped up out of their seats to get in the middle of their fight, and just like that, all three men immediately came off their highs. Moses grabbed Richard, and CJ caught his mom. With blood running down his face, Richard pulled away and went on a tirade.

"Who the fuck are you calling a bitch ass nigga? Only a slimy ass, piece of shit, bitch ass whore would call someone else a bitch, and by the way, ain't going to be too many bitches coming out of your mouth. And if you ever hit me with anything again, I will forget that you are a woman and beat your ass like an annoying ass Karen."

Neither Monique nor Richard was listening to Moses or CJ. They continued to say the ugliest and most vile things to each other, that was until they heard a roar like no other.

"GOD – DAMNIT. I SAID SHUT THE HELL UP – NOW!"

Silence covered the room. Moses said this was way too much and shouldn't have gotten to this level. He apologized to CJ and told him their meeting as father and son shouldn't have ended on such a sour note. Both Richard and Monique tried to speak, but when they saw the scowl on Moses' face, they immediately looked down at the ground. There was a sadness floating in the air and on Moses' face. CJ walked over to him and told him that it didn't matter how the meeting ended; what mattered to him was that the two of them could see each other and create a path to getting to know each other as father and son.

They embraced each other with such a force that you could tell they were already full of love for each other. CJ announced that his car service had arrived, so he had to go. He looked at Moses and said with a smirk, "Best friends?" Moses told him that it was complicated. CJ looked at his mother, hugged her, and said he loved her despite her past. She cried, thanking him as she hugged him again. Finally, CJ looked at Richard and told him that he needed to apologize to his mom, Richard did so slowly. CJ then looked at his mom and said, "You apologize to Richard as well," and Monique reluctantly apologized to Richard. CJ smiled at Richard and told him that it was a pleasure to have met him; they embraced, and as he walked away, Richard said to him that he hoped to see him again soon; CJ then stopped to look at Richard and smiled as he called him Unc! Richard's face beamed with pride toward his newly discovered nephew.

Moses looked at Richard and told him he needed to go to an emergency room to get a few stitches. Monique looked at the two of them and told them both to leave. Moses told them both how disappointed he was in the two of them. As for Monique, Moses said to her that his interest was only in Renee, and there wasn't anything she could offer to change his feelings. Moses explained that he wasn't a little high school boy any longer, and his members didn't make the decisions for him. He continued to speak, telling her that her selfishness caused her to lose a husband and his family, material things, and her social standing in Charlotte. Instead of blaming everyone else, he suggested Monique take a long look at herself and her behavior and decide what she needs to change. He explained to Monique that he didn't need to go to Richard's level to call her out of her name, but he understood why he felt the need to do it. He grabbed his hat and walked towards the door. Richard and Monique stood there looking shocked.

They spent all night in the E.R. to get Richard's face stitched up, and while Moses was waiting, he managed to change both of their flights to an earlier one. They had enough time to pack, shower, and get to the airport after leaving the ER. The men were exhausted and snored so loudly that the flight attendants had to wake them up several times because they were disturbing everyone on the plane.

Finally, they landed at Tampa International Airport, and once they gathered their luggage, they drove to Moses' home. Richard had one month left before returning to work at the college for the fall semester, so he decided to hang out at Moses' home while Moses took care of Renee. Moses called Renee to tell her they had made it home and that they were tired and needed to sleep.

He told her they would be over first thing in the morning. They both said I love you before they hung up for the evening. Moses showed Richard to his room and gave him towels to shower. They didn't feel like sleeping any longer. They thought about going to Renee's but decided to have man time. Moses grabbed two of his favorite cigars along with his whiskey and two glasses. They stepped out to his deck to relax and talk about the craziness of the previous night.

Monique thought about what Moses said and wondered if he was right. Here she was in that big house alone. She knew CJ loved her, but he was making his own life on the West Coast. Her two oldest and dearest friends were no longer her friends, and after what happened tonight, she knew that there was no turning back. It'd been a long time since she felt alone, and Charlotte, North Carolina, was closing in on her, she thought.

She woke up the following day still wearing her irresistible dress that became resistible. She forgot that her dress was suitable to wear for a short period. She could barely breathe, then noticed one of her breasts fell outside her top while she slept. She ended up with makeup everywhere on her pillowcase and sheets. At that moment, Monique no longer cared about being polished or part of a social society; she ran her shower and cried as she washed her face. This cry was different because her heart was saying goodbye to everyone. She no longer wanted to function within her environment.

After her shower, Monique pulled herself together after deciding to make some changes to her divorce. She called Stephanie to inform her that she would move out of the home sixty days earlier and would only take what belonged to her, including her jewelry. Monique immediately began looking at places around the world to start her journey now that she was fully vaccinated, and most countries had reopened. One month later, the ink was dry on her divorce papers, and her alimony payments were set up to be directly deposited in her bank account each month. Monique decided now was the time for her to leave, and since no one would miss her except CJ, there wasn't any need to tell anyone her plans.

She had decided to start her journey in Dubai, and she was getting excited about putting her plans into action. Monique bought a first-class plane ticket and found a hotel in Dubai. Now it was time to find a storage place for all her belongings. She placed her expensive jewelry in a safe deposit box the next day. She could wrap up everything in a few weeks, just days shy of when she had to be out of her home. As she watched the moving truck drive up, she got a little choked up, her life was stored in boxes. They contained a lifetime of memories, and it was bittersweet to see how her life had dramatically changed from being a wife and a member of one of the most prominent families.

She was now the single mother of an adult son and ousted from every social circle and her childhood friends. She called CJ to tell him her plans but only got his voicemail. Finally, she left a message for him to call her back, saying it was necessary. She hoped to hear from him before leaving town, but he never called. She tried again on her way to the airport but got his voicemail again. This time Monique left a voicemail message informing him that she was on her way to the airport, no longer lived in the house, and was taking an exceptionally long and much-needed vacation to see the world alone. Monique boarded the plane and silently said goodbye because now that she was worth several million, she would never return to the United States, at least not to Charlotte, North Carolina. It would take CJ to need for her to return to the U.S.

Until Death

One year later, love was still in the air for Renee and Moses. They were heading to their wedding destination spot. After reconnecting at the class reunion, they both found what they longed to have for so many years: love that only a few have ever experienced.

They went from each other's homes, each finding something about the other that they preferred more than their own. They decided to sell both of their homes and purchase one together, which would give them the extra cash to have the wedding of their dreams. They bought a four-bedroom ranch-style house with a pool, sauna, and gym. Renee kept exercising, joining Moses on his daily run in the morning out on the causeway. Her jewelry business was taking off, keeping her busier than ever. Renee finally felt like all the missing pieces of who she wanted Renee Morgan to become were falling into place. It was an exciting time as Renee and Moses embarked on holy matrimony.

Since it was going to be the two of them, Jessica, Richard, her twins, and CJ, they wanted to make it fun, so they decided to wed in Rome, Italy. Moses remembered a place that he said was breathtakingly beautiful and would be perfect to have their wedding. Renee found photos of the site on the internet he was telling her about, and she agreed that it was beautiful and a perfect place to get married. He still had connections at the base and pulled in a few favors to ensure that Renee had the most beautiful wedding ever.

Moses thought about his visit with CJ at Monique's home last year and how he had told Renee everything the following morning, explaining why he and Richard decided to end their trip early. At first, Renee found herself becoming upset but quickly realized Moses had not done anything wrong. Renee confessed that she knew that Monique was going to try something, and her first instinct was to tag along, but it wasn't about her or Monique. It was about Moses and his son. She had no idea how sexy she was to him at that moment. He loved seeing her confidence. He officially proposed to her two months later. On one of their morning runs along the causeway, right when the sun was rising, a woman who was jogging saw what he was doing and offered to take pictures with one of their phones.

Renee smiled and gave the stranger her phone. He kneeled on one knee with the ring box in hand, Renee's back was facing the sun rising, and the woman managed to snap beautiful pictures of his proposal. She also took pictures of him putting the ring on her left finger – after she said yes – and of him kissing her. By the time they started kissing, the sun was up and shining bright. They were interrupted by the woman handing Renee her phone back. As they listened to the sounds of celebration, Moses and Renee realized they had attracted a crowd of onlookers clapping and congratulating them.

The newly engaged couple decided to cancel their run; neither one of them was in the mood, and all Renee wanted to do was call Jessica. As Moses drove, Renee looked at the pictures the stranger had taken and was amazed at the beautiful backdrop the rising of the sun had created. It was simply breathtaking. So instead of calling, she cropped one of the pictures showing her two-carat Cushion Cathedral Petite Pave Engagement Ring.

Renee was happy to see that her nails still looked fresh in her photo. She sent the photo of her engagement ring on her finger to Jessica and, immediately, her phone rang. She and Moses chuckled.

"That was quick," Moses stated.

"Hello," Renee answered her phone.

"Hello? Renee, you need to stop playing, you knew the second you sent me that photo of your engagement ring I was going to call! When did this happen? Today? Have you guys set a date? How many people have you told so far?" Jessica was firing out her questions so quickly that Renee didn't have time to respond.

"Slow down, breathe. We just got engaged a few minutes ago, and you being my best friend, I wanted to share with you first. Moses is driving and hasn't even had the time to let Richard know," Renee said.

Moses interrupted and said that he had forgotten that he talked to Richard last night and told him that he was going to propose in the morning. Jessica snarled at Moses because she wanted to be the first to know. Renee said to her that she was the first to find out officially and to see the ring. When Moses tried to correct what Renee said about being the first to see the ring, Renee waved him off and mouthed I'll explain later. Renee told Jessica she would call her later because they were at their favorite breakfast restaurant.

"I don't know why we entertain those two characters," Moses said.

"They are our oldest and dearest friends we love like family?" Renee said, as she grabbed his face and kissed him.

They went to breakfast and enjoyed their food and each other's company.

Six months later, it was time. The wedding was happening in Rome, Italy, and Renee was a stunningly beautiful bride. When Moses saw her walk down the aisle with both of her children, he felt a little choked up. He wiped his eyes, and this time, Richard didn't say anything clever.

Richard found himself thinking back on his wedding to Jessica, how happy they were then, and how they managed to now only be friends. He made his decision four months after Moses and Renee became engaged to give Jessica what she had been asking for, space and time. He found his new passion, taking pictures. He discovered how much taking pictures calmed him down and gave him so much peace.

He took lots of photos during the wedding; afterward, he wanted to capture every beautiful moment. He took pictures everywhere and of everyone he could, including the bride and groom and their families. He took one photo by the chapel where the two got married. He noticed a woman who resembled Monique wearing sunglasses and a big floppy hat. Richard wondered if it was her, but quickly decided that she wouldn't crash their wedding. The ceremony was beautiful, and Richard was glad he had a chance to be there for his best friend, standing as his best man.

For a while, he thought Moses would ask his son CJ to be the best man, but Moses told him that it didn't feel right to have him as the best man when they were still getting to know each other. His best man was that young boy he grew up with, fought, and cried with; the one he protected, defended, laughed, became angry with, and most of all, became a man with; and that was Richard J. Palmer. Friends for life. Richard loved Moses like a brother, and there wasn't anything that he wouldn't do for him, and he knew that Moses would do the same thing for him.

After he returned from Rome, Richard wasn't feeling well. He thought he may have eaten some bad food and developed poisoning. Richard made an appointment to see his doctor, and after a few tests, they called him to come back into the office. He knew that wasn't a good sign. He tried to brace himself for the worst, but he didn't want to bring lousy juju to him either. Richard walked into the doctor's office, and they asked him if had he brought anyone with him. He told them that he had no one to call. Richard didn't want to bother Moses, who was still on his honeymoon, and he was no longer Jessica's problem in sickness or health – or anything else since they were divorced.

The doctor suggested recording their conversation because he wouldn't be able to hear another word once he told him his diagnosis. Richard told the doctor that he was making him nervous with all this doom and gloom talk. He did what the doctor suggested and pushed play to record the visit on his phone, and the doctor was right. He didn't hear another word after saying to him, "Richard, you have Stage 3 prostate cancer." What he heard stunned him; confusion replaced shock, then fear quickly took over. He fought back the tears and asked him how this had happened.

The doctor didn't want to lecture him, but it was necessary, especially for African American men who had a high probability of getting prostate cancer. He explained to Richard that it was vital for him to get his prostate checked once a year, and he had missed the last three years. He explained that catching this cancer earlier increases the chances of a better outcome. The good news, though, was that his cancer was still where it was treatable but would require a more aggressive intervention plan. He strongly suggested that Richard find someone who would be able to become his caretaker, and the sooner, the better.

Richard left the doctor's office, where he had held his emotions in for as long as he could. But the second he sat down in his car came a heartbreaking sound that would leave no eyes around him dry. He stopped by the church to talk with the pastor who married him and Jessica what seemed like a lifetime ago. The pastor gave him some encouraging advice and prayed over him. Richard thought about calling Moses when he left there but decided to wait until he got home. He noticed that Moses had been trying to call him a few times and finally Moses texted, telling Richard to call him. Richard wasn't ready to talk to anyone now. He needed time to digest the news of having cancer. Richard knew that the sooner his treatment started, the better his chance of survival would be. But he couldn't ask Moses to interrupt his time with Renee to come and help him through this time, not knowing how long it would take.

A month went by, and he still hadn't called or texted, and he knew that Moses was worried. Moses reached out to Jessica, asking her to stop by and check on him. Jessica decided that she wouldn't reach out to Richard, who was probably still in his feelings about her not wanting to get back together, and this was his last attempt for attention. Richard just didn't have the energy after his chemotherapy and radiation. Then one day, out of the blue, this huge bald man knocked on his door and looked at Richard, and for the first time, Richard saw his friend's face change to fear and concern.

Moses knew Richard was sick. He didn't know what was wrong, but if he had to guess, it was cancer. He had seen it too many times with his military friends and dad. Richard, who had come to the door with a cane, told Moses to come in and get out of the cold.

"Why didn't you tell us? Does Jessica know?" Moses had so many questions.

He played the visit that he had recorded with this doctor and Moses listened as Richard was getting dressed. Moses asked if he was getting dressed for a doctor's visit today and Richard said yes. Moses insisted that he accompany his friend. Richard gently smiled feeling thankful for the arrival of his best friend. Moses decided to call Renee after the appointment to give her the bad news. He knew that Renee would feel the same way, that they should have Richard stay with them during his treatment. On the way to his appointment, Moses brought it up to see how Richard felt about his suggestion. Richard agreed, but with one stipulation; they couldn't tell Jessica about his condition. He made Moses promise and made it clear that when he told Renee, he needed to make her promise.

While in his doctor's office, Moses asked the doctor if he could recommend a facility and doctor in the Tampa area who specializes in cancer with a high success rate. He explained that he and his wife would be Richard's caretakers and asked if he would send a referral to the insurance company for approval. Two weeks later, because of the intense treatment required and he otherwise had no one to help him, Richard received approval from his insurance company. The insurer approved the out-of-network doctors and facilities to be paid as though they were in-network.

The fact that Richard would not have had a caregiver was a unique circumstance and the reason the insurance coverage was approved that way. They rarely approve of anything these days. God is a way-maker; that was what Renee said when Moses told her the news the following afternoon. Moses was bringing his brother to live with him and his family to take care of the only best friend he ever had. Renee knew that when Jessica found out, she would feel hurt that she had been left in the dark, but Renee couldn't worry about that now. It was essential to keep Richard calm and without drama, so that was what she planned on doing.

After a month had gone by and she hadn't heard anything from Renee or Moses, Jessica decided to check on Richard. After all, she was worried that he hadn't responded to her calls or text messages once her conscience got the best of her. She decided to stop by his home after work, and it looked as if he hadn't been there in months. His home was dark, the curtains were closed, and some stranger was cutting his grass. She decided to ask him if he lived at the house.

 The older guy said he didn't and was the neighbor; Richard asked him if he wouldn't mind looking after his house for a while because he was leaving town and wouldn't be back for a few months. When he mentioned how skinny Richard had gotten, Jessica felt a sharp pain in her stomach which almost caused her to bend over in pain. She thanked the man and tried to call Richard, but still no answer.

 Jessica finally called Moses, and the only thing that he could say was that Richard was staying with them for a while. When she tried to press for more information, he told her that she needed to talk to Richard. Frustrated with the entire conversation, she hung up and called Renee, and when she got the same pushback from her, she hung up and grabbed the next flight to Tampa. Renee knew her friend well and knew she would come to see what was happening. She was glad that Jessica had called because she hated keeping secrets from her. The next day when their doorbell rang; it was Jessica. She pushed past Moses looking for Richard. She finally saw him and was stunned at how sick he looked. Richard looked at her face and told her he had prostate cancer as he fought back his tears. She fell to her knees and cried.

Renee and Moses left them alone as Richard and Jessica held each other, crying in each other's arms. After Jessica wiped away her tears, she sadly asked him why he wouldn't tell her he was sick. He put his head down and said to her that he didn't want to bother her. He was no longer her responsibility and didn't want to mess up anything if she was dating.

"What the fuck do you mean you didn't want to bother me? I'm the nurse, not Renee or Moses, ME! I should have been the one you called," she yelled.

Richard waited until she finished yelling and calmly told her to stop. He had no energy to deal with her anger. He reminded her that she had no right to be upset with him, especially since she adamantly told him she needed space. After calming down, she laid her head on his chest, but he politely pushed her away.

He apologized but also told Jessica that she needed to leave. He needed to focus on his health and couldn't do it with her under the same roof. He continued to tell her that he would always love and be in love with her – until his dying day – but what he couldn't do was fight anymore. It wouldn't be good for his health, and he realized just how short life was. So, if she wanted to be there for him, she would have to stop all that hostile cussing and leave in the morning.

"Please let me take you back home so I can take care of you," she said.

"Nope," he replied.

"What do you mean No? You don't want me to take care of you?" Jessica sadly responded.

"Baby, listen, ain't no way I'm moving back to cold-ass Rockford, Illinois when I can have fun in the sun every day. I had Moses call my realtor to place my home up for sale. I will stay with them until I'm better and can find a home."

Once Richard was cancer-free, he would put in for retirement at the school. "I'm not of age, but I have been there long enough to retire. I'll work as a sub-teacher as supplemental income, and if my cancer progresses, then I have a different retirement," he said.

"Please stop joking about dying, Richard!" Jessica screamed and ran out of the room, crying.

Richard felt terrible that he had made her cry, and went to try to find her, but found himself so weak that he crashed to the floor. Everyone came running to his aid, asking if he was okay. Richard laughed and said yes. He told them that Jessica had his ass chasing her all their lives, so why would this be any different? Moses grabbed his buddy and helped him back into bed. He stayed in the room with him for a little while, still asking him if he was okay, and Richard assured Moses that he was fine. Jessica asked if they had room for her to stay. Renee told her of course, but to respect Richard's request. The two ladies hugged, and Jessica walked back into the room where Richard was lying down.

As Moses passed Jessica, they embraced each other, and she could see that he was just as scared as she was that Richard wouldn't make it. After apologizing for making her cry, Richard thanked her for coming to see him. She softly broke down and cried; he could barely understand what she had said and asked her to repeat it. She wiped the tears from her face again. Jessica kissed Richard and told him that she loved him. She wasn't going to fight him to come to stay with her, but she promised that he would see her often.

Renee was in the kitchen putting dinner away when Jessica walked in, face beet red, and she could tell that her friend was having a difficult time. When Renee asked how she could help, Jessica told her to take care of Richard. Jessica conceded that he didn't want to come back with her. It broke her heart, but she understood. Renee asked if she had eaten, and

Jessica shook her head no. Renee fixed her a plate and warmed it up in the microwave and gave her friend a full glass of wine. They sat in the kitchen talking until she had finished. Renee showed Jessica to her room, and they hugged, but neither one was ready to say good night to the other. So, Renee grabbed a bottle of wine and two glasses as they made their way to the patio outside. The ladies talked and cried until they could see the sun beginning to rise. Jessica decided to leave instead of getting some rest. She said that it was too painful for her to stay.

 She said her goodbyes and kissed Richard on his forehead, then kissed him on his lips. Jessica knew that their relationship had changed and the man she knew who would always love her, now he sees her with different eyes. It was clear to Jessica that their relationship was barely as friends and that there would be no rekindling romance like Renee and Moses. A young man was waiting in a car ready to take her to the airport. As a tear rolled down Jessica's face, she waved goodbye. Her relationship with everyone in that house was forever changed and not in a good way. Maybe it was the exhaustion or the truth about Richard's illness making her feel betrayed and brokenhearted. Renee wasn't the woman or friend that she knew. Since her marriage to Moses, she stopped caring about Jessica's feelings, and that their relationship continued to develop unfixable cracks. She would have never imagined that the three little girls from the hood, who developed an unbreakable bond, found ways to break it, and possibly forever.

The End